The Ravine

The Ravine

A NOVEL OF EVIL, HOPE, AND
THE AFTERLIFE

Inspired by a True Story

Robert Pascuzzi

Hope Messenger

The Ravine
www.theravinebook.com

Hope Messenger
www.theravinebook@gmail.com

This is a novel and entirely a work of fiction. Names, characters, businesses, organizations, places, events, and incidents are the product of the author's imagination or, if loosely inspired by any actual event, such event has been transformed entirely into fiction by the author and should not be read to portray any actual persons, living or dead, or locales or events.

ISBN-10: 0615982999
ISBN-13: 9780615982991

Cover design by Elizabeth Mihaltse
Cover image (c) Roy Bishop/Archangel Images

To our friends

There are some who bring a light so great to the world that even after they have gone, the light remains.
—Author Unknown

Contents

Lord, help us realize that everything that happens to us happens for a reason. Help us realize that every sorrow or setback we experience can be transformed into a blessing, if we but trust in you. Help us realize that if we trust you, all things—even tragedies—will work out for our good.

Amen.

Prologue

HER HEAD ACHED the ache that always came when she saw things too clearly, when it was impossible to push the images and sounds out of her mind. It was especially difficult at this time of day—4 a.m., just before dawn, when the darkness grudgingly ceded its power and the veil was most transparent. This was a particularly angry dawn.

The cries of the little boy swirled through her head, ferociously bringing her to her knees and then all fours. The sound she uttered began as a growl and grew into shouts of an otherworldly language, before finally reaching a pleading howl. "No, dear Lord. Don't let this happen. Stop him *now!*" But she knew it was too late. She could see the dark figure lurking at the top of the stairs, manipulating, dictating, and preventing the slightest hope of reprieve. There was only one place to go, one thing to do, and now it was done.

By the time the sun rose, Joanna was seated in her chair by the window. Watching, just watching. The breeze brought some sense of relief. The most intense pain had passed, but she was drained and weeping. Not for herself, nor for those who were gone, but for the people for whom this awful day was just beginning.

How cruel a beautiful day is for the unfortunate few suddenly plucked from their mundane existence, she thought. The rest of the world goes about its business, the more fortunate unwittingly mocking their fellow travelers, unaware of how grateful they should be for their traffic jams, quarreling kids, the dress that's too tight, the annoying talking heads on the morning news. *Go ahead. Offer up your prayers for protection, and throw in a "thank you" to purchase a little extra insurance for your loved ones. Perhaps today will not be your day. But my day is every day.*

God had given Joanna a special gift, or burden. She'd lived with it for as long as she could remember. She knew things and saw things that did not make sense to those who lived in what she called "the natural." But now it was time to get to work. She usually felt an odd peace right at the beginning, but there was something about this time that just didn't seem right. She waited. Then the reflection in the window came into focus. She nodded and said, "Okay, now I'm ready."

Chapter 1

Out of the Blue

Life changes in an instant.
The ordinary instant.
—Joan Didion

PARADISE ON EARTH has a name: Sorrento, Italy. That's what Tony Turner said to himself as he breathed in the warm, salty air and gazed at the deep-blue water lapping into the Bay of Naples. He'd been humming that catchy melody to the famous Dean Martin song since he woke up that morning, and it wasn't about to stop playing in his head.

Though he'd slept through what was reputed to be a spectacular sunrise, he was planning to catch that evening's sunset—that is, if he wasn't napping after a day that would include a visit to Pompeii and perhaps a side trip to Mount Vesuvius. Then he and Emily had reservations for a late dinner at Don Pedro, arguably the best restaurant in all of Sorrento. For now, he was content to sit on the veranda, sip his first cup of coffee, kick back, and try his best to forget about business for a week.

It wasn't an easy sell, but he'd convinced Emily to leave the kids with her parents, get away, and take some time alone, together, for the first time in a long time. They had even made a pact: Emily would try not to worry about the kids if Tony wouldn't talk about work—and so far they had pretty much stuck to it. The deal was cinched when Tony had agreed to unplug from all the devices to which he was addicted once he stepped on the plane at Hopkins.

So when the house phone rang, shattering her calm, Emily lunged for it, certain something had happened with one of the kids. Just then, Tony leaned back to soak in the sun, and so was oblivious to the "I told you so" stare she aimed at him, irritating Emily even more. She'd deal with him after she sorted out whatever was going on back home in Ohio.

"Hello, who's this? Is that you, Mom?" Emily asked.

"Hel-lo, Emily? It's not your mom. It's Nick. I need to talk to Tony, about business. Is he there?"

"Yes, he is Nick, but we're really trying to get away from things. Can't this wait till we get back?" She tried to sound annoyed for Tony's benefit, but she was relieved it was just some work issue.

"I'm really sorry, Emily, but it can't wait! Can you put him on, please?"

"Okay, Nick, calm down," Emily said. "Tony, it's Nick. He says he has to talk to you right away. You better talk to him before he has a stroke or something," she said, handing him the phone.

"Tony, it's Nick. Hey, man, I'm really glad I got you. I tried to call your cell. Didn't you get my message?"

Tony hated when people asked him if he'd gotten their voice mail, when they were speaking on the phone and it obviously didn't matter any longer. Tony's first inclination was to unload on Nick, but the beautiful vista had started to work its magic, so he hesitated.

Tony had busted his butt over the years and now had a small chain of fifteen sports-supply stores, called Steve's Sporting Goods, throughout northern Ohio. It didn't take a genius to be successful at it, but it took some guts, lots of hard work, and the ability to make common sense decisions all day long. Nick was a childhood friend who had been his right-hand man for years now. True, Nick didn't practice quantum physics in his spare time, but he was honest and could be counted on to show up, work late, and usually make the right call. By now, Tony expected him to be able to deal with personnel issues, late shipments, markdowns, and any of the usual problems they encountered.

"I turned the stupid thing off last night so I might actually enjoy my vacation. This better be important, buddy. You know I promised Emily I'd forget about work for a week."

"It is, it is, man, I swear, Tony. There's somethin' really weird going on with the Little Brother, really weird. Ya gotta listen to me; it could be really serious. Danny's done something freaky and we can't find him."

Tony wasn't surprised that the issue had something to do with Danny. Unfortunately, Danny was always finding one way or another to screw up his life, from bad financial decisions to marital problems to a less-than-exemplary work ethic. The truth was that Tony had pulled Danny's chestnuts out of the fire more times than he could remember. However, since Danny had married Rachel—really, since his two boys had come along, around ten years ago—for the most part, he'd seemed to get his act together. Tony now even trusted him to run five of his stores, under Nick's supervision.

Tony's irritation turned to concern. "Okay, could you just tell me what you're talking about already?"

"You know that Logan kid who works for Danny at the Copley Street store?"

"You mean that sleazeball creep he was supposed to fire?"

"Yeah, yeah, that's the guy. He's here with me now and he's really freaked out. He says he just came from Danny's . . . says he was there all night, and—"

Tony raised his voice, starting to lose it. "Why would Logan have been at Danny's all night? I told Danny to fire that jerk because he said he caught him red-handed. Why would he let that loser stay at his house after he fired him? That makes no sense."

"I don't get it either, but he says he was there all night, and Danny did some really weird stuff. The dude is freaked, man, really. You better talk to him."

"Okay, then, put him on."

"Hey, Tony, sorry to bother you," Logan said, "but I'm kinda freaked out and not sure what to do."

Tony pictured the skinny creep, with his hat on sideways, probably high on something, stogie in his mouth, trying to get over on him with some BS story.

"What's this all about, Logan? Just be straight with me."

"Umm, well, I met up with Danny last night at the Copley store. And, well, he told me, ya, know, to follow him to his house and wait in the garage until he needed my help. So, ya know, I did that, but then I fell asleep, and I don't know what Danny did, but he woke me up this morning and told me I had to leave right away. So I did, but he was acting real strange—spooky, ya know?"

"No, I don't know! Asked for your help with what?"

"I don't really know, man, but I don't wanna put ya on. I can't really say. It's so crazy, you wouldn't believe me anyway. I just stayed in the garage all night; I didn't do anything, but I just thought you should know, because he was acting real strange."

"I still don't know what the hell you're talking about, and none of this makes any sense. Did you pay him back the money you stole? Where's Danny now?"

"I don't know, but I think you oughta call him. I'm gonna pay you back in a—"

"You're damned right I'll call him," Tony said and slammed down the phone.

"Just when I think I'm gonna get a few days off, Danny has to do something stupid," he shouted to Emily.

"What's going on, Tony?"

"I don't know! Maybe nothing, maybe something. These jerks just call me out of the blue and dump this on me. I have to call Danny."

He turned on his phone and discovered a flood of activity since he'd turned it off the night before: two new voice mails and a bunch of new e-mails. He skipped the voice mail from Nick and went directly to the one his brother had left the night before, at ten o'clock, Ohio time. Tony tapped the screen and heard Danny's voice through the speakerphone.

"Tony, it's Danny. I just fired Logan here at the Copley store. He admitted he took the money and said he was sorry, but said he couldn't pay us back. He begged me not to fire him, but I told him I didn't have no choice—first he sorta started cryin', then he got really pissed off, and said he was gonna kill me. I'm driving home now, and I think he might be following me. He sorta went nuts, and said he was gonna come to my house and stuff . . . I think the guy could be dangerous, so I thought you should know. I don't know what to do; so, if you get a chance, call me back."

Now Tony was even more annoyed. Either Danny or Logan was lying because the two stories just didn't add up. *So much for my peaceful morning,* he thought. But now he was roped in; he had to get to the bottom of things.

He checked his e-mail and, sure enough, there was one from Danny. It had come in at 4:48 a.m., Danny's time, a little over two hours ago. And that was when Tony realized that something was very, very wrong.

As Tony read Danny's e-mail, panic washed over him: "Life insurance—MAC Mutual/AGG. Take care of Evan and Christopher."

Life insurance? Take care of the boys? "What the hell?" he shouted.

"Babe, what's going on?"

"I don't know. Look at this," he said, handing the phone to Emily. Now they both started to panic.

"Oh, my God, what does it mean? You better get him on the phone."

"That's what I'm doing," he said, pacing the floor, while Danny's phone kept ringing with no answer. At last, he got his voice mail.

"Danny, what the hell is going on? What's this about life insurance? Call me back, right away, you understand? Right away!"

"Tony, that sounds serious. What could he mean by that?"

"I don't know, but it's certainly not good. He's not answering his cell. You call Rachel's cell and I'll try their house.

They had no luck with either place. The message at his brother's house played sharply in Tony's ear: "You've reached Rachel . . . Danny . . . Evan . . . and Christopher." The tone and pitch of voice changed as each Turner family member called out his or her name. "Please leave us a message," they ended in unison.

"Guys, it's Tony and Emily. Pick up, right now, if you're there. We need to talk to you right away." He waited. No answer. "Okay, when you get back, give me a call right away, on my cell, so I know everything's okay," he said, trying to reassure himself. Five thousand miles away, back in Ohio, his voice echoed through the silent house.

Tony always fixed problems and he would figure out how to fix this one. It was probably just a mix-up of some sort, but he couldn't disguise the quaver in his voice when he got Tom Schroeder on the phone. Tom was one of his best managers, and lived a few miles from Danny and Rachel. True to form, Schroeder picked up on the first ring.

"Tom, this is Tony. Thank God. I'm really glad I reached you. I need a really big favor. I'm on vacation, and it's probably nothing, but I think that Logan creep might have done something to Danny. He called and left some strange messages, about life insurance and stuff—"

"Tony, what are you talking about? I just saw Danny yesterday."

"Yeah, but something's wrong. Nobody's answering; can you drive over there right away? I'm really worried about him."

"You got it, bud. I'm in my car now, on my way to work out, so I'll just swing by. I'll call you back in a few minutes. Chill out, and go back to enjoying Italy. I'm sure everything's okay. I'll check it out. *Ciao,* boss! Stop worrying!"

⇢⊨◉ ◉⊨⇠

Tom gazed in his rear-view mirror as he backed up to make a U-turn. He was about a mile or two from Danny and Rachel's house, so he planned to shoot over there and then head directly to the gym. He was a little put out because it meant he would have to cut his workout short, but really, he had to admit to himself that he just generally resented Danny. For whatever reason, it seemed that anything that had to do with the guy usually turned into some sort of needless problem. His brother owned the company, and so Danny had five shops under him. But everyone knew that the only reason he had so many shops was because he was related to the boss. Behind his back, he was "the Little Brother" to Tony and all the managers, who usually had to suck it up and cover for Danny when he forgot to put in his orders on time, or just didn't show up for work and stuff like that. On top of that, Danny would always use his trump card as Tony's brother if he wanted to one-up one of the other employees.

Tony was famous for his common sense, except when it came to Danny. Everybody else knew he couldn't be trusted, messed around on his beautiful wife, Rachel, and, for a forty-three-year-old man, still acted like a kid. Tom only managed three shops and probably made half the commission Danny made, though he could run rings around him. It just wasn't fair. When Tony got back, he planned to sit down with him and give him a piece of his mind. Things had better change, or he'd tell Tony to take his dopey Steve's Sporting Goods job and shove it.

Suddenly Tom laughed out loud to himself, letting out a big, self-deprecating guffaw. A few seconds before Tony's call, he'd just finished saying his morning prayers. It hadn't been two minutes since he'd asked for God's help in being patient and understanding that day—in feeling love for all the good and great people in his life. He'd even specifically mentioned Tony as someone for whom he was grateful. But the first little curve he was thrown, and he was off to the races, wallowing in self-pity, jealousy, and plots of revenge. "Okay, Lord, let's start this day over," he said, as he made the turn onto Danny and Rachel's street.

Little did he know that he was going to need every ounce of God's grace to cope with the scene he was about to encounter.

CHAPTER 2

A Brother's Love

God dislikes evil
And no happiness can be built on hate.
Love one another as brothers.
—Josephine Baker

DANNY TURNER HAD it all going for him when he was in high school. His stunning blue eyes and crop of blond, wavy hair gave him the sort of bad-boy look that the girls just seemed to love. He wasn't a big guy at five foot nine, but he was one of the strongest and fastest players on the football team. He'd worked out diligently since that day when he was thirteen and was humiliated by the neighborhood thug, Al Rocco.

Al was an oversized Neanderthal who liked nothing better than grabbing some smaller kid so he could pin him down and taunt him. That day Al not only pushed Danny to the ground, but held him there, digging his knees into his shoulders and letting his filthy spittle drip slowly and repeatedly onto Danny's face. The other kids gathered, cheering and chanting each time another glob landed on Al's latest victim.

It was payback time pretty soon for Al when Danny's brother, Tony, heard what had happened. Tony jumped into their dad's pickup truck and bolted to the school yard faster than a speeding bullet, while Danny tried to explain why he'd let that Rocco kid get the better of him. Sometimes Danny thought Tony was a lot like Superman, because he could always be counted on to swoop in and save the day. Tony's jet-black curly hair and blue eyes lent even more credibility to the image Danny had of his brother.

Over the years, this incident became a valued piece of Turner-brother family lore. Whenever the brothers recounted this story (which frequently happened while perched on barstools), they would invariably begin by mimicking the wide-eyed, guppy-swallowing expression and squeal that escaped "Fat Al" the second he turned around to see Tony barreling down on him.

Tony was taller than Al; while he didn't weigh as much, at six foot two, 175 pounds, his athletic build was solid muscle. So it wasn't hard for him to grab Al by the throat and pin him to the fence with one hand while punching him smack in the center of his stomach, sending him tumbling to the ground.

"Get up, you fat turd, and apologize to my brother."

Al just sat there with a scowl and said, "I didn't do nothin', ain't gonna apologize to nobody, ain't no way, and you can't make—"

Tony grabbed him by the hair, brought him to his knees, and slapped him full across the face. The wallop raised a big red mark on the kid's cheek.

"Come on, get up and fight somebody your own size."

Al just kneeled there with a stunned expression. He wiped the snot off his nose; otherwise, he didn't dare move or say a word. When it became apparent that the excitement was over, the group of kids who had just been egging on Al quietly began to disperse, afraid Tony would turn on one of them.

"This guy's just a punk," Tony said to Danny. "Let's go home."

With that, Tony turned and marched out of the school yard with Danny trailing behind, feeling vindicated and protected.

But Danny decided then and there that he was never going to let anyone push him around again. Even if it took hard work, he was determined start a workout program and bulk up, and that's just what he did. He dusted off his dad's barbells and bench, and worked out every day. Pretty soon he started to see ripples in his biceps. The squats and leg raises gave him lower-body strength, and he would spend half an hour every day doing sprints to build up his speed.

So by the time Danny was a sophomore at Geauga High, he was the starting halfback, and Tony, by then a senior, was the quarterback. In football-loving Cuyahoga County, the Turner brothers were local celebrities in that magical year of 1978, the year they went all-state but lost in the finals. The Geauga Arrows had never gone so far, and never would again.

The Turner family moved to their ranch-style home in 1967, in the part of Chesterland that was not as bad as Streetsboro (which was literally on the other side of the railroad tracks), but not as nice as Clover Hill, the development that was built in the early '60s. The kids whose fathers worked in the office at AE's Jayomar plant, or at one of the other big manufacturers, or were local professionals, tended to live in Clover Hill. The kids whose fathers worked in one of the factories or at one of the stores on the main drag, Mayfield Road, lived near the Turners in the area commonly called the Junction.

Most of their neighbors kept up their houses and the lawns were usually tidy, but every once in a while you could find a house with a junker in the front yard, weeds pushing up through the rotted steel. Steve Turner had two healthy teenage boys who kept his yard in great shape, for which each earned ten dollars a cut. It was his way of teaching them responsibility and giving them some spending money. When it was time to cut the lawn, Tony always had to bug his brother to do his part, but a few smacks upside the head would usually do the trick.

Steve and Debby Turner had a traditional marriage. He'd worked his way up to foreman at Jayomar and she ran the house and mothered with the best of them. Tony and Danny took a special pride in friends' comments that going to their house was like walking into the TV show *Father Knows Best*. Visitors were usually greeted by the scent of a cherry pie or a pot roast at the front door, and Debby had a way of making their friends feel welcome, even when she was preoccupied with one of her projects. She would always praise their new haircut or cool sneakers, and then break out the cookie jar.

Steve would arrive home after work around five, read the paper, drink his one beer, and then sit down to dinner and say the blessing. After the dishes were cleared, the family would gather around the television set to watch Walter Cronkite and the *CBS Evening News* at 6:30. Ever since that day in November 1963 when ole Walt took off his glasses, hesitated, glanced up at the clock, and choked out the exact time President Kennedy had died, Steve felt like he knew the man personally. The country could be at war, preparing to dodge nuclear missiles, rioting in the streets, landing on the moon, or queuing up at the gas pump; all would be put right or at least explained when the Turners settled into their living room to perform their simple family ritual with the rest of America.

Of course, a hardworking guy like Steve would get frustrated with those fools in Washington, New York, and Los Angeles who flew over Ohio (except during the presidential elections) but otherwise didn't care about Ohio, and didn't give a damn about the farmers, plumbers, auto workers, and the other "Steves" who were the backbone of the country. It seemed the politicians just couldn't figure out how to get along, and Steve would often remark, "they're like three bald guys fightin' over a comb." This would always get a laugh out of Tony and Danny, though they never could quite figure out what it meant.

They looked up to their father and knew they were lucky to have the mother they had. When 1978 rolled around and the boys made their parents proud, all was good.

But the truth was that Tony and Danny, like most teenagers, had another life, a secret life their parents didn't know about. That's the way it's always been and always will be. In most cases, teenagers grow up and life moves on, but with the Turner boys, things always went a bit too far. The more they got away with, the more they pushed the envelope.

Tony was the leader, and Danny liked it that way. He found it impossible to resist whatever adventure was on the agenda. When Tony decided it was time for Danny to become a man at age sixteen, he brought him downtown to Cleveland and got the matter settled for fifteen dollars with a buxom Spanish girl whose kids were crying in the next room while she told him to "hurry up and get it over with." Tony taught Danny how to smoke cigarettes, roll a joint, snort coke, and hotwire a car, as well as the most efficient way to cut through a chain-link fence while breaking into a stockyard.

However, by the time Tony and Danny graduated from high school, and were passed over for the football scholarships they had presumed would come their way, they no longer needed wire cutters. They had discovered the simplicity of the inside job.

Both brothers found employment in the warehouse at Tager's Lumber. Tager sold every tool known to mankind, along with construction materials, paint, and everything a homeowner or carpenter could ever want. The brothers wore blue overalls with their first names emblazoned on the pockets so that customers could call them by name when directing them to cut wood or load items into their station wagons. The job wasn't fun, but they had big plans for the future. The prize they had their eye on for their first big score was a new shipment of circular saws that Danny had shelved not more than twenty feet from the back door earlier that day.

This time it was Danny who came up with the scheme. Tony listened intently as his brother described how they would climb in the window he'd unlocked, unlatch the back door, grab a case of DeWalts, and scoot out to their waiting pickup. Easy peasy.

"You didn't think of one thing, Einstein," Tony said with a grin. "That stupid mutt Barney who sleeps there all night will be all over us."

"Damn, you're right! What are we gonna do about that mangy pain in the ass?"

"Well, we can either risk it tonight or wait a day."

Danny gave Tony a quizzical look. "What good's it gonna do to wait a day? He'll still be there tomorrow."

"Or maybe he won't," Tony said with a mock evil grin followed by his best ghoulish laugh.

The brothers high-fived, and Danny had to hand it to Tony yet again. How lucky he was to have such a smart brother. He was like a master chess player, always thinking several moves ahead. He was definitely going places, and Danny would be right by his side.

The next afternoon, the whole warehouse was in an uproar when Barney's body was discovered lying next to his water bowl. Danny and Tony stood off to the side and watched the spectacle unfold. It felt good to be in control while those goons freaked out over a lousy mutt. "How'd you get him to swallow the Seconals?" Danny whispered to Tony.

"I just split them open, sprinkled them on a piece of chopped meat, rolled it into a meatball, and gave it to the dope. He gobbled it up."

Phil, the warehouse manager and titular owner of Barney, was so distraught and preoccupied with the burial out back that he didn't think to make certain all the windows were locked. Normally he wouldn't have had to consider such things with Barney at his post, but without Barney's presence the brothers easily managed to lug four cases into the truck and speed away into the night. Tony knew a guy in Chardon who would pay fifteen bucks for each saw, so with eight to a case, they would bring in a total of around five hundred dollars. They drove home and hid the boxes behind the shed and covered them with a tarp. Tony sat on the top of the pile and proposed a toast: "To the Turner brothers and the easiest haul ever made in the history of Chesterland." They chatted excitedly and acknowledged their brilliance in planning the whole thing. *Too bad about the dog, collateral damage, ya know . . . what the hell, we're just making minimum wage . . . we were just getting our due.* Finally they ran out of accolades and headed in to catch a few winks before getting up for work.

Old Man Tager was more pissed off than anyone had ever seen him the next morning, when he ordered the troops to gather near the back door to listen to his tirade.

"I know one of you punks stole those saws. Probably was a couple of you workin' together." He seemed to look at Danny and then at Tony as he said this—or maybe it was just their imaginations working over-time. Tony didn't show any emotion, but Danny felt his heart pounding like a jackhammer and his face go flush. He might as well have been wearing an "I DID IT" sign, he thought.

Just then two cops came through the back door and, in feigned *sotto voce*, told Tager they knew the make of tire of the getaway car, and would need to look at all the trucks in the employee parking lot. *Oh no!* Tony thought. *They've already narrowed it down to a truck. Man, are we screwed!* He knew he could keep his cool, but had his doubts about Danny. He snuck a glance at him, and his brother's panicked eyes confirmed his worst fears.

The taller of the two cops stepped forward. He had the mean, narrow, no-nonsense look of a military guy who was used to dealing with the lower elements, and was itching to crack one of these imbeciles in the skull and beat the truth out of him.

"Okay, listen up. I'm Officer Colby, and I am going to expect all of you to cooperate in this investigation. I'm going to make three points, and I'm only going to say them one time. One, it's obvious that someone climbed in that open window, unlocked the door, and took off with four cases of saws with a retail value of close to five thousand dollars. Two, it's also obvious that the same person, or persons, planned this and went so far as to poison the guard dog yesterday. Three, this could only have been done by an employee, which means that several of you know who did it. So, we can do this the hard way or the easy way. The easy way is you come clean now, return the merchandise, and deal with the consequences. The hard way is you stand there and keep your mouth shut, and try to make me look like an idiot. But I guarantee you that is a mistake because that will make me very unhappy, and believe me, you don't want to do that. So, what's it going to be?"

After a few seconds of silence, the group started to murmur, and then a few guys said straight out "wasn't me," "I wouldn't kill no dog or steal nothin'," "don't blame me, I had nothin' to do with it." Pretty soon it got very loud with more than a few men saying that anyone who would kill a dog was the lowest form of scum, and they planned to beat the crap out of the guy when they figured out who killed a harmless dog like Barney.

So Danny and Tony joined the chorus, shouted out their innocence at the top of their lungs, and cursed the killer of the innocent dog. They reasoned that only a guilty person would keep his mouth shut, and each made the independent decision that the best way out was to lie. Thus was set a pattern in the life of the Turner brothers, which, for one of them, would have fateful consequences at the most crucial moments of his life.

Eventually it became clear that no one was going to fess up to the crime, so Colby took each of the nine warehouse workers to a glassed-in room for an interview, one at a time. He leaned across and stared into their eyes, nose to nose, pounded the table and kicked over a chair or two for effect. When he interviewed Danny and Tony individually, his antennae shot up, but neither cracked, and Colby just naturally gravitated toward the two black guys because one of them had a record, and, well, they were black. Colby actually didn't have any tire tread evidence, or any evidence to speak of. His main tool was intimidation, and when that didn't work, he didn't have many arrows left in his quiver. The truth was, this level of criminal escapade was pretty much beyond his sleuthing powers. Danny and Tony breathed a sigh of relief as they watched the patrol car turn out onto Fairmount Road and head off to parts unknown. Of course, had Colby and his partner thought to delve into this mystery a little deeper and actually bothered to visit the home of each employee, they eventually would have discovered the saws beneath a tarp behind the Turners' shed. But lunch beckoned, and that put an impromptu end to the investigation.

That night Danny and Tony unloaded the saws in Chardon. They didn't get five hundred but rather one hundred and fifty bucks. On the drive back, they started arguing about how stupid it was to risk jail over such a low take. They blamed each other, and then sat in silence until Tony burst out laughing.

"Man, did you see the look on Old Man Tager's face this morning?"

"Yeah, and that cop thought he was spooking us, but I knew all the time, he didn't have nothin'," Danny lied.

And this was pretty much the way things went for the next year on their petty crime spree. Good old Turner luck kept them going until it finally ran out.

CHAPTER 3

There Are No Coincidences

But I have promises to keep,
And miles to go before I sleep.
—Robert Frost

DURING THEIR HIGH school years, throughout football season, Friday was the best day of the week for the Turner brothers. And, of course, the best part of the day was Friday night. It seemed as though Tony and Danny had some form of mental telepathy on the field, particularly when the team was in dire need of a score. Their specialty was the broken play. Just when things looked most desperate, Tony would sense where Danny was on the field, toss the ball in the air, and, like a heat-seeking missile, it would drop into his hands. Then Danny's legs would do the rest. After the *Cleveland Plain Dealer* ran a feature on the brothers, they became a source of pride for the entire community. For a few years, Steve Turner's money was no good at any Chesterland pub.

It was after one of these games that Danny was introduced to Rachel McKenna by Carolyn Hamilton. Carolyn knew Danny because her dad had coached his Little League team, and her brother Kenny palled around with him

Carolyn was convinced Danny and Rachel would make a great couple, and was excited to introduce them. However, Danny breezed by after the introduction, in pursuit of the keg party that was also part of the Friday night tradition.

"Nice meeting you," he said as he walked away. "What did you say your name was? Renée?" But Danny was gone before Rachel could answer.

Years later, after they were married, Rachel never tired of telling this story, and, as if on cue, Danny would look chagrined, raise his hands in a gesture of innocence, say "I love you, Renée," and plant a big kiss on her cheek.

Logically, Rachel and Carolyn did not seem like great candidates to become acquaintances, let alone develop a lifelong friendship. Rachel was outgoing, boisterous, seemingly self-assured, and melodramatic. She came from hard-drinking Irish stock who defined the phrase "dysfunctional family" before it was in vogue. Carolyn was raised by strict parents who took their Roman Catholic faith seriously, sending Carolyn to elementary and middle school at Sacred Heart in Mayfield Village. Studious and shy, she liked her routine and was uncomfortable with change. She lined up her pencils at home in order to be better prepared to do her homework.

So when Carolyn suddenly found herself attending Geauga High, an enormous public school where she hardly knew a soul and coolness was clearly the highest priority, she felt totally invisible. Then one day all of that changed.

Much to Carolyn's horror, wacky Mr. Ercolano, the language arts teacher, who wore his hair a bit shaggy to complement his mutton-chop sideburns, declared that everyone in the class was to immediately select a partner, because today was the day they were going to learn how to "really talk about themselves with another human being." Ercolano had spent a summer on a commune during college and this was one of the things they did with the aid of hallucinogens. He'd come up with this brilliant idea last night while he and his girlfriend stared at the night sky from their beach chairs sharing a joint. This was going to be heavy.

Of course, the kids instantly gravitated toward their friends, elated at the opportunity to spend the next forty minutes joking and gossiping rather than listening to that windbag Ercolano drone on about dangling participles, the dangers of homonyms, and other nonsense they would never put to use. The room instantly came alive with activity.

Carolyn didn't really know anyone, and would never have just walked up to a veritable stranger, so she slowly rose and stood next to her desk, mortified as the rest of the class paired up. She felt a jolt of fear in her stomach that would doubtless explode into that horrible red blotch that erupted on her throat whenever she was embarrassed. She was certain that within seconds she would be derided as the most uncool person ever to exist in the history of the universe. Then she heard a sweet sound.

"You look like you could use a partner. I'm Rachel. What's your name?"

And so were spoken the first of many millions of words they would share with each other during their lifetimes. Neither of them could remember what they talked about on that day, but talk they did, non-stop, until the bell rang. Then they exchanged numbers at the classroom door. Each knew they had found someone special. Carolyn never forgot Rachel's simple act of kindness. She knew Rachel was one of the "cool" kids who easily could have matched up with someone else, but, as Carolyn was to learn, Rachel always followed her heart and her natural instinct was to reach out to help someone in need.

For her part, Rachel discovered that Carolyn was someone she could trust with her deepest secrets, which was amazing, because she spent so much of her time hiding the truth. At fourteen, Rachel's life was already filled with darkness that she spent much of her time hiding from the world. But for some reason, when she looked into Carolyn's eyes that first day, she began to learn how to trust a friend.

A few months after they met, Rachel did something with Carolyn that she almost never did with anyone; she brought her home.

⇢▬◉ ◉▬⇠

Home for Rachel was always a roller coaster ride. There were times when things were peaceful and almost cheerful for days at a time. Rachel was close to her two younger brothers, Sam and Petey, and very tight with her older sister, Terry. Her mother was sweet and loving, but completely incapable of controlling the chaos her alcoholic husband brought into the household.

Ted McKenna learned how to drink at an early age, and for the first part of his life booze was his friend. It helped him loosen up and chat up the girls, and it gave him the courage he needed when the Polish guys who shared a border with the Irish on the east side of Cleveland would make some slur about how it was too bad all these Micks had moved into town and were stinking up the place.

He loved to tell the story of how this behemoth of a Polack came at him one day in O'Healy's, and he had the presence of mind to smash the bottom of his beer bottle on the bar and stick it in his fat, round face.

"That big moose was like a giant compared to me," he would brag, "but he backed down because he seen the look in my eye that I was serious. I musta looked like a crazy guy to him. He ran outta there and never set foot in O'Healy's again."

Because Ted was actually a skinny little runt, he usually didn't fare too well in barroom brawls; when things would erupt, he'd normally hang back. Those stories, though, didn't often make it home.

Under his roof, however, things were different. Here, Ted was all-powerful, and he could demand strict obedience from his kids and his wife. He saw himself as a benevolent sort of parent, who would give a kid a second chance with the warning "don't make me take my belt off." But all too often the kids would push things too far, and Ted would have to take action to keep the little brats in line.

They just didn't appreciate how hard he worked, or how lucky they were to be living in a place like Newberry, rather than in Cleveland, particularly with how it was those days. Nor did they realize the skill it took to maneuver a forklift truck along the factory floor, moving hubcaps from one warehouse to the other, making sure they were lifted to the right location, without dropping them or otherwise screwing up. And they certainly didn't understand what it felt like if you happened to have had a little too much to drink the day before, but had to haul your butt out of bed, toss your cookies and then show up for work, putting up with an idiot of a boss all day. These kids just had it too easy, and, if he didn't keep them in line, they would wind up going bad.

He'd often remind them that he hadn't planned on signing up for this deal.

"Where the hell would you all be," he would ask, "if I hadn't done the right thing by your mother when she got pregnant when she was nothin' but a kid? Where would you be without me? Nowhere! Who would put food on the table? No one!"

This was the usual sort of dinnertime conversation around the McKenna table. Of course, no one dared mention that Dad had had a hand in getting their mom pregnant, and that, in actuality, Ted had planned to leave town the night before the wedding, but got too drunk and found himself pretty much propped up at the altar by his brother.

It was during moments like these that Rachel felt the shame radiate from her mother, and she would wonder why she didn't just pick up and go far, far away. But shame that deep has a way of rubbing off on children, until everyone silently agrees that it's best just to pretend everything is fine and, most of all, to protect the family secrets from the outside world. This was a lesson Rachel never forgot.

Rachel's mom would try to placate Ted, bringing him a beer and encouraging him to relax and let the kids be kids. Sometimes, much to her relief, that would work, and he would be the "old" Ted—the guy she fell in love with, who could tell a joke with the best of them, dance up a storm, and fix just about any gas engine ever invented.

One of the lies Rachel's mom told the kids, in order to justify why she ever had anything to do with their dad in the first place, was that she'd never seen him drunk until after they were engaged. And by then it was too late. She said it so many times, she started to believe it.

And so Rachel learned that her job was to take care of everyone else. She was the one who comforted her mom when things were really bad, she was the one who made her younger brothers tiptoe around Dad, and, along with her mom, she was the one who worried about Terry when she didn't come home at night. And then she would head off to school, put on a happy face, and make believe she was like all the other kids, with loving parents and a happy home.

So it was a big step to bring Carolyn home one day after school to show her the new blouse she had bought downtown at Higbee's and was saving for the upcoming April dance.

The girls were sitting in Rachel's room, thumbing through a magazine, giggling as they debated which hairdo to wear to the dance, when all of a sudden they heard a loud crash come from the kitchen.

"Don't worry about that; it's nothing," said Rachel.

"What, are you kidding? It sounds like somebody fell down out there," Carolyn said, and she was out the bedroom door before Rachel could stop her.

Rachel's dad was lying on the floor, trying to pull himself up, and cursing the cops in Newberry for not having the damn sense to just leave a guy alone when he was driving home from work. Just then there was a commotion at the front door and two uniformed police officers came in, lifted Ted up, cuffed him, and dragged him into the squad car, kicking and screaming.

Carolyn did her best to pretend she hadn't seen what had happened, but when her eyes met Rachel's, they both began to cry and Rachel ran into her room, followed by her friend. Carolyn insisted that Rachel come home with her, have dinner with the family, and stay the night. She would not take no for an answer.

That night they sat up talking in Carolyn's room until three in the morning, and that was the first time Rachel told the truth about her life to another person. Perhaps that wacky Mr. Ercolano wasn't so wacky after all.

Of course, it wasn't too long before Carolyn's mother figured out what was going on with Rachel, and without so much as saying a word, she pretty much adopted her. So, when the two girls became women, it was natural to say they loved each other like sisters.

⇥⊫◉ ◉⊨⇤

One day later that year, Carolyn's doorbell rang and Rachel was standing on her doorstep, a great, big smile on her face. She was bubbling over with excitement.

"You'll never guess what happened!" she said to Carolyn.

"What, what? Tell me!"

"My dad moved out! He met some woman at the bar, got her pregnant, and they're moving to her brother's place in Minnesota. He told us the news last night, and he's already gone!"

"What? What did your mom say?"

Rachel laughed when she thought about how cool her mom had been when she heard the news. "My mom looked at him and said something like, 'Well, I didn't know you still had it in you.' And then she said, 'Which suitcase do you want? Take your pick.' I haven't seen my mom look so happy in years!"

Carolyn thought about how strange this was. She loved her dad with all her heart, and couldn't imagine feeling anything but tremendous pain if her mom and dad split up, but she was happy for Rachel because at last it looked as if she would have something that resembled a normal home life.

The next several months were peaceful in the McKenna household. Terry had graduated from high school and was working full time and contributing most of her paycheck, and Rachel's mom worked at the A&P where Route 6 crossed 44. Rachel got a part-time job after school at the same A&P, to help make ends meet. The truth was that Ted tended to drink away a good portion of what he earned, so even though they had a little less money in the house, they were managing. The one good thing her father had done was pay off the house when he inherited some money a few years back, before he stumbled off to Minnesota. Everyone was enjoying no longer waiting for the other shoe to drop. But then it did.

Rachel noticed that her mom had seemed distracted for a few weeks, and then she took a day off from work, which wasn't like her. That night, she just sat at the kitchen table by herself and stared off into space.

"What's the matter, Mom?"

"Oh, nothing. Nothing I need to bother you kids with," she said, but Rachel persisted.

Finally her mom told her she had been to the doctor because she was feeling tired all the time, and she had something called lymphoma. All the kids gathered around the kitchen table, and she told them the doctors had assured her she would get well, but was going to have to go for some treatments.

The next day, Rachel went to the school library, took down the K–L volume of the *World Book Encyclopedia,* and looked up the word she would come to despise. She slammed the book shut when she learned it was a form of cancer that was most often fatal.

So her mother began chemotherapy, but she seemed to get sicker and sicker as time went on instead of getting better. Finally she had to quit her job. Terry and Rachel sat down with their mom and told her they had come to the decision that Rachel would work at the supermarket full time.

"How are you going to do that and still go to school?" her mom asked.

"That's just it, Mom. I'm going to have to quit high school until you get better."

It took a few weeks of debate, but as time went on, Rachel's mom just didn't have the strength to fight about it, and in her heart, she knew Rachel was right. And someone had to take care of Sam and Petey.

To Carolyn, the fact that Rachel would have to drop out of school, on top of her mother's illness, was just about the worst news she could hear. She was worried about what would happen to Rachel in the future without so much as a high school diploma. Carolyn planned to attend college, and Rachel was working at a supermarket, helping to support her family. She felt guilty for having it so much better. And really, she couldn't imagine going to school and not seeing her best friend every day.

But there was nothing Carolyn could do about it, and that was what happened.

When Rachel's mom died, Terry and Rachel moved into a two-family house on Mayfield Road, above an auto parts store. Her dad came back for the funeral and claimed ownership of the house, which he eventually sold before moving the two boys to Minnesota. Rachel found a job as a receptionist at a dentist's office, and it was there that she met a woman who worked for Jenkins Realty. This woman convinced her to become the office manager, took her under her wing, and made sure she got her license.

Rachel was a natural at real estate. She truly enjoyed helping people find just the right home, allowing them to envision how their house would look with new wallpaper, curtains, and the right places for their furniture. Despite her lack of a diploma, she was a whiz at math, and could estimate the monthly mortgage costs better than most mortgage brokers could. At this time, with interest rates up around 20 percent, it was tough to sell houses, but Rachel was always one of the top performers in her office.

So Carolyn enrolled in college, at John Carroll University, but lived at home and commuted to school. She saw Rachel at least once a week, and they made a point of talking on the phone every single day. They helped each other through all of the travails of life as only sisters could. Mrs. Hamilton insisted Rachel get her GRE, and Carolyn drilled her the night before the test, which Rachel passed with flying colors.

By this time, Rachel could afford her own place, which was fortunate because Terry had moved in with Tommy Staziak, a hard-drinking Polish guy who—guess what?—drove a forklift truck for a living. It wasn't long before she was pregnant with Tommy's baby. The sins of the mother were visited upon the daughter. Rachel tried her best to like Tommy, but he just reminded her too much of her father. By the time baby Cheryl was born, Tommy was starting to dabble in hard drugs and would disappear for days at a time.

In order to support herself and the baby, Terry had to work several jobs, so Rachel fell into the same old pattern of taking care of others, only this time it was a little baby girl. By the time Cheryl was walking, she was spending as much time with Rachel as with her mother, and that meant she was spending a good deal of time with "Aunt Carolyn."

By Wednesday of most weeks, Carolyn would call and ask, "Rach, what do you want to do this weekend?"

"I don't know, sweetie, what do you want to do?" was the usual reply.

Often they would double date, or just go to the movies together. Neither of them had found anyone special, but both were confident that eventually the right guy would come along.

Then one Saturday morning, upon entering a diner to have breakfast, they noticed a familiar face on the top of a stack of newspapers. There, right on the front page of the *Cleveland Plain Dealer*, handsome as could be, was Danny Turner. He'd finally made the big time.

CHAPTER 4

The Price of Fame

Fame is a bee.
It has a song—
It has a sting—
Ah, too, it has a wing.
—Emily Dickinson

ABOUT A MONTH after Barney died, and the saws were stolen from Tager's, Tony decided it would be a good idea to nip a twenty-dollar bill from the cash register while the manager, Phil, had his back turned. Unfortunately, something told Phil to turn around right at that instant, and he grabbed Tony's hand before he could stash the bill in his pocket.

"What do you think you're doing, bozo?"

"I wasn't really gonna take it. I just wanted to see if I could trick you," was the best Tony could muster on such short notice.

Tony couldn't believe Phil would be such a rat as to tell Tager about a minor infraction such as this, but it was the very next thing he did. He'd had it in for the brothers since the events of the previous month, and was keeping a close eye on both of them. It took Tager about three seconds to tell Tony to get the hell out of his store, and to take his scheming little brother with him. So off they stormed, huffing with indignation that anyone would have the nerve to fire the two greatest sports legends in the history of Cuyahoga County.

When they told their father that they had decided to quit without another job lined up, it made Steve curious, so he went over to Tager's and discovered the real reason they were no longer employed. By this point, he knew this was the sort of thing his boys were capable of, and he was getting used to apologizing for them, so that's what he did, and then he headed back home.

He couldn't believe how radically things had changed in just a few short years. He'd given them everything he had, and it wasn't that long ago that they were pretty much the toast of the town, but now that was starting to feel like a dim memory. He thought all of their problems could be traced back to that group of guys they were hanging with at Barton's Pub, but they wouldn't listen to him about that crowd. They were good boys at heart, but he was going to give them a piece of his mind.

Of course, when he got home and confronted them, a big argument ensued, and in the end Tony and Danny marched out the door, threatening never to return, which was fine with Steve. But Debby was terrified something awful would happen to her sons "out there on their own." Steve assured her they would be back once they ran out of money and were hungry, and of course he was right. Besides, they were now at the age when they *should* be out on their own, but neither he nor Debby had the heart to toss them out into the street.

There was something to Steve's idea about the crowd at Barton's being part of the problem, but the fact of the matter was that Tony was pretty much the ringleader whenever they would go out on a petty crime spree. If they knew someone was going to be away for the night, then a few of them would figure out how to break a window, sneak in, and steal anything of value. The problem was that most items were too big to haul away, and even if they were able to snatch a watch or a necklace or some jewelry worth a few hundred dollars, they would only get a fraction of the value. So, even with a little job here and there, Tony and Danny were broke most of the time.

Despite being out of pocket, when one of the guys would suggest a B&E at a house they knew would be vacant, Tony would usually find a reason to nix the idea. They'd had too many close calls over these stupid little hauls. He had the good sense to realize their luck would run out eventually. He knew the answer was cash. Cold hard cash. But how to get that? A bank job was too risky. Gas stations and convenience stores had cash, but that was almost like robbing a place in broad daylight, and you never knew if the guy behind the counter had a gun or some other weapon. They were bound to get busted or worse.

Then one day their luck started to turn for the better.

Tony and Danny were friendly with this tall, skinny, frizzy-haired kid named Jimmy Bagneski, who drove a truck for a local delivery service. He liked to call himself "the Bagman," because he thought it gave him a certain criminal cache, but to most folks he was usually just "Bags." Bags was one of the Turner groupies who attended Geauga High back in the glory days, and he still thought Tony and Danny might one day find great fame. Tony thought Bags was an idiot, but he put up with him because he always picked up the tab—and he enjoyed reliving the days when he was the big man on campus.

One night he showed up at Barton's as excited as a dog at dinnertime, convinced he had found just the ticket they were looking for.

"You know that antique shop over in Novelty, the one that sells all that crap like old clocks, paintings, tables, and stuff?" Bags asked smugly. He didn't know it, but he had just asked a rhetorical question.

"Yeah, what about it?" Danny said. "What would we do with that stuff even if we could get that junk out of there?"

"Well, here's the deal. I deliver to that place every day, and I got friendly with that old bald dude, Jack, who hauls the stuff around for the two old farts who own the place. He says they do a lot, I mean *a lot*, of business in cash, and that they take it home to their house in Chagrin Falls, and have it stashed there in a safe."

Tony started to get interested. "Okay, that sounds good, but how are we going to actually get it out of the safe, if we don't know the combination?"

Bags was ready with the answer he knew would impress the guys. "That's the best part. This guy Jack says he knows the combination, and he'll give it to us if we cut him in. He won't help do the break-in, but he'll give us the combination. Better yet, he says they're going down to Florida for a few months in January, and if we give him a thousand bucks up-front, he'll make a copy of the key and tell us the code to the alarm system!" Bags had really done his homework, covering all the bases.

Tony and Danny couldn't believe their good fortune. This was going to be like taking candy from a baby. It felt just like the good old days, when the Turner brothers would snatch victory from the jaws of defeat and score a touchdown in the final seconds of the game, striding off the field like the gladiators they were meant to be.

⇢▸═◉ ◉═◂⇠

Danny, Tony, and Bags managed to scrape together the thousand bucks, and met with Jack the day after Christmas behind the bandstand with the cupola at the park in the center of town. Snow was falling, which was something the folks in Chesterland took for granted this time of year. "Lake effect," they'd say knowingly to one another.

Jack handed over the key as well as the combinations to the safe and the alarm system. He told them the safe was bolted to the floor in the upstairs bedroom. He also made it clear that he knew for a fact there was at least $50,000 in it, so he expected his take would be a minimum of $12,500 and not a penny less. Of course Tony and his buddies had intended to beat Jack out of his share.

Tony stared right into Jack's eyes, giving him his most sincere look. "You don't think we'd cheat ya, do you?"

Jack had a few years on Tony and wasn't about to be taken. "Sure I do, which is why I will be far, far away, out of Ohio, with a rock-solid alibi when you guys do this, and if I don't get my full cut, then I promise you the cops will be tipped off about you three and you'll be toast." If Jack had had an ace on him, he would have pulled it out of his sleeve at that instant. Even Bags could figure out that his cut just went way down.

"A deal's a deal," Tony assured him, annoyed with himself for thinking he could trust a thief to trust a thief.

Now that they had the address, the key, and the combinations, all they had to do was wait for the owners to pack up and go to Florida. With any luck, they wouldn't even discover that the money was missing until they returned a few months later.

⇢⊨◉ ◉⊨⊷

The house was on Maple Street in Chagrin Falls, one of the most picturesque, quintessentially American towns in the country. Downtown Chagrin during the Christmas season could have been the set for *It's a Wonderful Life*. With the enormous white face antique clock smiling down at the end of the square, you half expected to see James Stewart and Donna Reed arm in arm, viewing the spectacular falls where the Chagrin River had a natural drop of fifty feet, and the icy rush of the cascading water created an immediate hypnotic daze. At that time of year, snow usually coated the ground, and the square was ablaze in colorful lights. For families in surrounding towns, it was a tradition to make the annual pilgrimage to Chagrin Falls to get a taste of old-time Christmas. There was no better way to transform a grinch into a good-natured, patient, and generous man or woman.

However, the trio of Tony, Danny, and Bags couldn't have cared less for the festivities and wholesome feeling of the town. They had a plan, and they were starting to get pretty annoyed with the home owners, Don and Linda Grant, for still being in attendance as late as the fifth of January. Jack said they always closed the shop the first weekend after Christmas, packed up the car, and headed south almost immediately. If they didn't leave soon, there might have to be a change of plans, Tony thought.

The Grant home was a classic colonial, bracketed by massive brick chimneys on either side with a generous porch that surrounded the front of the house. The landscaping was immaculate, and the Christmas decorations were tasteful, yet meaningful. There was a manger on one side of the front lawn and a reindeer on the other. The ground was covered with snow, which only added to the simple beauty. At eleven o'clock at night, when the Grants' decorative lights shut off, the nearby street lamp stretched a surreal silhouette of the reindeer that resembled a giant black stallion.

On that particular night, the nefarious trio was brazen enough to pull up in front of the house just after the outdoor lighting went dark. They sat silently and stared into the windows. They could see the movements and hear the sounds of a household shutting down for the night: the TV flickering off, dishes clattering in the kitchen, pillows being fluffed, a phone ringing, muffled conversation, laughter in the distance. Eventually the lights went out downstairs and were turned on upstairs. There wasn't much to see, but the simple act of watching from the shadows gave the guys a thrill. Somebody said he felt like Charles Manson, and they all had to struggle to stifle their laughter.

After all the bedroom lights were turned off, Tony suggested they get out and take a walk around to get the lay of the land. "Make sure you keep your mouth shut," he warned, "and don't knock anything over." They silently worked their way through the front gate and onto the porch. A peek through the window convinced them the Grants had some serious money. This wasn't the usual type of place they hit; this was a real step up. They noticed that the next-door neighbor's house turned slightly toward the Grants', and Tony made a mental note of that. He decided that, when they robbed the place, it would be prudent to wait until around three in the morning, when everyone in the neighborhood would be asleep, and not to turn on the houselights.

They were exhilarated when they got back into the pickup truck. Danny pulled out a pint of vodka, and they passed it around. They knew this was going to be a piece of cake, so they were chomping at the bit to get this party started, and actually put their hands on the cash. The amount of money they were going to pocket in a matter of days would be more than any of them could earn in a year.

Bags lit up a smoke, while Don Grant, who had gotten out of bed because he thought he heard footsteps on the porch followed by the slam of a car door, looked down from his bedroom window and watched the beacon from the cigarette swirl in the darkness. He thought it was a pretty odd scene, but then the truck drove away, and he shrugged and went back to bed. He and Linda had plans to finish packing the next day so they could leave for Florida by the end of the weekend, and he was exhausted.

The gang drove by on Sunday afternoon and the manger and reindeer were no longer in the front yard. The three agreed that Danny was the most respectable-looking of the group, so they parked around the corner while he walked up to the front door and rang the bell. If anyone answered, he would just pretend he was looking for directions. No one answered. Tony still wasn't convinced, so they drove around the front and rear of the house later that night, and it appeared that only a small lamp in the hallway was on, probably managed by the same timer the

Grants used for the Christmas lights. Tony felt they needed a little more preparation, so he decided they would wait one more day to do the job. It was a fateful decision.

→━◎ ◎━←

Around seven o'clock the next night, Danny, Bags, and Tony met in the Turners' finished basement, ostensibly to play cards and have a few beers, but the real reason was to review their plans and gather their equipment for the night. Because they had easy access to the house, they would not need the usual glass cutter or other tools to bust a lock. Tony pointed out that they would not need to take the pistol they had stashed in the shed or any other weapons, because the house would be empty and they would be in and out in a matter of minutes.

Danny shut the basement door and locked it. He went over to the stereo and turned it up a few notches so his parents wouldn't hear what they were talking about. Bags lit a bowl and passed it to Tony, trying to hold in the hit for as long as possible. Robert Plant began quietly singing "Babe I'm Gonna Leave You," and the guys were completely stoned by the time Jimmy Page started his famous riff. Before long they were on their feet, playing some mean air guitar.

"Okay," Tony said, "let's get down to business." They would all dress in dark clothes and wear knit caps. He laid out three flashlights. "We can't turn on the lights. The neighbors might see, and they'd be suspicious if they saw the lights on. We'll have to do this in the dark, with just the flashlights." Tony then took out three pairs of white surgical gloves. "Make sure you put these on before you leave the car."

Bags started to get a bit concerned. "What if the neighbors see the flashlights in the house and call the cops?"

"Yeah, and what if your ass falls off?" Danny said. "We can do this; we just have to use our heads."

Tony and Danny would drive their pickup, and Bags would bring his beat-up Volkswagen Bug. Most important of all, Tony and Danny would bring the two gym bags sitting in the corner for the cash.

"Okay, we'll leave at two on the dot, and take two cars over to Chagrin," Tony whispered in his best conspiratorial voice. "Bags, you park across the street and Danny and me will park in front of the house. When we leave we'll go in opposite directions, and meet back at your apartment." As an actual matter of fact, Tony and Danny had decided they would stop at home first, leave some of the cash behind, and then meet up with Bags at his place. However, they didn't call him "the Bagman" for nothing; Bags had already decided to bring his backpack, so he would get his fair share. By now, he'd spent enough time around the Turner boys to know that honesty was not one of their strengths.

With the plans laid out, they hid everything in the closet, unlocked the door, and played a few hands of poker. Danny made a point of loudly protesting the bad hand he'd been dealt so his parents wouldn't think anything suspicious was going on. The Monday Night Football game was on and Howard Cosell droned away in the background. It was just a month ago that he was the first to announce John Lennon's death to the nation. Now the shock was starting to wear off. When Mrs. Turner came down with bowls of potato chips and popcorn, it looked like a typical Monday night. They're not such bad boys after all, she thought as she headed back upstairs.

At roughly the same moment, over in Chagrin Falls, a car was pulling into the Grants' garage. Kevin Grant and his wife, Missy, had driven from Chicago that day, and were planning to head to Florida on Wednesday. Kevin's parents had helped him and Missy get a start in the antique business, and every January they too would close their shop and go down to Boca for a visit to escape the Windy City at the worst time of year. The young couple was especially excited because they planned to surprise Don and Linda with the news that they would be grandparents before the end of the year. They smiled at each other as they watched the garage door open, relieved to have arrived safely after their harrowing eight-hour drive along some very icy and snowy roads.

Once inside, they disarmed the security system, and they sat down to relax and have a sandwich and a slice of the crumb cake Linda left out with a note: "We can't wait to see the two of you. Don't forget your bathing suits! Love, Mom." At around eleven, Kevin checked all the doors and re-set the alarm system. Missy turned off all the lights (including the lamp on the timer), and the couple went upstairs to Kevin's old room, which now served as the guest bedroom. As they slid under the cool sheets, Kevin said he expected to "sleep like a stone," and Missy came back with "like a log!" Kevin laughed and gave her a goodnight kiss. Within a few minutes they were both dead to the world.

At the same time, at around eleven, Tony and Danny got antsy, and decided to do another drive-by just to make one last check. The coast was clear. "Measure twice, cut once," Tony said as they drove off to their destiny. Tonight would be the night.

⊷┅▦ ▦┅⊷

Tony cut the engine as he glided into the space in front of the Grants' home. A few minutes later, they heard the signature grind of Bags's Bug coming down the road, and Danny and Tony rolled their eyes at each other as their fear that they might have a weak link in the chain was confirmed. Now that they were there, really there, ready to do the job, much of their bravado was gone, though neither would admit it. There was no turning back now, in any event, and besides, an easier job was never going to come their way. That magnificent fifty-thousand-dollar figure had burrowed its way into their minds and wouldn't let go.

Yet the unspoken, or perhaps unrealized, sense that it was all too good to be true hung in the air. If they had taken the time to think things through, they would have realized that the entire plan rested on a stranger whose last name they did not even know, who was now hundreds of miles away, along with one James K. Bagneski, who barely would have qualified to carry their spikes a few years earlier. But greed, ignorance, and delusion kept those nettlesome thoughts tucked away, out of site, and made certain they were delivered to this very moment.

So, on the short journey from their home to the Grants' house, as the pickup seemed to drive itself, the brothers sat in silence, each lost in his own thoughts.

Tony planned to take his share of the cash and move to another part of the country. He wasn't quite sure where, but a girl he'd dated had moved to Monterey, and the last time they spoke he promised he would come out for a visit. He figured that was about as good a place as any, and now he would have the money to do it. Who knew? Maybe he would stay there for a while, or go someplace else, but it sure was time he got out of his parents' house. He needed to start over where no one knew him and had all of these big expectations. He hated the look of disappointment when he told local folks what he was up to these days, which was basically nothing, or nothing he could talk about. Tony knew there had to be something better for him out there, but at twenty-two, he didn't yet know what it was.

Danny looked out the window and started to think about the voice. That's what he called it: "the voice." This was the voice inside of him that told him what to do and what not to do. He wasn't sure where it came from, but he knew it was there, knew it was real, and knew it was his friend. When he was alone, driving the pickup or walking in the woods, he would talk out loud to it, but most times it was just there in his head. It really came alive in '78, on the field, when all of a sudden something would seem to take control of his legs and tell him to "cut right, turn left"; he would put his head down and run, and a few seconds later look over his shoulder to see the pigskin about to land in his hands.

He remembered one day when he was a little kid, maybe around nine or ten, and was in the supermarket. He had a Hershey bar in his hand and was heading for the cash register, when the voice said "just put it in your pocket and walk out," and he did. "Just walk like nothing's wrong," it said. He walked to the corner, convinced the store owner was on his heels, but he did what the voice said to do. He resisted the urge to run until he turned the corner, and then he scooted behind a building. Much to his relief, no one came after him, and he squatted there, trembling, eating his free candy bar. As time went on, things like that became easier, because he came to rely upon the secret guidance he knew was his and his alone.

Once, when he was doing fifty-five on Mayfield, in a stretch where the limit was thirty-five, he looked into the rear view mirror and saw the flashing lights behind him. He thought, "I'll make a break for it," but the voice shouted, "Just pull over; I'll make sure you get off." And sure enough, the cop turned out to be the father of the kid who played center on the team, and there was no way he was about to give a Turner boy a ticket. "Just try not to have such a heavy foot, Danny," he said. The voice knew.

So when Danny got a very strong message to reach under his seat and take the tire iron with him, he knew it was the right thing to do.

Tony looked at him like he was out of his mind. "What the hell are you bringing that for? You know the place is empty. We have to get in, open the safe, take the cash, and get out of there as fast as possible. You won't need that!"

"Who knows if we will? What's the difference? I'll just leave it in the gym bag, just in case."

"In case of what?" At times like these, Tony knew there was no talking sense to his brother, who could be so thick-headed. Anyway, Bags was on his way across the street, pulling on his gloves; it was time to get to work.

Tony unlocked the front door while Danny and Bags pressed into the shadows, following him inside once it was open. Great! The key worked. They shut the door. Now it was up to Danny to punch in the security code while Bags shined his flashlight on the keypad. It beeped a few times, but they were done in a flash, and, amazingly, good old Jack had given them the right code.

The plan was for Tony to take the lead, using only his flashlight to illuminate the way. They would head directly to the master bedroom, open the safe, take out every last dollar, scoot down the stairs, punch in the exit code, and close and lock the door. There would be no stopping to look for jewelry or pinching something one of them might want to grab. By the time the robbery was discovered, the crocuses would be forcing their way up through the earth. So far things were going just as planned. It bothered Tony that the lamp he thought was on a timer wasn't on. The bulb must have burnt out, he reasoned.

They crossed the foyer and started up the steps. The house was old, so the steps creaked, but that didn't concern them because they knew the house was vacant. In a hushed voice, Danny said, "Remember, we have to turn left at the top of the stairs." He could hear his heart pounding and the blood rushing through his head; he barely could find the breath to speak. Suddenly he wanted this to be over with. Something was wrong; he knew it, but he dared not say anything to his brother because Tony hated it when Danny had one of his stupid "feelings."

They gathered at the landing and the beam from Tony's flashlight hit the chrome of the bathroom faucet, and then lit on the door to the master bedroom, which was closed. They were at the door in a few seconds, and it clicked open when Tony twisted the knob. Kevin stirred in the guest bedroom, mumbled something to Missy about hearing the alarm go off, and then turned over and went back to sleep.

Tony saw the three of them reflected in the blackness of the mirror, and thought how young and frightened they all looked—Danny in particular, with those big eyes poking out of his head. He silently pointed to the closet door. "That's the one," he whispered. When they opened the door, it was just as they had imagined.

This was the real deal. The safe stood about two feet high, was gun-metal gray, and was bolted to the floor. There was no way anyone was ever going to carry that baby out of there. Bags was reputed to have nimble fingers, so it was his job to turn the combination lock to the correct numbers. He squatted down, and Tony realized for the first time that he was wearing a backpack.

Danny shined his light on the piece of paper Jack had given them the day after Christmas. Bags's hand was shaking so badly that Danny had to reach down and hold his wrist. But within a few turns they heard the cylinders click into place. Bags turned the handle and pulled out one of the drawers; it was filled with piles of neatly stacked cash.

"All right!" Bags exclaimed. "We hit the mother lode!"

In their excitement, they forgot their promise to keep the noise down, but it didn't matter. What mattered was getting the cash into the bags and getting the hell out of there. Tony unzipped his bag and started feeding the cash into it.

Missy and Kevin both bolted upright when they heard voices down the hall.

"Somebody's in the house," she whispered. "We better call the cops."

"The only phone up here is in Mom and Dad's room. I'm going to go check this out."

Missy groped around, found a kids-size baseball bat, and whispered, "Here, you'd better take this; maybe it will scare them away. Be careful!"

Kevin crept down the hall in the dark, reached around the wall, and turned on the bedroom lights. He saw three men gathered around the open safe, and they turned around at once, clearly startled and shocked.

"What the hell are you doing here?" he shouted, lifting the bat above his head.

"We were just leaving," Tony said. "Don't do anything stupid and no one will get hurt." He tried to sound menacing but knew this was a bad situation about to get much worse. He put his hands up as if to imply that he was giving up, but now he was glad Danny had prepared and figured he would know what to do.

Danny was kneeling next to his bag; he slid his hand in and gripped the tire iron. Then a woman in a nightgown appeared at the door, and the guy with the bat said, "Missy, go downstairs and call the cops, right now."

When Kevin moved a step closer, Danny whipped out the tire iron and clubbed him around the knee, and the guy brought the bat down on Danny's head. Tony jumped in and tried to grab the bat, but the man was swinging it furiously. Somehow Danny managed to stand up and wildly swing the tire iron. He caught the guy on the side of the neck, which knocked him down and out cold, but then Danny started beating him on the back, shouting, "Bastard, don't you ever hit me!"

Tony jumped in and said, "Stop! We've got to get out of here." Bags grabbed the gym bag with the cash and ran down the steps and out the door.

When Tony got to the bottom of the steps, he saw the woman dialing on the phone in the kitchen. He ran in the room, pulled the phone from her hand, and ripped it out of the wall, inadvertently sending her flying across the floor. Holding the phone like a club, he leaned over her and threatened to kill her if she called the cops; then he turned and ran out the door. Missy sat crumpled on the floor, trembling and calling out for Kevin to come downstairs. Eventually, when she found him, her shrieks echoed throughout the neighborhood.

CHAPTER 5

Crossroads

Our lives are the sum total of the choices we have made.

—Wayne Dyer

DANNY AND TONY rushed off to track down Bags and get their fair share (and beat him to a pulp), but he was nowhere to be found. It turned out the bag he ran off with contained around ten thousand dollars. That's roughly the amount the police gathered up after it went flying through the windshield, along with Bags, when his VW Bug took off like a missile and collided head-on with a big oak on Winding Way in Gates Mills. The police estimated he was going at least seventy miles per hour. In his obituary, it was noted that he was a graduate of Geauga High and an avid football fan.

By the time Danny and Tony reached their street, the sun was coming up. There were several police cars in the driveway. The brothers backed up when they saw the twirling lights, but made it only as far as Mentor before they were apprehended. Missy had attended Geauga High and recognized Tony and Danny for the stars they used to be. The Chesterland police were not at all surprised, but they were mighty disappointed in the Turner boys. The officers who were assigned the duty of breaking the news to Steve and Debby did so with the great delicacy and sympathy only another parent could understand.

Kevin Grant spent almost a month in the hospital and suffered a brain injury at the base of his skull, along with numerous broken ribs and a punctured lung. A few more strokes with that tire iron and he probably wouldn't have recovered. Don and Linda Grant flew back that day and were horrified to see the condition of their son, their house, and their daughter-in-law. Linda began to cry when she saw Kevin, and didn't stop until that night when Missy took her aside and told her the good news about the baby that was due later that year.

Because of the ghastliness of the crime—and the bitter irony of the fleeting fame once enjoyed by the Turner boys—it was the top news story in the Cleveland area for a few days back in January of 1981. The court proceedings were handled quickly; because there were two eye-witnesses, Tony and Danny were advised to take a plea bargain. And so they were each sentenced to a minimum of ten years and a maximum of twenty-five. The Grants, and in particular Kevin, thought they had gotten off too easily, but they wanted to get on with their lives, so they finally agreed with the prosecutor and the sentence was passed.

For the first year, they were held in the same part of the Chillicothe Correctional Institution and had some contact, but then Danny was moved to a unit on the other side of the prison, and they could only communicate by letter or by an occasional phone call.

Tony, in particular, seemed to mature while in prison. He realized that this was an opportunity to take a new direction once he was released, and, if he played by the rules, he might get out early. He was determined to make something of himself. While in prison, he attended anger-management classes and constantly read books on business and self-improvement. He even began to develop a sense of gratitude about his situation. He knew they had come pretty close to killing someone that night, and if not that night, it would have happened another time. He accepted the fact that they were fortunate they were caught.

He felt sorry for Danny, and somewhat responsible, but there wasn't much he could do for him.

Danny, on the other hand, couldn't get over the fact that the Grant kid picked that night to "sneak" into his house right before they showed up to rob the place. He was angry about his rotten luck, didn't think life had given him a fair shake, and refused to discuss his real feelings with the prison psychologist or anyone else who might have helped him. There were a few other guys in the prison who were equally angry about their situations, and they fed each other a steady diet of resentment. They all agreed they were entitled to their bitterness because it helped them to keep their dignity, which was one of the few things they had left—and they were not about to let anyone take that away.

After Danny was relocated, Tony started to write to him to encourage him to make the best of his time in prison, and to try to admit that what they did was wrong, really wrong, and that he was lucky he hadn't hit that Grant guy three inches higher on his head, because he would have killed him. At least now he had a shot at getting out and another chance to make things right.

Danny wasn't convinced, and told Tony that he was going to play along with the system because it benefited him, and earned him certain privileges that made life a little more tolerable. He resented having to take the classes on anger, and thought the psychologist he had to see was a sucker. So he enjoyed pretending that he had seen the error of his ways and was going to change. He tucked a Bible under his arm when he went to his sessions, and started to quote scripture. Every once in a while something he read would strike him as a real truth, but then his inner voice would tell him he was being played for a fool, and he'd quickly reverse himself. No, all he wanted was to get out and stay out. In that respect, he learned something: crime really didn't pay and he needed to pick up some skills. One of the things his voice told him was that he shouldn't listen to Tony: if he hadn't done his bidding in the first place, he wouldn't be sitting in prison.

He discovered that he was naturally good at auto repair, and so he learned as much as he could about that subject. He even took a class that was offered, and decided it was something he could do when he got out—if only that day would come.

Steve and Debby Turner visited as often as possible. Debby always told herself that she was not going to cry, but then she would spend a good deal of the visit tearing up, blurting out things like "What did I do to cause this?," "If only we had gone to church more often as a family, but your father had no interest," "Anthony and Daniel were such good boys when they were young," and, her favorite, "It's really a shame you boys got mixed up with that bad apple, James Bagneski."

Most of the time, Steve would just sit quietly, unable to say what he thought because he really didn't know what to think. He preferred to stick to his memories of his two sons playing ball in the front yard until it was so dark they couldn't see a thing. He remembered leaning over Tony's shoulder as they sat at the kitchen table and diagrammed the plays they invented. It was satisfying to watch their excitement, but it was the love Tony and Danny had for each other that truly gave him confidence in a secure future. Getting them to do their homework was another matter, but Steve didn't care too much, because some part of him bought into the fantasy that his kids would one day play pro sports, or at worst get athletic scholarships to college.

Life was so simple then. Pajamas, football, family dinner, more love than any two kids could expect from the best mother in the world—and yet here they were, sitting in jail. Steve was planning to retire early because he just couldn't stand the way people looked at him down at Jayomar. Either they smirked and whispered to each other or gave him a look of pity. But what Steve didn't realize was that most of the decent folks didn't like to think about what had happened to Steve and Debby, because, as parents, it frightened them. If this tragedy could happen to the Turners, maybe it could happen to them. So, if they thought about it at all, it was to tell themselves that this horror came about because of something that lurked behind the walls of the Turner home, which would never invade their household. It was sort of like asking if the person who died of cancer had been a smoker.

Tony and Danny endured these visits from their parents, but except for the small items they were allowed to receive, such as toothpaste and books, there weren't too many positive things that came out of these sad get-togethers. Both sons hated to be reminded of the pain and shame they had brought upon their parents, and they were truly perplexed as to how their lives had gone from good to bad to horrible so quickly.

As Tony grew in his faith, he was able to see that things had gone downhill little by little, because of the numerous bad decisions he had made. Pride had played a big role in his decline. After all, by the time he was a junior in high school, he was used to being the most popular kid in school; he believed this was his due and expected it would continue throughout his life. One day, when his mom came alone for a visit, he told her about some of the lessons he had learned, and honestly asked her to forgive him. It was the first time he saw her truly smile since that night in January. That's when Tony realized these visits were for his mother and his father, not for him and Danny, and he needed to see them in a new light. He also saw that the truth was very powerful.

Danny, too, felt a responsibility to try to cheer up his parents when they met. He could always get his dad to talk about the rivalry between the Browns and the Steelers, or gripe about how poorly the Indians were doing, but it was a mistake to go near reality. Once he slipped and said, "The first thing I'm gonna do when I get out of here is go down to Cleveland Stadium to see the Indians or Browns. Whatever time of year it is." The awkward silence that followed spoke volumes, and then his mom began to weep.

The topic of just how long they would have to stay in jail always brought the discussion to a sad ending. The reality was that it was possible they would be in prison for another twenty years. To young men in their twenties this prospect was horrifying. While other young men their age were starting families and building their careers, they were stuck in this place, for "one stupid mistake," as Debby often said, concluding with "it's just not fair." The prospect that they might not be free until they were in their forties was daunting.

And so it went for several years. One of the reasons Tony was able to change and grow was thanks to the regular visits from Joe Hamilton, Carolyn's father. He knew the boys from coaching them in baseball and, as a man of faith, felt it was his obligation to visit them and, by his presence, let them know that someone cared about and forgave them. He visited each of them and encouraged them to find the strength every day to get the most out of life, despite their situation, and never to give up hope, because miracles were always possible. Both Tony and Danny appreciated his visits, and even Danny, who was usually uncomfortable talking about his feelings, would sincerely thank him for coming. Mr. Hamilton never failed to bring each of them a few copies of *Sports Illustrated*, and they would pore over these pages again and again.

Then one day that miracle Mr. Hamilton had been talking about happened. They each received an identical letter from Kevin Grant. Yes, the very same Kevin Grant whom Danny had clubbed in the head, whose pregnant wife had been shoved to the floor, whose parents' house they had robbed, and who had spent a month in the hospital and another year recovering from the wounds they had inflicted.

He wrote that after years of hating them, he had come to the conclusion that the only way he could be free of his misery was to forgive them. He wanted to write to their warden and ask for a meeting with them, so he could personally forgive them. He needed to do this for himself, not for them, and he wanted their permission before he wrote to the warden.

Imagine that, thought Tony. *Here we beat the crap out of this guy and, four years later, he's asking us for permission to come and forgive us!* There was honesty in that letter that was undeniable. Jesus taught that unless you can forgive those who have harmed you, you will never be free. Tony remembered the verses as: "And forgive us our debts, as we forgive our debtors" and "forgive our trespasses as we forgive those who trespass against us." He realized how powerful these words were when they were lived, not just recited, like he had done in church as a little boy. Tony wrote back to Kevin to tell him how touched he was, and that he would, of course, be happy to see him.

Danny read the letter over about six times. He couldn't believe his eyes. Why would a guy he almost killed want to come to see him to forgive him? At first he was touched, and he even found himself holding the letter and tearing up a bit. He started to talk to God, and a newfound sense of freedom began to come over him. But then the voice began to whisper: There was something fishy about the whole thing. This Grant guy must want something. Maybe he was just doing this to make himself look holier than thou. Maybe he wanted to go to the press and say, "Look at me! Look at what a great guy I am." Just because Danny was in prison didn't mean that anyone was better than him. *But Kevin Grant could be useful,* the voice advised him. *Meet with him. Maybe he'll help you earn a "get out of jail early" card.* Danny thought using some of the scripture he'd learned might do the trick. Always mix in some truth with a lie. He looked in the mirror. *Never forget who you are, Danny,* he said to himself, *and never again let anyone take advantage of you.*

His psychologist was pleased that Danny wanted to ask for forgiveness and helped him write his response:

Dear Mr. Grant,

I was very touched to receive your letter. Of course I would be happy to meet with you, but I don't know that I am worthy of such forgiveness. I have studied the Bible, and have come to love Jesus, but I am nowhere near being a forgiving person. The truth is that I am bitter about being in jail and seeing my life slip away, unable to do the simple things in life because of my mistakes. I hope we can meet soon because I want to reach the point where I can be free of my anger, and I am sure that just seeing you and being forgiven by you would help tremendously.

I am very grateful for your offer.

Yours in Christ,

Danny Turner

⋅⇥⟩⟨⇤⋅

The warden was a little suspicious of Kevin Grant's true motives. After all, it would be pretty embarrassing if Mr. Grant actually had retribution on his mind rather than forgiveness. But after meeting with him, he agreed to permit him a supervised visit with Tony and Danny.

He arranged for them to meet in a small conference room that was reserved for family visits. The meeting would be private, except for the presence of a prison guard.

Danny was the first to arrive. He was lead into a nondescript room that was painted the sort of muted color he had come to expect in institutions. He sat there in the room alone, and looked out the window. It was clear, except for the wire embedded inside the glass. In the distance, beyond the prison wall, he could see the town of Chillicothe, the church spires rising up above the surrounding buildings. It was two in the afternoon; outside the sun was shining and he knew the temperature was in the nineties. The air conditioner hummed away, so it was almost chilly in the room. He was glad he would see Tony, but had his doubts about how things would go with Grant. He still could not believe the guy was for real.

The door opened, and in walked Tony. They had not seen each other in over a year, but they had spoken on the phone a few times. They hugged and then stepped back to look at each other.

"Man, you look great," Danny said, a little envious. "You look like you've been on vacation in the Caribbean or something!"

"You look good, too, Little Brother," Tony replied, but he was a little alarmed by the stilted sadness he detected in his brother's eyes.

They knew they only had a few minutes before Kevin Grant arrived, and so they talked quickly back and forth about how amazing it was they were having this meeting. Tony was totally convinced Grant was sincere. He had developed a regular practice of praying and reading the Bible himself, and understood the concept of forgiveness. "We need to forgive ourselves for our mistakes, first of all, bro," he said, putting his hand on Danny's shoulder, and looking him straight in the eye. "This isn't BS. I've really changed."

Danny was about to say he could see that something was different about Tony, when the door opened again and there stood Kevin Grant. He hadn't been able to attend the court proceedings due to his condition, so the last time these three were in the same room was on that fateful night, when they were clubbing and swearing at one another.

The officer who escorted him into the room suggested they shake hands, and then said they should sit across from one another at the conference table in the center of the room—Danny and Tony on one side, Kevin on the other. The officer stood off by the window, but his nightstick swung by his side and he reminded the group that there would be no shouting or any other violent action. This was a highly unusual meeting, and they were only doing it "because of the persistence of Mr. Grant," he added.

Kevin looked different from the person Tony and Danny remembered seeing that night. He seemed older. That may have been due to the fact that the newspaper articles always included a picture of Kevin from his college yearbook or his wedding, and that was a long time ago. He was a clean-cut sort of guy, six feet tall, with dirty blond hair and dark eyes. He had grown a mustache, and that made him look a little older as well. However, he seemed imbued with a definite happiness, and greeted them with a wide smile that broke the ice.

"I know you guys must think I'm crazy or some sort of religious fanatic, but I want you to know that I'm neither, and I appreciate this," he said, gesturing as though inviting them to sit at his table for dinner, and then sitting down himself. "They're only going to give us fifteen minutes to meet, so I want to say what I have to say, because I've been thinking about this moment for a long time."

Feeling incredibly uncomfortable, the brothers mumbled something along the lines of "no, we really are grateful, go ahead, and say what you want to say."

"Well, as I said in my letter, I spent the first few years after that night being driven crazy by my anger at the two of you and that other guy who killed himself in Gates Mills. I just couldn't accept that anyone could be so horrible and selfish and brutal as to break into someone's house, steal their money, and then beat me almost to death and throw my pregnant wife on the floor." He looked at Tony when he said the last few words. This was not going the way the brothers had expected, and the officer moved a step closer to the table.

"I would lie in bed at night and replay the incident, wishing I had taken the bat and smashed both of you in the head, and just put a stop to the whole thing. Why didn't I defend my wife? I was angry at myself, and I felt like a coward, because when I turned on the light and saw the three of you, I was terrified for me and my wife."

"Listen, man, we're sorry—" Tony started, but Kevin cut him off with a wave of his hand.

"I know you are, because you got caught, but it easily could have gone the other way. I might have been killed, and Missy too, and it could have been a lot worse. But I wasn't able to see that for a long, long time. After I recovered and could go back to work, and our son was born, I thought I would be able to get back to normal, but instead, I started sinking deeper and deeper into a depression. My wife made me see a shrink, but all he did was make me talk about my rage, and that just made it worse.

"Then one night, I left my shop around eight o'clock, and I saw this guy Harold, who often slept on the grate outside my store to keep warm. He was talking to this very unusual-looking woman with long, white hair, who seemed to be very excited and then suddenly gave Harold a big hug. I like Harold and all, but, well, he was filthy, and I would never have even shaken hands with him, let alone hug him. But there she was, treating him like a long-lost relative. She was clearly a very spiritual person."

Danny now figured the guy for a religious nut who imagined he had seen the Virgin Mary or Mother Theresa on the street in Chicago, and he figured he knew where this was going. Kevin started to remind him of the sort of sucker who gets pulled into a church and winds up giving away the family jewels.

"So, I was just walking on past them, and I gave Harold the wave and nod I usually gave him, when he called out to me and said, 'Kevin, this is Joanna. Slow down, man. She wants to talk to you.' Then the woman turned to me and said, 'You must be Kevin. Harold has told me about your sadness, and I see it in your eyes. I have to tell you one thing. Let go of your anger. Give it to God. Go home tonight and pray for the men who hurt you. Do it every day, and really mean it. Speak out loud to God. Pray that these men you hate will be happy, and one day free, and pray for God to allow you to forgive them, because that is the only way *you* will ever be free. And, one more thing: your plan for tonight is a very bad idea.'" Kevin continued to speak, but tears started to run down his cheeks.

"You see, when I met this woman, I was heading to my car to take all of the pills I had brought from home that morning. I planned to just sit in my car and die. I couldn't see all the wonderful things I had to live for, like Missy and my son, my parents, my friends, and everything else in my life. I hated the way I felt, and I was filled with so much hate for the two of you, and for myself for not being a man that night, that I couldn't even see what my death would do to all the people who loved me, and how much I had to live for.

"Then this woman gathered me into a circle with Harold, and the three of us prayed. She gave me this very intense stare, like she could see into my mind, and I went weak in the knees and almost fell over, but Harold held me up. Finally, when she was through praying, she held my hands and looked even more deeply at me, and then she touched my cheek. It was so gentle, like a mother touching her child. And then she just walked away.

"When I got to my car, I looked at the bottle of pills, but instead of swallowing them, I prayed out loud like she said to do. I even prayed for you guys to have good lives, and I prayed to be able to forgive you, and I prayed for forgiveness for myself. And then the most amazing thing happened. I started to feel free. I felt God come into my life and I knew I had been blessed."

By now, all three men were weeping, and they just naturally reached out their hands and touched one another. The officer struggled to hold back tears. He knew this was a moment of grace like none he had ever seen before.

Kevin asked if it would be okay for him to say a prayer, and the brothers both nodded. "Lord, thank you for bringing the three of us together today," he prayed. "Help us to forgive one another, and help our wounds to heal. Please give my brothers, Tony and Danny, happy, productive lives with all the freedom your world has to offer. Amen."

They all leaned back in their chairs. The time limit had expired. The police officer took off his cap, put both palms flat on the table, cleared his throat, and said, "Gentlemen, I'm afraid our time is up. Mr. Grant, I'll escort you out."

He broke protocol and turned his back while the three men hugged at the door.

⭑⭓⭑

A battle raged inside of Danny later that night, when he was alone back in his cell. The voice threatened, screamed that Grant was just a kook, and that Tony hadn't really had any sort of conversion. But Danny could not deny how he had felt the moment they held hands and said that prayer. He also had a vision of a woman with long, white hair and olive-colored skin, who was looking at him with the most beatific smile. He only knew her through Kevin Grant's description, but when he closed his eyes he could see her as if she were standing right there in the cell with him.

Danny knew something was different; it was like a wind had passed through him and wiped him clean. He didn't want to be a cynic any longer. All night he tossed and turned, and had crazy, vivid dreams. When the morning light came through his window, he awoke. He was lying there, half awake, half asleep, when he heard the sound of beautiful music, like a mother singing a lullaby—only he knew it was meant to wake him up, not put him to sleep. Then he spoke to God. He rejected the voice he had heard in his head all these years. He acknowledged it for what it was: It wasn't his friend. It was his enemy. It was evil.

⭑⭓⭑

Danny and Tony were released roughly a year later. It seemed that everyone around them noticed a genuine change had taken place. The officer who was in the room that day was an old friend of the warden's, and he told him his life had been changed when he watched those three boys pray.

When they were given a hearing for early release, the committee considering their cases read letters of support from Linda, Kevin, and Missy Grant. Don Grant wanted nothing to do with it, however. Throughout their years in prison, Danny and Tony had maintained exemplary records, so they were on very solid ground. The decision to grant them early release was unanimous.

As it turned out, Tony was released a day before Danny, so he was there with his parents to greet Danny at the prison gate the next day. Later that day, they went to a restaurant to celebrate, and Danny and Tony felt as if a miracle had happened. Everyone smiled, laughed, and cried with relief. Then Tony, ever the pragmatist, said, "I wonder if anyone will hire us, given our record."

Steve and Debby looked at each other and smiled, as if they knew a secret. "Well, boys," Steve said, "I guess *I* could take a chance on you."

Then he explained that he had decided to leave Jayomar, but had saved enough money to start the sporting goods store he'd always wanted to own, and he wanted his sons to help him run it. The name even had a nice ring to it. He would call it Steve's Sporting Goods. It was time for all of them to start over, he said. "Everyone deserves a second chance, boys. Let's give it our best shot and see if we can't make a success out of the place."

-→-►━⊙ ⊙━◄-←-

"So, how are you doing, Danny?" asked Mike Berger, Danny's probation officer.

"Well, I knew you were gonna ask me that, Mike, and I was wondering how I could honestly answer you. The truth is that things are better than I ever could have imagined. Working with Tony and my dad has been really good, and I have to admit that I'm just trying to keep it simple."

"Have you met anyone yet?" At their last meeting, Danny had mentioned he was pretty lonely, and that most of the decent women didn't want anything to do with him. He had met a few girls, but just for fun, and he felt like life was passing him by. He was about twenty-six now, and most of his friends had gone to college, gotten into the workforce, and were married or about to get married. He didn't want to settle, however. He wanted to meet someone he could count on as a life mate, so just getting involved with someone to pass the time was something he had decided to avoid. This was all part of the new Danny, the grown man who was honest with himself.

"Well, Mike, that hasn't changed much. It seems that a guy with a prison record isn't seen as such a great catch. I guess I'm just gonna have to be patient."

Danny didn't realize it, but his patience was about to pay off.

That night Danny met up with Tony and a few of his buddies for their regular Thursday night game of hoops. They would generally get around ten or twelve guys on a regular basis, and play for about two hours before calling it quits. Of course, these were competitive men who played to win, but the idea was to get some exercise and have some fun. Danny and Tony got involved with this group shortly after leaving Chillicothe, when they met Mitch Bianci. Mitch was a young architect who designed the interior of the first Steve's Sporting Goods store and, as luck would have it, became a trusted friend.

Mitch had graduated from Geauga High a few years before Tony and Danny, and had gone out of state to college, so he wasn't around town at the time of the incident in Chagrin Falls. After school, he had taken a position with an architectural firm in Boise, and had recently moved back into the area. He didn't know the first thing about the Turner brothers' past when he met with Steve Turner to discuss the interior design of the store. When Steve let something slip about his sons' prison time, Mitch noticed his embarrassment.

"Look, Steve," he said. "I don't feel that I'm in a position to judge anyone. I've learned that I'm better off leaving that to God." Mitch said this in a way that impressed Steve. Here was a young man who wasn't afraid to come right out and talk about his faith.

"That's how I try to live my life," Mitch continued. "I don't always succeed, but I try. I've certainly made my mistakes, and I don't expect others to judge me, so I try to stay away from that. In my business, you go into people's homes and you learn a lot about folks, even if they are only talking about adding on a bedroom or something. If there's one thing you find out, it's that nobody's perfect."

Tony came into the room a few minutes later as Mitch was packing up to leave, and Steve introduced them. Mitch took one look at Tony and knew he was just the sort of guy who would fit in at the basketball meet-ups.

"Tony, if you're ever looking for something to do on a Thursday night," Mitch said, "a bunch of us have a pickup game of basketball every Thursday over at the gym at St. Francis on Mayfield. We start around seven, and play until we're ready to fall over." Mitch sized Tony up as a pretty good athlete, at first glance, and they could always use another player for hoops. "Give it a try sometime," he said, as he headed out the door.

So the following Thursday night, Tony and Danny went over to the gym and, frankly, wowed the other guys. If there was one thing the Turner boys knew how to do, it was play ball of any type. They immediately formed a genuine friendship with Mitch. Once they got comfortable with him, Tony mentioned something about their past. Danny always avoided the topic, but Tony took it for what it was. Like Mitch, he'd read several self-help books, and knew that hiding behind your secrets just brought you down.

"Tony, can I ask you something personal?" Mitch said as they were toweling off one night.

"Sure. Let me guess. You're probably going to ask what it was like in prison, right?"

"No, actually, I wanted to know what you'd learned from the experience."

Tony looked down for a minute, and laughed to himself. "You got about a week to listen to my story? I learned a lot, but it's almost impossible to put it into words. I knew I was heading the wrong way for a long time, but, to tell you the truth, I think it started with simple things, like laziness and arrogance, or pride."

Mitch nodded. He knew what Tony meant because he had grappled with the same issues in his young life.

"Things just came easily to me when I was young. I didn't have to study much, but always got good grades. I was usually the best player on any team we had, and sports was pretty much my life. Then, when I discovered that the cute girls and the easy girls in school went for my bad boy act, I just played that up.

"Before I knew it, I was out of high school. When I didn't get an athletic scholarship, I was pretty surprised. So rather than paying to go to school, I figured, screw them, I don't need to waste my time with that. When I look back, I can see that if I hadn't let my pride get in the way, things would have been different.

"It's no one thing, Mitch. It's lots of little things put together. So, I accept that prison may have been the best thing ever to happen to me, and now I intend to work my ass off to make something of myself instead of feeling sorry for myself. You get it?"

"I get it," Mitch said, and he really did.

⇢═ ═◖═

Around that time, Tony met a smart and attractive young woman named Emily, and it was clear they had fallen in love. She accepted him for who he was, despite his past mistakes, and she encouraged him to grab life with both hands and go for it. She was a big fan of his Thursday night hoops because she knew how good it was for him to excel at something again, and frankly it got him out of her hair for a night. He was nuts about her, and the feeling was mutual. Danny and Mitch were both a bit envious, which meant they teased Tony endlessly about Emily.

Time wore on and Mitch and Danny continued not to be so lucky in love. Because Danny was such a good-looking guy, he didn't have any trouble getting dates, but when he saw the relationship Tony had with Emily, he knew that real love was worth the wait. Mitch was a bit of a perfectionist, and was convinced he would know the right woman on sight when she came along. Danny told him he had been reading too many of those weird books he was always talking about, but Mitch was unshakable in his conviction. So there they were, both reasonably good catches in their twenties who had outgrown the dating game. And that's how they found themselves on a Friday night with nothing to do.

After hoops that night, Danny mentioned he'd run into a girl he knew from his childhood, who had told him about a club up in Put-in-Bay, on Lake Erie, where they had terrific live music every Friday night. It was called Lakeside Bar, and she had suggested they check it out. Initially Mitch wasn't very interested, until Danny told him that Macon Peach, an Allman Brothers cover band, would be playing. They were supposed to be incredible; the two guitarists could knock off the harmonic lead guitar parts note for note. Mitch liked Southern rock a lot, but he absolutely loved the Allman Brothers, so he was sold.

As they expected, the dance floor was crowded when they got there, and Danny looked around for his friend, Carolyn Hamilton. Danny felt a special bond with Carolyn because of her father's visits when they were at Chillicothe, though they never talked about that time. Finally he spotted her across the floor, with an entourage of guys circling her. When she saw Danny, she ran over and told him how glad she was that he had made it because she had someone she wanted to introduce—or rather reintroduce—to him.

"Reintroduce, what do you mean?"

"A long time ago, when you were leaving the field after a game, I introduced you to my good friend Rachel, but you were too busy running off to a keg party to notice," she said, with a laugh.

"Well that sounds like me, back then. By the way, I want you to meet my friend, Mitch."

All this time Mitch had been standing there, admiring Carolyn's golden hair, deep-blue eyes, and great shape, feeling a little like Michael Corleone when he was struck by the thunderbolt. He was smitten just looking at her, but then when she laughed and smiled, and he heard her voice, he literally felt a flash. He felt as if he had known her all his life, though he had yet to say a word to her. He knew she was the one he had been searching for.

Mitch, who was normally quite talkative, was speechless. He opened his mouth and out came a sort of croaking sound, leading Carolyn to cup her ear and shout, "What did you say?" The music was pretty loud, so that gave him a chance to regroup.

Danny jumped in to save his friend. "Mitch is a great guy. He's an okay basketball player, but just about the best architect you'll ever meet. He went to Geauga a few years ahead of us."

Mitch got back to his natural footing and started talking about the high school, and some of the teachers there. Carolyn said her favorite was Mr. Ercolano, and Mitch mentioned that he'd heard he quit teaching to go write the Great American Novel, and on it went. Then Carolyn spotted Rachel, and said excitedly, "Danny, there she is. Come with me."

For the rest of his life, whenever he heard the opening licks to "Sweet Home Alabama," Danny would think of Rachel. Because the instant he took her hand, that's the song the band broke into.

Rachel let out a screech of delight and started dancing to the music. "I just love this song! You want to dance?" she asked Danny, grabbing him by the hand as they disappeared onto the dance floor, not to be seen again for hours. Mitch and Carolyn eventually made their way outside where it was quieter, to a veranda that overlooked Lake Erie. They began the conversation that would continue to this day, fifteen years of marriage and three boys later.

Danny and Rachel, however, beat Mitch and Carolyn to the altar by three months.

For the next ten years, the couples were inseparable. Mitch and Carolyn bought a house in Chesterland, and it wasn't long before Danny and Rachel found a place two blocks away.

When Rachel was pregnant with her first boy, Evan, Rachel and Danny wound up adopting Maryann, Rachel's cousin, who was then twelve years old. Maryann's parents had died within a year of each other, when she was six, after which she had been shuffled around from foster home to foster home. When Maryann called Rachel to tell her that her latest foster family was going to move out of state at the end of the month, and she wasn't sure where she would wind up, Rachel did a typical Rachel move.

"Well, then you have to come live with me and Danny."

"I couldn't do that, Rachel. You're pregnant, and what would Danny say?" But Maryann had been hoping that Rachel would offer to have her live with them, so she held her breath.

"Don't worry. I'll talk to him and call you back later."

Rachel couldn't stand the idea of her cousin being alone and unprotected. She knew what it was like to be a young woman without a safe home. When she broached the subject with Danny, she was delighted that he was instantly behind the idea. He understood that sometimes you just did the right thing even when it didn't make sense on the surface. That was a lesson he had learned from Kevin Grant.

The years went by in a whiz, filled with work, kids, school, sports, holidays, birthday parties. Rachel watched Carolyn's kids and vice versa. Their boys thought of one another more like cousins or extended family than neighbors. And Maryann was like a big sister to all of them, and a great babysitter to have available. There was a bond between the two families that could not have been tighter.

Tony turned out to be exceptionally industrious, and bought out his dad when Steve was ready to retire. About a year later he had an opportunity to purchase a small chain of sporting goods stores from a fellow in Akron who was nearly bankrupt, and Tony closed the Chesterland store and moved to Akron. He named the new chain Steve's Sporting Goods, after his father's store, and convinced Danny to join him, with the offer of two shops to manage at the outset; Tony had plans to expand, and he needed his brother's help.

When Rachel told Carolyn that she and Danny had found the most wonderful house in a development in Akron named Wingate, on a strange-sounding street called Caves Road, the reality hit them, and they both started to panic.

"Rach, I don't know how I'm going to make it without seeing you every day," Carolyn said.

"I feel the same way, sweetie, but you know we're going to talk every day, and we'll make sure to get together at least once a month, you know that."

And so the day came when the big green and yellow moving van was packed and the two families watched it drive off to Akron with all of the Turner belongings.

Their SUV was sitting in the driveway, with the engine running. Evan, Christopher, and Maryann were in the backseat, excited to be going to their new house, but sad to be leaving their friends. Luke and Joey Bianci ran around both sides of the car getting in some last-minute jibs and pokes, which was their way of telling their friends they would miss them.

Mitch and Danny broke into a man hug. "We've been through a lot together, my friend," Mitch said.

"I know, I know," Danny replied. "Don't worry, we're not that far away. We'll still get together for hoops." They both turned and looked off into the distance, so they wouldn't see each other tearing up.

"We'll meet at the stadium to watch the Indians invent a new way to lose real soon," Mitch offered, to break the awkward silence. Then they turned to look at their wives.

Carolyn and Rachel were holding hands and looking into each other's eyes. Of course they were both crying, and making promises to stay in touch and speak every day. Finally, Danny and Mitch had to pull them apart. They climbed into the car, with Rachel mouthing "every day, every single day" to Carolyn, and then Danny pulled their big maroon SUV out of the driveway and they headed off to Akron.

When they were just about twenty feet down the road, Rachel screamed "wait!" and suddenly the car screeched to a halt. She jumped out and ran over to Carolyn; she had forgotten to give her something. She handed her a piece of paper, and then ran back to the car and off they went, this time for real. Carolyn opened the paper and recognized her own handwriting, and the phone number she had written on it the day they met.

CHAPTER 6

November Sky

What's done cannot be undone.
—*William Shakespeare, Macbeth*

EIGHTY-THREE CAVES ROAD, Danny and Rachel Turner's new home, was set back on an acre of land, like all the other houses in the Wingate subdivision. Its long, curving driveway made the house feel isolated and remote. Tom Schroeder reduced his speed as he rolled up the driveway, until the house came fully into view. Unlike the other homes in the neighborhood that were bustling with activity on this typical Wednesday morning, the Turner house was completely dark, which was the first thing to strike Tom as odd. What was it that Tony had said about the weird voice mail or e-mail he'd gotten from Danny?

The barren trees that framed the house gave an already bleak November morning more of an ominous feeling, sending a shiver through Tom. His whole body shook uncontrollably for an instant. "Where the hell did that come from, Schroeder? Goose walk across your grave?" he said out loud in an attempt at frivolity meant to counter the creepy sensation that had suddenly descended upon him.

Before getting out of the truck, Tom scanned the windows, room by room, hoping to see even a single light. But every room was black. For an instant he thought he saw a figure at the window of the master bedroom, but when he glanced back it was empty and dark. Something told him he might wind up having to shimmy open a window, so he rummaged around in the glove compartment until he found a screwdriver; however, he knew he really was hesitating because of an overwhelming, irrational desire to leave.

He instinctively felt for his cell phone as he stepped out of his truck, and tried to figure out what it was that didn't seem right. Why would the whole family have taken off in the middle of the week, when the kids were due at school and Danny at work? It wasn't like Tony to jump to conclusions or worry unless there was a good possibility something was up. He tried to reassure himself that there could be any number of reasonable explanations as he shuffled through the leaves and headed for the front door.

He rang the bell several times. No answer. He knocked hard, hammering on it.

"Hello, Danny? Rachel? Anybody home?" Still no answer.

Tom circled the house, cupping his hands to peer into a few windows, and then punched Danny's home number into his phone. He could hear it ringing from outside the window, and then the Turner voices answering through his phone. It was downright eerie. He hung up, frustrated, and was about to try a window when he glimpsed something scurry across the foyer floor. It looked like one of the kids, but he couldn't be sure; whoever it was had just whisked by and was now out of sight. But someone was in there for sure. Why hadn't they responded? What the hell was going on? He rapped on the window with the handle of his screwdriver and shouted as he sped around to the front door.

Suddenly he heard the sound of feet coming toward him, down the steps and across the floor. From inside a child's voice shouted, "Someone's at the door! Are we late for school?"

Tom let out a sigh of relief. "It's Tom Schroeder. Can you let me in?"

The mahogany door instantly swung open and there stood Christopher Turner, Danny and Rachel's eight-year-old son. He was wide-eyed and very excited, but looked scruffy, like he had just rolled out of bed—yet he was dressed for school in jeans and a white Cleveland Indians T-shirt.

"Chris, where are your mom and dad?" Tom asked while shielding his eyes from the sunlight that was streaming across the foyer.

"I don't know," Christopher said, blinking. "Are we late for school?"

"Christopher, where are your mom and dad?" Tom repeated, louder.

Without answering, Christopher turned and ran back up the stairs. Tom followed after him, taking two steps at a time, and reached the hallway on the second floor. The boy was standing outside his parents' bedroom, excitedly waving his hand toward the darkened room. Tom put his hands on Christopher's shoulders and gently moved him aside as he gave the door a poke and it wobbled open. He took a few steps forward and then stopped at the threshold, frozen in place. There, in the stillness, the morning sunlight shone upon a crumpled mass of covers, saturated in blood. Next to the bed, splayed grotesquely across the floor, her head crowned by a pool of blood, lay Rachel Turner, motionless and obviously dead.

Tom looked at Christopher, whose trusting expression implied that he thought this grown-up would fix the bad thing that hurt his mommy. Schroeder shuddered as he glanced back over his shoulder, into the room, and then hurried Christopher down the stairs, babbling "everything will be all right," because he had no idea what else to say.

His quivering fingers could barely find the numbers as he dialed 911.

"This is Tom Schroeder, I'm at the house of Danny and Rachel Turner," he told the operator. "Something very bad has happened; we have an emergency; we need an ambulance; please send someone right away, right away."

"Can you be more specific, sir? What is the address?"

His mind could not process the information. "Please, you must be able to trace the call; send someone immediately." Finally the street popped into his head.

The dispatcher, in her trained noncommittal voice, assured him someone was already on the way. He turned to Christopher, who was standing passively at his side.

"Christopher, where is your dad?"

"I don't know."

"Where's your brother, Chris? Where's Evan?"

"I think he's upstairs in his room." With that he took off again, ran up the stairs, and stood in the hall, pointing into the room next to where Rachel lay.

"There he is!"

Praying he would find Evan sleeping soundly, Tom's heart sank when he noticed a faint, bloody handprint on Christopher's shoulder. He held the boy firmly to him as he looked into the bedroom to see Evan, lying on his back, his covers a deep purple, a dark red streak arcing up the wall behind his head. His face was almost unrecognizable. He did not need to enter to verify his condition. It suddenly dawned on Tom that whoever did this might still be in the house, and that, in any event, he had seen enough. With that, he scooped up Christopher and carried him outside, into his car. His smallness made the awful magnitude of the situation excruciatingly real.

In the distance he heard the sound of sirens approaching. He took off his jacket and wrapped it around the little boy, kneeling down beside him to hold him close. Tom repeated his reassuring lie like a mantra: "It's gonna be okay, little guy. I know it's gonna be okay. Don't worry, it's gonna be okay." But in his heart, he knew he was praying for the child in his arms to somehow find the strength to overcome the events of the most awful day of his life.

⇥➡◉ ◉⬅⇤

A few hours earlier, as the sky began to fill with light, a black Cadillac Escalade pulled to a stop approximately thirty feet from the edge of the cliff at Nicholson's Quarry. Danny Turner had come here many times in the past when he had no other place to turn and needed to be alone. He loved the beauty of the vista, the crunch of the granite under his tires; he had come to believe he had a spiritual connection to this place. The official town history always included a mention that the Cuyahoga Indians had revered this lookout as sacred ground and somehow had pushed two enormous boulders up the cliff to create a natural gateway of astounding beauty. Whenever he stood in the center of the opening, looking over the precipice, into the ravine, Danny would be overtaken by the awesome power, not of God, but of the random nature of life. Occasionally, he would pause to ponder the big questions.

How can there be a God? If I wanted, I could just jump off of here and end it all. Am I in charge, or is He? And if He is, then why has He let things get so out of control? If only . . . if only this, if only that. How can this beautiful world be so cruel? Danny always had more questions than answers. He knew one thing. He knew love existed because he loved Christopher and Evan, and, most of the time, he loved Rachel. But then life got in the way, and things had gotten so complicated. Where was God when he needed Him? Maybe some sort of God existed, pulling him to this spot, or maybe this was just one of those gifts of nature. After a cigarette and a few moments' contemplation, he would return to his car, determined to confront whatever dilemma was before him. But most often, he would just go home, have a few beers, and watch the game. It was better not to admit there was a problem, because then he might have to do something about it.

On this morning, as the sun rose and poured through the windshield, the time for philosophical debate had ended. It was too late to undo the horrible things he had done, and so he placed his head on the steering wheel and sobbed uncontrollably, praying to the God whose existence he doubted, hoping He would forgive him. The thing he'd plotted for so long, the plan that seemed so logical just the day before, had gone as wrong as wrong could be. He looked over at the passenger seat as if listening to someone, and then opened all the windows so he could hear the wind one last time. The leaves scattered on the ground and a few blew in through the window.

Danny leaned over, picked up the shotgun resting on the Escalade's floor, inserted it barrel-up between his knees, and delicately placed his chin on the round, metal rim. He swallowed hard. Then, with his left hand on the steering wheel and his right thumb on the gun's trigger, he pressed the accelerator to the floor.

The truck took off, gaining speed as it scaled the embankment leading up to the quarry, until the speedometer read over eighty miles per hour. At the precipice, the car narrowly passed between the two large boulders, snapping the trees at the mouth of the quarry as it became airborne. As the Escalade propelled off the cliff, Danny closed his eyes, braced himself, and with one final cry, pulled the trigger of the powerful gun.

A single shot rang out and echoed against the quarry walls as the heavy weight of the engine pulled it down into a dive. The vehicle bounced off the jagged side of the one-hundred-foot ravine before crashing into the quarry's watery bottom. There, the car rested on its side and quickly engulfed Danny. Little did it matter.

He was already in the hands of the Lord.

CHAPTER 7

Forever Young

Brief is life,
But love is long
—*Lord Alfred Tennyson*

NOVEMBER 17, 2004, began as a normal weekday for Carolyn and Mitch Bianci. He charged out the kitchen door dressed for the gym a few minutes after seven, juggling his dress clothes and briefcase with an apple clutched in his mouth, cradling his cell phone to his ear and somehow managing to wave good-bye. Carolyn raced around and, by some motherly magic, was able to whisk Luke and Joey out to the bus stop in front of the house just before the doors closed. She then ran back inside and wrestled Frankie into his winter coat, despite his protests that it made him look like a little kid. She drove him to his kindergarten class, dropped off the clothes at the cleaner, stopped at the supermarket, and finally started to relax when she pulled into the driveway, envisioning the steaming cup of coffee she presumed was in her immediate future.

As she was coming in the door, she heard the tail end of a message her mom had just left on the answering machine "—so, you need to call me back right away." That was Carolyn's first inkling that today was not going to be just another day.

"Well, that doesn't sound good, whatever it is," she said under her breath, as she dialed her mother without first listening to the message.

Her mom definitely did not sound like herself, so naturally Carolyn started to conjure up a dozen scenarios that might be the cause of her mother's call.

"Hi, Mom, it's me. What's going on?"

"I don't really know all the details, sweetheart, but like I said on the message, it's about Danny and Rachel and the boys."

"What do you mean? Were they in a car accident or something?"

Silence. And then her mother began to weep.

"Mom, Mom, what is it? Are they okay?" Adrenaline shot through her system, and the receiver began to shake in her hand.

It took another minute for Rosemary Hamilton to collect herself, and even then she couldn't quite believe the words she was about to say to her daughter. They didn't make any sense. They were too foul and despicable to say out loud. She didn't want to speak them, because somehow that would make this horrible thing real, and she wanted it to be a dream—but she knew it wasn't. Every instinct in her body told her to protect her daughter, yet she knew what she was about to tell her would shatter her life.

"Mom, Mom! What is it? Tell me!" Carolyn shouted. She backed up and tripped over a toy, landing softly on the rug in the family room, as if an angel sister had caught her and gently sat her down.

"Rachel's gone, and one of the boys . . . and Danny, too."

Carolyn couldn't comprehend what her mother was saying. Clearly there was some misunderstanding, because earlier that morning, she had listened to a message from Rachel about passing her real estate exam, and how they would get together that weekend, and how grateful she was for Carolyn's pep talk.

"No, there has to be some mistake," Carolyn objected. "I just heard from Rachel!" She tried her best to block out the truth. She knew the message was from last night, but didn't want to admit it. Yet the fact came worming back to the forefront.

"Mom, I don't get it. Tell me this isn't true! Rachel, one of the boys, and Danny dead? I don't believe it!"

"I'm sorry, honey, but it's true, and I'm afraid it's even worse."

"Worse than that? What? What could be worse?" Carolyn was starting to feel numb.

At this point, Rosemary could no longer contain herself. She began to sob in great heaves, finally gathering up the strength to say these horrific words: "Danny shot and killed Rachel and one of the boys, and they found his car at the bottom of some quarry down in Akron, so the police think he drove it off the cliff and killed himself."

Carolyn did not believe what she was hearing. It didn't compute. Danny wasn't violent. He loved Rachel and the boys. He didn't even own a gun as far as she knew. Why would he drive his car off a cliff and kill himself?

"Oh, my God, Mom, this can't be true. Who told you this? There has to be a mistake—this doesn't make any sense. Danny doesn't have a gun, and he never even yells at the kids. He and Rachel never fight, and if they were having trouble, Rachel definitely would have told me—"

"Honey, I'm sorry, but it's true. I wish it weren't, but it is!"

Carolyn's heart was pounding so hard she thought it was going to leap right out of her chest. She started mechanically shaking her head "no," and then she began shouting, over and over, "No, no, no, no, no!" She fell to her knees and began to sob uncontrollably. Throwing the phone down as if it were some vile creature, she dropped her head to the floor and screamed into the rug. She began to gasp for air and felt as if she were drowning; then a horrendous pain shot from the small of her back to the top of her head. Carolyn thought she was about to pass out. Suddenly she sat up, leaned back, and forced herself to take a deep breath. Now she felt better; she had it figured out. She crawled to the phone lying on the floor. It wasn't true. Her mom had gotten it wrong. She probably saw something on TV, about a murder in Akron, and just thought it was about Rachel and Danny. That was it. Just one big mistake.

She felt relieved now that she was about to get to the bottom of things. She was almost smug when she said, "How do you know, Mom? Who told you?"

"Dixie Clemons. She lives in Akron, one street over from Rachel and Danny. Remember she was at their cookout last summer? She heard all the police cars and ambulances this morning and went over there. There was a big crowd in front of the house, and when she found out what happened, she called me right away because she didn't want you to hear about it on the news, or from someone else. One of her neighbors in the crowd told her what happened, and then she spoke with a police officer, and while she was talking to him, a report came in about Danny's car being in a quarry because he drove it off a cliff. I'm sorry, honey, but it really happened."

"Oh, my God, Mom! Rachel . . . Danny . . . dead? And one of the boys? Danny killed them? Which boy, Mom? Christopher or Evan?" Carolyn felt like she was having an out-of-body experience. The question she just asked sounded surreal; she had the sensation that she was standing across the room watching herself speaking on the telephone.

"I'm not sure of their names—I always get them mixed up—but Dixie said she saw the younger boy sitting in an ambulance, and he looked like he was in shock, but he wasn't hurt. Then the ambulance drove off with him."

"That means that Evan is dead. That can't be; he's only ten years old!"

"I know. It's so awful. That poor little boy. And dear, dear Rachel. Oh, I wish it were a mistake, but it's not."

"Then that means Christopher saw it all, and he's all alone," Carolyn mumbled.

"Carolyn? . . . Carolyn? Are you still on the phone?" She could hear her breathing, but there was no response.

"You stay there; don't go anywhere. I'm going to come over right away." Rosemary wished she could just jump through the phone and hold her daughter, but forced herself to hang up and run out the door to her car.

Carolyn continued to hold the phone to her ear and listen to the dial tone as if it were a sound she had never heard before. She stared straight ahead and abruptly stopped crying. She put the receiver back in the cradle, and calmly walked to the steps leading to the upstairs bedrooms. She had an overwhelming desire to hold the high school photo of Rachel and her that was sitting on her dresser. *The one where Rachel is planting a kiss right on my cheek,* she thought. *We always get a big laugh out of that!*

She felt Rachel's presence and pictured her wide eyes and welcoming smile that first day. "You look like you could use a partner. I'm Rachel. What's your name?" Like a little girl reciting a rhyme, with each step she climbed, she repeated out loud: "I'm Rachel." *Step.* "What's your name?" *Step.*

She bargained with God to let this chant reverse what had happened and wake her from this nightmare. However, the instant she touched the photograph, the brutal reality consumed her and she collapsed on the bed.

→═◉ ◉═◄

Mitch had just walked into a meeting with a client who had travelled from Oregon to meet with him and his team. Mitch would lead the pitch about why he should select Xanadu Architects, Inc., to design his new chain of organic food supermarkets, which hoped to compete with Whole Foods. This account presented many challenges, but could be quite lucrative if the idea took off. The client was interviewing several firms and made it clear he could devote only one hour to meeting with

XAI because he had a plane to catch. He appeared tired, bored, grumpy, and impatient—just the sort of challenge Mitch relished.

At the outset of Mitch's presentation, he felt his cell phone vibrate in his pocket, but chose to ignore it. A minute later, just as he was launching into the second slide, it buzzed again, and he ignored it again. The client was already starting to look antsy and Mitch couldn't risk losing his rhythm once he got his mojo working. He was just starting to get to the part about why their unique mix of creativity and practicality would be a perfect fit for this project when his phone rumbled again. Now he was concerned, so he asked a colleague to take over the presentation. The client made sure Mitch noticed he was annoyed as he excused himself and stepped outside the glass-walled office to check his phone.

His father-in-law, Joe, had called three times. That wasn't like him, so Mitch guessed something important must be happening. Joe picked up on the first ring and got right to the point.

"Mitch, you had better go home right now. Mom's over at the house with Carolyn, and she is not doing well."

"What? What is it? Did something happen to one of the kids?" Mitch felt panic about to set in.

"No, son, but there has been a terrible tragedy with your friends Danny and Rachel, and Carolyn is going to need all the support she can get."

When Joe told him the details, Mitch ran to his office, grabbed his car keys, shouted to his assistant that he would be gone for the rest of the day, and headed out of Cleveland in a complete state of confusion. Danny, Rachel, and Evan all dead? Danny killed them all, and then killed himself? What in God's name could have happened? He knew Danny was struggling with some financial issues, and that Rachel had caught him cheating, but that was a few years ago, and they had seemed fine the last time they had dinner together up at Johnny's.

He slowed down a bit on I-91, after he cut off a semi driver who blasted his horn. He realized he wasn't thinking straight in his desperation to get home. He was upset, but he knew that Carolyn must be devastated. He couldn't imagine how she had taken the news, and he feared that his wife would never recover. Then his thoughts went to Christopher. *Oh, my God, that poor little boy was left in his house alone. Who knows what he witnessed, before his father abandoned him to the horror he created?*

For the first time, the enormity of the situation enveloped Mitch, and he banged the steering wheel and screamed, "Danny, you rotten coward, how could you? What would make you do something so horrible? Why? Why? Why? Oh Lord, why do you allow such misery to happen in our world?" He felt crazed and carried on like that for the rest of the drive home, but composed himself as he pulled into his driveway. He would be no help to anyone if he was out of control.

When Mitch entered the house, he hugged Rosemary, and she told him Carolyn was upstairs lying down.

"How is she?"

Rosemary shook her head and said, "Not good." She was very worried about her daughter.

When Mitch walked into the room, Carolyn gazed at him with a look of utter disbelief. They simply held each other and cried.

Finally, Mitch got up and said he would call—whom? Not Tony, given the circumstances. Rachel's mother and father were gone. He would call Maryann—she would know about the arrangements. Maryann had now moved out, but had been legally adopted by Rachel and Danny; so, in essence, they were her parents and Evan and Christopher were her brothers.

"Do you know if we have her number, honey?"

Carolyn shook her head and said, "It's in the address book downstairs."

Mitch reached Maryann and learned that the funeral service would be in three days, and that there would not be a wake. "I don't think anyone could bear it, Mitch."

She suggested that he contact Tom Schroeder, the man who worked for Tony and was friends with Danny, and who first discovered the murders. She believed he knew someone in the police department who was planning to sit down with her and a few other close friends at Tom's house tomorrow afternoon.

"I know Rachel would want you guys to be there," she said. "I'll see you then." Maryann gave him the number, but her monotone made it obvious she was as stunned as everyone else.

He went back to the bedroom and told Carolyn about the plans for the next day. Little by little Carolyn was starting to accept that this had really happened and knew that the only thing to do was to help with the plans however she could. She couldn't bear the thought of going through this, but she was going to be strong for her friend. She didn't know how she felt about Danny, however. It was too early and there were just too many unanswered questions.

When Carolyn came downstairs her mother offered her the cup of coffee she never got that morning, and they sat in the kitchen in silence. Joe had come over while Mitch was upstairs.

Mitch stepped outside the kitchen door into the breezeway and dialed Tom Schroeder.

When he picked up, Mitch introduced himself and explained how close they were to the Turner family. Tom reminded Mitch they had met once at Danny and Rachel's place, at a Christmas party.

"Mitch," Tom said, "you guys should know that Danny and Rachel talked about what good friends you all were, and how much they missed being near you. Danny mentioned to me that you were sort of like another big brother to him."

Mitch didn't quite know what to say. He was like a big brother to a man who had just killed his wife and child. He didn't feel like a very good friend at that moment, so he changed the subject.

"Tom, I understand that someone from the Akron police department is going to be at your house tomorrow. Is that right?"

"Yeah, I know the homicide detective on the case, and he agreed to talk with the family and a few close friends for a few minutes and answer any questions we might have. You wouldn't believe how many TV trucks and reporters have shown up. Everyone thought it was best not to make the family walk in and out of the police station."

Mitch thought it was unusual that the police would do this, particularly so soon after the crime. But he had a million questions, and his nature was to pursue things until he thoroughly understood them, so, as much as he dreaded the meeting, he was grateful that he and Carolyn were asked to attend. He was relieved Tom did not choose to go into the details of his discovery that morning. Obviously this was a subject no one wanted to go near.

He jotted down all of the pertinent information, got the directions, thanked Tom, and said he would see him at two the next afternoon. It was a relief to talk about something like directions, rather than the reason for the call.

Joe, Rosemary, Carolyn, and Mitch chatted about the upcoming plans and how difficult the next few days were going to be for everyone. This was safer territory than discussing the actual murders; that subject—all the whys and what ifs—would come in the future. Now was too soon.

Mitch and Carolyn each knew they had a serious chore in front of them—how and what to tell their three boys—but neither was ready to discuss it. It hung in the air, like a giant balloon, unspoken, yet on everyone's mind.

Finally, Joe said, "I know you two are thinking about what to tell the boys. I know you have a policy of always telling the truth, and I won't pretend I know what to do, or that it's my place to give advice. The only advice I'll give is that the two of you pray for guidance before you speak with them."

"Dad, do you think we have to tell them now?" Carolyn asked, ignoring the fact that her father had just said he didn't know what to do. She always went to him with her problems, and he and her mom always gave her solid advice. For example, the first time Mitch came to the house to pick her up, Joe, who was naturally suspicious of young men around his daughters, let Mitch babble on without saying anything in response. Rosemary instantly liked him.

When they got to the car, Mitch said, "Whew, I hope I didn't say anything too stupid. Your dad just looked at me and didn't say anything, but I think your mom liked me."

Carolyn laughed and said, "He liked you. If he didn't, you would have known."

That night when she came home, her father was sitting on the porch, waiting up.

"Hi, Dad, what are you doing up so late?"

"Waitin' for you. I wanted to tell you something. That fellow, Mitch, do you like him?"

"I really do, Dad. I think I might actually love him."

He looked at her and smiled. "That's good, because I stayed up tonight to tell you I think he's a keeper. He seems like a fine young man to me." That was all. With that he got up and walked into the house and up to bed, and Carolyn watched his rocking chair sway to and fro until it stopped.

She looked up at him now and waited, hoping he would encourage her and Mitch to wait to speak with the boys.

Joe wasn't given to needless sentiment, but he was in foreign territory and knew bad news didn't get better with age. "I don't think it's going to get any easier in a few days, and it's possible they will find out from someone else."

Mitch agreed. "Honey, we'll speak with them tonight after dinner. They'll know something is up anyway, and we'll be in Akron at least until Monday."

Joe and Rosemary decided it was time to let Carolyn and Mitch be alone, and so they hugged them and said good-bye at the front door. Fortunately the boys could stay with their grandparents while Mitch and Carolyn were gone, and they would know how to handle their concerns.

Mitch and Carolyn looked at each other across the table. "As usual, your dad gave us some good advice," he said. She nodded. "I mean about praying for guidance," he added.

"Mitch, I'm not ready to talk to God just yet. Can you do it?"

⇥⚬ ⚬⇤

Dinner was an odd affair, and as Mitch suspected, the kids knew something was up. Luke, their eleven-year-old, noticed his mom had been crying, and asked her why. She tried to put him off by saying it was just the change in seasons, and her allergies were acting up, but at dinner when Carolyn suddenly excused herself, the pretense started to crumble.

"Dad, what's going on? Are you and mom getting a divorce like Tommy's parents?" Luke asked. He looked like he was on the verge of tears.

"No, son, nothing like that. Let me get Mom, so we can have a chat."

Mitch knew the moment had finally come, and said another silent prayer for God to put the right words in his mouth as he went to retrieve

Carolyn. Their three boys thought of Danny and Rachel more as a big brother and sister than as friends. Heck, they even called them by their first names. Rachel and Danny had insisted on that. And Evan and Christopher were like family as well. You couldn't be closer without being blood relatives.

Carolyn was in the upstairs bathroom. Mitch could tell that she was inconsolable. It broke his heart to do it, but he tapped on the door and told her it was time to talk to the kids. They couldn't wait any longer. Carolyn walked out, nodded bravely, and said, "Tell me one thing, Mitch. How, just *how*, do you tell your children one of their friends is dead, and that he was murdered by his father, who also killed his wife and then committed suicide? None of this makes sense, even to an adult, let alone to three small children."

"I don't know. But we'll do our best."

When they sat down at the kitchen table, all three boys were wide-eyed and clearly frightened. Their nine-year-old, Joey, thought for sure Mrs. Furlong had called his mom like she said she would if he got out of his seat one more time, and six-year-old Frankie thought they were going to have to move because one of the kids in his kindergarten class had to move and he was crying about it all that morning. Frankie didn't really know what "moving" meant, but he knew it wasn't good, and he hoped that wasn't why his mom and dad looked so serious.

Luke was just confused and worried.

"Listen, boys, we have some really bad news we have to tell you," Mitch started, "and, well, there just isn't any easy way to say it." Uncharacteristically, the three boys were silent. Carolyn's sobs were the only sound in the otherwise silent room.

Mitch took a deep breath to steady himself and said, "Danny, Rachel, and Evan died today."

Now that it was out there, the news was greeted with a chorus of confused questions all around the table. Frankie started to cry; then the other two boys followed suit. Finally, Luke turned to his mother for confirmation and said, "Mom, is Dad right? Are they really dead?"

"Yes, I'm afraid it's really true."

"What . . . what happened?" he replied as his lip started to quiver.

Carolyn wished for any other answer than the one she had to give. A plane crash, car accident, house fire, even that they were murdered by some stranger—as awful as all of those explanations would have been, they paled in comparison to the truth. But she and Mitch had agreed they owed their children the truth. She tried to be honest while she softened the blow, but there really wasn't a way to sugarcoat the reality regardless of what she said, so she told them in as few words as possible.

"Danny was sick," she began. "I mean sick like in his mind, and he shot Rachel and Evan, and then he was so sad about what he did that he killed himself." Once again, Carolyn had the sense that someone else was talking while she was saying these things, that she was watching herself sitting at the kitchen table telling her children this horrible news.

It took almost a half hour of answering questions, hugging, and crying, and then all five of them curled together on the couch and held each other. After a little while, they all sat quietly; even little Frankie (who was known for talking nonstop) was speechless, because words were inadequate at that moment. Eventually, the family headed upstairs to go to bed.

Finally the boys climbed in their beds, and said their nightly prayers. Each asked God to bless the souls of Danny, Rachel, and Evan. When it was Frankie's turn, he looked at his father who was kneeling beside him.

"Dad, is it okay to ask God to forgive Danny for what he did?"

"Sure it is, son. We know that with God all things are possible, and Jesus died for all of our sins, so we can all be forgiven." He sounded to himself a little like a preacher reciting something of which he was trying to convince himself.

"Okay, then . . . God, I know Danny did a really bad thing today, and I don't know why he did it, but I hope that when he tells you he's sorry, you will forgive him and let him go to heaven. Amen."

Mitch averted his eyes while he pulled the covers around Frankie and kissed him on the forehead.

While Carolyn and Mitch dressed for bed, they made small talk about how exhausted they were and tried to feign a conversation that was in the realm of normal, reaching for any topic other than the black cloud that had descended upon their home that day. Both in their private thoughts were grateful this horrible day was finally coming to an end, but dreaded the night and what lay ahead in the days to come.

They settled their heads on their pillows, but through the silent language of old friends, agreed they were not yet ready to turn out the light. Sleep was not likely to come to either of them, despite the fact they were entirely spent, so they lay there for several minutes, simply holding hands, staring at the ceiling, and waiting for the pain to subside. But it didn't.

Just as Mitch reached over to turn out the light, he noticed Luke standing at the door. His two younger brothers then appeared behind him and they stood in a cluster. Each clutched his respective pillow, blanket, and favorite stuffed animal. With the innocence, honesty, and wisdom that only children possess, they had devised the best and perhaps only plan that would allow their family to navigate the darkness and safely arrive at daybreak.

The oldest brother, Luke, spoke for all three: "Mom, Dad, can we sleep in here with you tonight?"

CHAPTER 8

Reality

Grief teaches the steadiest minds to waver.
—*Sophocles*

MITCH DIDN'T MAKE it to daybreak. He awoke a little before five, while it was still dark outside. Once the ugly reality settled in, he knew sleep was out the question. He silently grabbed his sweats, stepped over the boys, and crept down to the kitchen. Sleep, blessed sleep, was a gift on this day, so the last thing he wanted to do was to wake anyone prematurely. He was grateful for the rest he did get, because he expected the day ahead would be emotionally grueling. In this instance, ignorance *was* bliss. Mitch didn't know how right he was about the day to come, nor did he realize that the reality of yesterday's events was far worse than had yet been revealed.

He curled up in his favorite easy chair and sat quietly with a glass of orange juice, gazing through the sliding glass doors. Little by little daylight overtook the night. He hoped Carolyn would sleep in a bit, not only to spare her a few moments of pain but to give him a little time to sit alone and consider the jumble of facts that were plaguing him.

He was an architect by training, and so his initial instinct was to evaluate a project and try to figure out how it all fit together. A magnificent bridge was worthless if it couldn't support the weight it was intended to carry. As a child, he would spend hours building a structure out of blocks, and then slowly add more and more blocks, one at a time, until it inevitably came crumbling down, determining the load-bearing weight. Everything had a breaking point, a threshold. It was just a matter of how much weight or pressure was applied, and eventually it would collapse. So he looked at yesterday's revelations in much the same way, and was utterly confused. This felt more like a massive collision than a trickle, but what did he really know? And why hadn't he seen it coming? Had he just been too preoccupied with his own life to notice anything? With something so monumental brewing, how could he have been so unaware?

He prided himself on being observant. He paid attention to the little things because they were often indicators of major issues lurking just below the surface. These habits showed up in the way he raised his children and managed people, and in his keen ability to read the body language of a client or, more importantly, smell that a junior architect might have cut corners or been a little sloppy. Buildings needed to survive *all* eventualities, not most eventualities. When they didn't, disasters could occur—not the time to discover a structural problem. So Mitch generally followed his sniffer and, if something was amiss, he usually uncovered it.

The more Danny's actions sank in, the more confused he became. There were dozens of unanswered questions. He presumed he would get some clarity later today when they met at Tom Schroeder's house, but he just couldn't push away the image of Danny shooting and killing his wife and child. It was just too horrible to contemplate.

Unfortunately, Mitch knew that murder-suicides were all too common. The ritual was for television reporters to flock to the crime scene like jackals to prey, poke a microphone in the mouth of a hapless neighbor or relative, and probe for answers about the personality of the murderer. The public demanded to know "why." Everyone longed to uncover the motive, as if there would be one singular "ah-ha" moment that would explain why an otherwise loving father and husband would commit such a heinous act. Invariably, the bewildered individual would respond along the lines of "he was a nice guy, I never would have expected him to do something like this," which was not terribly comforting for the populace at large, because it meant that your next-door neighbor or perhaps even your Uncle Dave might be capable of the same sort of violence and was worthy of suspicion. However, had Mitch been asked about Danny, he certainly would have said he was baffled by the situation, and probably would have defended him until all the facts were known.

Twenty-four hours ago he believed Danny and Rachel had a typical suburban marriage. There were hints of trouble, but nothing major. He thought back to the last time he had seen them, two weeks ago in Cleveland for dinner at their favorite Italian restaurant, Johnny's Bar on Fulton Road.

It was just the four of them that night. Carolyn and Rachel focused on each other, their conversation jumping back and forth breathlessly, while Mitch tried to coax an unusually quiet Danny into opening up. Sports seemed to be about the only safe topic, and on that subject, Danny could astutely analyze the last Browns game or rate the depth of the Indians' bench. LeBron James was the topic of conversation for most of the night. Hopes were high for the Cavaliers with this nineteen-year-old phenom. Finally, Cleveland was getting some respect. Mitch loved sports as well, but had begun a period of self-exploration in the last several years that he felt had been instrumental in his growth as a father and a husband and had contributed to his success in business.

He had read dozens of books in his exploration of spiritual matters and the connection between personal satisfaction, spiritual growth, and achieving one's full potential. There was no doubt in Mitch's mind that this pursuit had allowed him to overcome barriers in all aspects of his life. He had always felt that the best self-help book ever written was the

Bible and that, for sheer simplicity, there wasn't a better guide to living than the Ten Commandments. Faith was the bedrock of his existence, and he tried to follow the section in the second chapter of James, about how "faith without works is dead," to combine the spiritual with the practical.

However, when he was in his thirties, he purchased a Tony Robbins book after seeing him on a television show. At first he was put off by Robbins's excited attitude, but after listening for a few minutes, he started to understand that this person was sincere, and really excited about life.

It wasn't long before he'd purchased the CD program and then parted with a few thousand dollars to attend two seminars. He found them to be life-altering. One process in particular made a great impression on Mitch. He discovered he could walk across hot coals without experiencing pain or burning his feet! Even after he did it, he still thought it might be a hoax, so he volunteered to place the coals for a group later in the day, and discovered it was totally legitimate. After that, he gave up some of his skepticism and cynicism, and he began to recognize the self-limiting beliefs he carried around subconsciously. He started to see that what looked impossible often was very possible. And he wanted to share this newfound knowledge with his friend.

About a year ago, Mitch purchased tickets for Danny and one of his buddies to attend a Tony Robbins seminar when he was appearing in Cleveland. After Danny went, he called Mitch and thanked him for the tickets, but told him he hadn't gotten much out of it because he already knew most of the stuff they had presented, and he didn't see any reason to explore self-improvement because he was pretty happy with the way things were. Mitch got it. Some people didn't want to be bothered challenging themselves, and some of the concepts in the program were meant to force oneself to confront uncomfortable truths. It wasn't for everyone.

After his stint in jail, Danny's life had gone pretty well. He had a wonderful wife and two beautiful sons, and Maryann had become a devoted a daughter who completed their family unit. He was able to move to a comfortable house in Akron largely because his brother worked so hard to expand his small chain of sporting goods stores into fifteen locations.

Danny had a great gig managing a region that included five stores, which also gave him plenty of freedom to spend his days as he liked. Sometimes that included a round of golf in the afternoon, and sometimes it meant shacking up with a woman he'd met on the road. Despite the fact Danny wasn't known for his work ethic, Tony didn't seem to mind, and paid him handsomely.

Danny went to church regularly with his family, as did Mitch, and he and Rachel even attended a Bible study with Mitch and Carolyn, but they rarely had anything to say at those meetings. Every once in a while, Mitch would bring up God, and Danny would evade the question or just change the subject. He just seemed like a happy-go-lucky guy.

It was true that Rachel had found out about one of the girlfriends, and that seemed to be a bone of contention. A few summers ago both families rented a house for a week on Put-in-Bay. They arrived on Saturday; then, on Monday afternoon, after Danny and Rachael returned from the supermarket, Danny announced that he had a problem at work and had to head back to Akron that night. Rachel didn't seem pleased, and on Wednesday she decided to return. There seemed to be a problem, but neither of them talked about it.

Thinking back, Mitch could see the invisible moat drawn around his friend that was intended to keep people at bay. Rachel and Carolyn seemed to be able to explore their most personal matters, and their bond was immovable. Yet Carolyn hadn't a hint from Rachel that there were any serious problems, or at least nothing she had shared with Mitch.

Now he felt guilty because he had to admit he had allowed his relationship with Danny to drift apart after they moved to Akron. The last time they'd spent any real time together was when Danny came over and helped Mitch build a deck. That was the sort of guy Danny was. He would never turn you down even for something as unappealing as deck building. In that respect he was a true friend. If you were in a foxhole, Danny was the guy you would want next to you.

But thinking back on that hot summer day, after they had finished the deck, and were sitting on it having a few beers, he remembered a comment Danny made in passing.

"You know, Mitch, sometimes I wish I had it all to do over again."

"What do you mean? Your life has gone pretty well." Mitch presumed Danny was making an oblique reference to his time in jail, but knew enough never to specifically refer to that topic.

"It's just about freedom, man. You know, being able to do what you want when you want to, not being tied down all the time."

"Whoa, dude, do I hear a midlife crisis coming on?"

"I don't know, maybe. I guess I should just go buy a convertible, but some days . . ."

"Some days what?"

"Some days I just feel like pointing my car west and driving off to a place where no one can find me."

"Yeah, but you'd turn around at some point and go back to Rachel and the kids. You love them too much."

"Ya, think so, don't ya? Maybe yes, maybe no, but there's no doubt I'd land somewhere where at least the team in town had one decent starting pitcher!"

And that was how most serious conversations went with Danny. If you peeked under the hood a bit, it usually got slammed shut as soon as you veered too close to the truth.

Mitch took a sip of his orange juice and felt another pang of guilt for not having made more of an effort to reach out to Danny, now that he knew there must have been serious problems in his life. This was one time his sniffer certainly had not worked.

That night at Johnny's something had been different about Danny. He and Rachel had arrived early, and they were involved in what appeared to be a heated exchange when Mitch and Carolyn walked in. They both immediately went from pained expressions to happy greetings and wide smiles. However, when Mitch and Danny had their usual man hug, Mitch noticed a reticence from Danny, and, over dinner, he seemed guarded and withdrawn. He remembered thinking that Danny seemed preoccupied all evening. Was it possible he was already contemplating this horrible deed? Mitch preferred to think not—that something out of the blue had just happened to suddenly trigger a terrible series of events. It must have been some unexpected emotional explosion, rather than a plot. He would have been surprised but not shocked if Danny and Rachel had announced they were breaking up. And, while it seemed as though every segment of *Dateline* had a story about a guy killing his wife or vice versa, it was inconceivable that Danny would ever harm his children. He rarely even raised his voice to them; even when they were misbehaving and doing things that would anger most fathers, Danny would simply let them be.

He remembered his last glimpse of the two of them: that night, walking to their car down the hill from the restaurant, engaged in conversation. He waved, but they didn't notice. Mitch had the sense that something was wrong. For some reason, something told him just to stand there and watch them. They got smaller and smaller and finally turned the corner.

He said something to Carolyn about his concerns as he started the car, but they let the subject drop, involved in whatever issues were going on in their lives at the moment. He never could have imagined that when they disappeared into the shadows, it would be the last time he would ever see them.

Now Mitch didn't know what to make of the person he had known for more than twenty years. Was he a monster who plotted to murder his wife and child, or someone who was mentally deranged, who, for some incomprehensible reason, committed the ultimate evil and then punished himself by taking his own life?

He closed his eyes and said a silent prayer, and then dozed off for a few seconds. When he lifted his head he was astonished to see Rachel standing by the sliding-glass doors. She looked radiant, but the glare of the sun behind her made it hard to discern her features. He could recognize her face, despite it being obscured by her hair, which was gusting in the wind. She was smiling, almost laughing, and speaking, though her lips weren't moving. "We're all okay, Mitch, but I need you to ask Carolyn to do me a favor." He thought he heard her trademark giggle. "Tell her she has to speak at my funeral. I know she won't want to do it, Mitch, but tell her I will be with her all the way." He woke with a start, thinking someone had poked him in the shoulder.

As he shook himself awake, he heard stirring upstairs and knew the day was now beginning in earnest.

→→═ ═←←

Carolyn heard Mitch talking with someone downstairs and woke up. She lay in bed for a few minutes trying to remember Tuesday's phone call with Rachel, when it dawned on her that two of Rachel's messages were still on the answering machine. She and Rachel had spoken once but then missed each other's calls throughout the day. *What a gift,* she thought. *I can go downstairs and hear her voice!* She pretended for a moment that if the messages were still on the machine, all this horror would be undone, just like in the movies.

Why couldn't life be like her and Rachel's favorite movie, *The Wizard of Oz?* After facing the terrifying flying monkeys, creepy munchkins, wicked witch, and intimidating wizard who turned out to be a harmless old man who couldn't even help her get back to Kansas, all Dorothy needed to do was slip on a pair of ruby-red slippers, click them three times, and *poof,* there she was, back home where all was well. Whenever they watched it, by the time the final black-and-white part came on, Rachel and Carolyn would be scrunched on the couch together, handing each other tissues and bawling their eyes out. But this wasn't a nightmare from which she could awake; it was all too real.

The boys were still sleeping on the floor, so she quietly got up, threw on her robe, and tiptoed down the steps. She ran over to the answering machine without even noticing that Mitch was sitting in the family room. He started to say something, but Carolyn interrupted, "Not now, I just realized I have Rachel's messages on the machine!"

After fast-forwarding through three messages, she finally heard Rachel's voice: "Carolyn?" Rachel said in a lilting tone. "Hey, sweetie, it's Rachel. What are you up to? I'm calling you back and wanted to let you know that I'm going up to Cleveland today. We're getting nasty rain and I was wondering if it was raining up there, too. I want to know which coat to wear. Anyway, just give me a call when you have a minute. Love you, girlfriend. Bye."

On Tuesday, when she'd gotten the message, Carolyn was surprised and happy to hear Rachel would be in the Cleveland area, and thought she'd have a chance to spend time with her. But when she called Rachel back and invited her to dinner, it turned out she was only going to be in town long enough to take an exam for a job she had recently accepted. She wanted to get back home early so she could be ready to start the new job in the morning. The real estate broker she would be working for had assured her that if she passed the exam, the job would be hers. She still had her license, but this chain required all new employees to pass its test.

Rachel had been out of the workforce for a while, and she always said tests made her nervous, so she'd been studying quite a bit. Still, she was fretting over having to take the exam and called Carolyn while she was sitting in the reception area, waiting to be called in.

"You'll do great," Carolyn said. "You studied hard and you understand the material. You'll ace it, I'm sure!"

Carolyn reminded Rachel of all the things she had accomplished over the years, and how she had taken to real estate like a duck to water years before, and that, since she had studied and was prepared, she should just relax and expect to do well.

Rachel called and left another message while she was driving home. Carolyn's prediction had turned out to be correct.

"Carolyn! I'm thrilled! I passed the exam! I'll try you on your cell phone. If not, thanks for the pep talk. I really appreciate it. You don't know how helpful it was to hear all that right before I went in. So, anyway, I'll talk to you soon. Let's try to get together this weekend. Bye."

Listening to the message now, Carolyn regretted not calling Rachel back right away after hearing the good news about the exam. It brought up a whole bunch of other "what ifs." What if she'd taken Rachel to dinner to celebrate after the exam and then insisted she stay overnight to avoid the dark, rainy drive back? Surely Rachel would still be alive. She could have saved Rachel's life.

Why had she been so caught up in her own life that she hadn't taken the time to see her friend? She knew this was irrational thinking, but that didn't make her feel any less guilty. She couldn't have known what was going to happen Tuesday night. If she had, she would have hijacked Rachel's car and brought her home. But life doesn't work that way. True, Rachel had refused Carolyn's offer to get together, but hearing Rachel's voice on the answering machine, Carolyn simply couldn't stop wondering what else she might have done that would have changed everything.

But these meanderings were pointless. It wasn't as if Rachel had died in a car crash, leaving one to muse about how unfortunate it was she took the road with the black ice rather than a dry road. This wasn't happenstance, but a whole other level of tragedy. There was a predator waiting for her in her home, and, for whatever reasons, he was apparently intent upon killing her. Perhaps, if she hadn't gone home that night, whatever it was that made Danny do what he did would have passed, but Carolyn knew this was just wishful thinking.

In just a few hours, however, the truth would begin to unravel and the layers of deceit would be revealed. And the loathsomeness of this crime would be undeniable.

⟶▬◉ ◉▬◄⟵

They were silent until they turned onto I-271 to head down to Akron. Something about the sign with that name gleaming on it filled both of them with immense sadness. This was usually a joyful trip for a birthday celebration, a sporting event, one of the holidays, or just a casual lunch or dinner. Carolyn gripped the armrest and stared out the window, hypnotized by the mileage markers zipping by. She had never felt so helpless or so sad in her life, but she felt cried-out, without a tear left to shed.

"I think," she said, "I'd like to be doing just about anything else today than going down to Akron to meet with a homicide detective to learn all the details. I don't know if I can handle it, Mitch."

"I know, but in a weird way, I think we'll feel a little better just knowing the facts. There must have been a reason Danny would do something like this. I never even heard him mention having a gun, and he loved the boys so much. None of it makes sense. Something must have happened."

Carolyn couldn't talk about it anymore. She didn't understand why Mitch wanted to know the details. How would that help? She wanted to be angry at someone, but other than Danny, she didn't know whom to be angry at. It was all too new; it didn't seem real and at times it almost wasn't—and then it would come flooding back. She tried to preoccupy her mind with the things she had to do for her friend that day.

The burden of making most of the arrangements had fallen to Maryann, who was barely more than a kid herself, at twenty-two, and so she had asked Carolyn to help her prepare for the funerals. Today was Thursday; they had decided not to hold a wake, and both the funeral service and the burials were planned for Monday.

It was strange enough to be burying her best friend, but to think about burying her friend *and* her child (to say nothing of Danny, who was, after all, a friend for most of her life) was just bizarre beyond comprehension. However, Carolyn felt an odd comfort in being useful in some way. She knew Rachel would be there for her if the roles were reversed. *What would Rachel like to wear?* she wondered? *Oh, no! What a stupid thought! Oh, Rach, if only you were here. What a laugh you would get out of me sitting here trying to figure out what you'd "like" to wear to your funeral. You'd probably say, "I'm dead, girlfriend! I don't give a damn what I'm wearing!"* She couldn't laugh for fear of crying.

She glanced over at Mitch. He was concentrating on driving and she could tell he was trying to figure things out by the knit of his brow. Her husband. The father of her children. The person who shared her bed, burdens, and joys. How she loved and trusted him.

How awful to think that Rachel and her child were set upon by the man who should have been the protector of the family. Did he kiss her goodnight? Did he tuck the boys in? Did he lock the doors to make sure they were safe? What was it that sealed their fate? She wished she could stop these thoughts from rolling over and over, and concentrate on the tasks at hand.

Her reverie was broken when Mitch brought up the subject of the eulogy and his dream again. "Honey, I'm telling you that it was so real.

Like she was right there. She told me to convince you to do it, and that she would be there with you."

"Oh, Mitch, we're both starting to imagine things. It was just a dream. I don't think I could say more than a few sentences before I'd start to cry all over the place, and make a fool of myself, and make everyone feel really uncomfortable."

"I'm sure you would get through it. I know her spirit will be standing with you, and I know she wants you to do this."

"Well, it's probably a moot point, anyway, because someone else in her family will want to do it, or maybe the pastor will just say a few words, so I don't think it would be right to bring it up. If they want me to do it, then I'll consider it, but don't volunteer me."

"I'll bet that once I tell them about the dre—"

"Tell them about the dream? Don't do that! It was just a dream!"

They needed to have a little spat, just to try to talk about something else, though there was no escaping "it." Mitch stewed a little, and felt like he was letting Rachel down; then, a few minutes later, Carolyn tenderly ran the back of her fingers along his cheek and said, "Don't worry, we'll know what to do when the time comes. I just can't think straight."

⊷⊙ ⊙⊷

They left the interstate and headed toward a side road. The most direct route to Tom and Anna Schroeder's house would have taken them past Danny and Rachel's, but they went out of their way to avoid Caves Road. They both felt a mixture of dread and anticipation once they saw the sign for the road that led to the Schroeders' house.

In a few minutes they would be introduced to the detective assigned to the case. Normally such a meeting with the family would have taken place at the police station, but, because of the media presence camped out at all the logical locations, it was agreed to meet somewhere private.

All Mitch knew was that the homicide detective was named Thompson, and that Tom Schroeder knew him because their kids once played on the same basketball team. When Thompson had interviewed Tom about the discovery of the bodies, he had asked Tom to allow the family to meet at his house, and of course he had agreed. Maryann would be attending with Rachel's younger brothers, Pete and Sam, and she had asked Carolyn to come for moral support.

Before leaving the house that morning, Mitch had gotten a call from someone at his office, who had told him he heard a new report that Danny actually hadn't shot Rachel and Evan, but had stabbed them, and that he had committed suicide by shooting himself, even though he was found at the bottom of a ravine. That all sounded too bizarre, so Tom had put it out of his mind. He purposely hadn't turned on the TV at home or the radio in the car, because he didn't want Carolyn to hear these wild rumors. He always wondered how people got through these things when he saw them reported on the local news, but he had no idea how treacherous gossip and rumors were until now, when he was on the other side of it. He was determined to learn the facts, so if there was anything he could do to help the family, he could do it.

Mitch and Carolyn were both overcome with a queasy feeling when they parked behind a black cruiser and noticed the decal on the back window that read "Homicide Investigation Unit." Mitch took a deep breath and said, "*Homicide*. What an awful word." Carolyn glanced at it and looked away. Something about the car lent a horrible finality to the situation.

A brisk November wind greeted them as they headed up the driveway clutching their open coats. Tom Schroeder was standing at the door greeting Maryann, along with Rachel's brothers, Pete and Sam. When he saw Mitch and Carolyn he waved to them to come in out of the cold. They all huddled in the hallway and engaged in introductions and reunions, each coping with his personal grief, and privately mortified he might inadvertently say something inappropriate to the occasion.

However, since there were no appropriate words for such an occasion, they all took turns hugging one another and mumbling some version of "good to see you, I wish it were under better circumstances." Carolyn and Maryann held each other for an extra long time and started to weep while they were expressing their condolences to each other.

Maryann remembered all the times Rachael and Carolyn had counseled her on the trials and tribulations of her teen years. She had loved the fact they included her in their circle of two, because she knew it was a very special place. She could tell them anything, and they would always give her excellent advice, of the sort one could expect from older sisters.

Maryann was around five foot ten, with curly dark hair, a fiery temperament, and a slender yet fabulous shape, so back then the phone was always ringing off the hook with a nervous high school boy at the other end of the line. Their inside joke had been that any guy who wanted to take her out on a date first had to obtain the "RC seal of approval," or else he was out of luck. Now Maryann was twenty-two, engaged, and living with her fiancée. They were expecting their first child in the spring. Just a few weeks ago, Danny and Rachel had mentioned they intended to figure out some way to pay for the wedding that was planned for February. To Maryann, Danny had been her dad and Rachel her mom, and it was well known that the feeling had been mutual.

She was inconsolable. Not only had she been orphaned for the second time in her life less than twenty-four hours ago, but one of her little brothers was also gone, and her youngest brother had experienced something that was indescribably horrible. Worst of all, the cause of this misery was the man she had thought of as her father.

Rachel's brothers, Pete and Sam, were now both in their early thirties. Rachel kept in touch with them, but, as with many siblings separated by distance and busy schedules, they would only get together around the holidays or for weddings and funerals. Pete and Sam both had settled in Minnesota after their father brought them back there on that fateful day after their mother's funeral more than twenty years ago.

Rachel's father had died in 1999, five years ago. Carolyn remembered the occasion because Evan and Christopher had stayed at the Bianci home while Danny and Rachel were in Minnesota. She remembered how funny Rachel had been when she called to check in on everyone.

"You won't believe how many people showed up for my old man!"

"What do you mean, Rach?"

"I mean they are lined up in the street waiting to get into this place. They only should have known who he really was back in the day!"

In one of those fascinating twists of fate, Ted McKenna not only had sobered up when he was in his late fifties, but had become a paragon of sobriety. From that time until his death, he helped countless others overcome their alcoholism. Carolyn remembered the day Rachel called her to tell her the news.

"You'll never guess who just left my house! Never in a million years!"

"Let's see: Brad Pitt, Tom Cruise, or John Travolta?"

"Nope. Better than that. Ted McKenna!"

"No way, girl! Your father? Just out of the blue like that? Was he looking for money or something?"

Rachel started to cry, so Carolyn let up on the jokes. "Seriously, what happened? Why was he there?"

"Well, believe it or not, he took the cure a few years ago, went to a rehab out in Minnesota, and wanted to see me. So he came without telling me in advance. He was afraid that if he called, I wouldn't have anything to do with him. I mean, we haven't talked for fifteen years! So, I answered the door, and there he was! He didn't want anything; he just wanted to tell me how sorry he was for making a mess of my childhood, and that he wanted to 'make amends' and be a part of my life. He had it written out, and said a lot of things, but he ended with 'I am truly sorry for abandoning you.' I never thought I'd hear him say that."

So Rachel had gotten her father back for the last years of his life and, as it now turned out, the last years of her life as well. It seemed he really had become a different man. Years later, he took her to a little house in Akron where he said Alcoholics Anonymous had started. It seemed like he was old friends with the people who were the caretakers of the place, though he swore he'd never met them before. He was a changed man, and became a loving grandfather.

Rachel's brothers, Pete and Sam, had been fortunate enough to escape the family curse, and each had become successful in his own right. Normally, Mitch and Carolyn would have found it comical to see them together, because they were such an incongruous pair. Pete was tall and thin, with blond hair, and Sam was dark, short, and pretty thick around the waste. Most of all, however, their temperaments were completely different.

Pete had grown into a fairly conservative family man who made a solid living as a real estate lawyer, but Sam was independently wealthy. He had skipped college to play in rock bands, and then opened a recording studio. One day he got a call from Jerry Garcia's manager, wondering if Sam could squeeze in Jerry and a few buddies later that day. Jerry cut three tunes, credited Sam's studio as the "best in the Midwest," and the rest was history. Sam had a magical ear when it came to picking artists and had made a fortune staying ahead of the curve. He was opinionated and often disagreed with conventional thinking, which sometimes got him into trouble. Carolyn and Mitch hadn't seen either of them since Danny and Rachel's wedding, and, under normal circumstances, it would have been great to catch up. But today they all briefly hugged and made small talk in a fruitless attempt to overcome the awkwardness of the moment and to delay the true purpose of their visit. But, inevitably, the meeting had to begin.

Tom ushered them into his dining room and introduced his wife, Anna, whose puffy eyes betrayed her true state of mind, though she was determined to play the part of the hostess, in an attempt to make everyone feel as comfortable as possible. She had an array of pastries on the table and offered coffee all around.

When Carolyn saw the man standing at the end of the table, it was obvious he was the homicide detective. Sometimes life imitates art, and this was one of those cases. He was clearly sent from central casting.

Detective Dave Thompson was a tall, middle-aged, handsome black man, graying at the temples, with a matching, perfectly trimmed mustache. He wore black-rimmed reading glasses, which he nervously took on and off a few times as he greeted the visitors. His finely tailored charcoal suit, white shirt, and deep-blue tie with a perfectly wrapped Windsor gave him a dignified air. Mitch didn't get close enough to tell for sure, but he detected a hint of elegant cologne. He reminded Mitch of an older version of the right fielder and clean-up hitter from his varsity team and struck him as someone he would have gravitated toward had they been at the same cocktail party. However, he clearly wasn't there to make chit-chat. After all the introductions were completed, Thompson began. Though murder was rare in this suburb of Akron, he was a pro who had done this sort of thing before. The look on his face and his demeanor, however, made it clear this was not some run-of-the-mill barroom fight gone awry. He stood up and cleared his throat.

Chapter 9

Betrayal

The trust of the innocent
Is the liar's most useful tool.
—*Stephen King*

"Please accept my condolences," the detective began. "I'm truly sorry that we have to meet under these circumstances, and I know this is very difficult for all of you, so I will try to be as brief as possible. I should be clear that I can only release a limited amount of information, and I must also insist that you keep the details of what I tell you to yourselves, because it is privileged information, and once the media gets a hold of some of these details, they are going to have a field day."

They were all arrayed around the table, expecting to hear a simple yet awful story of a husband who lost it and went on a rampage with tragic results. Dave Thompson knew the truth was far worse, and so he hesitated, trying to find the right words with which to honestly convey such devastating information with the appropriate degree of sensitivity. That last comment, about the media, brought a gasp from Maryann, and everyone leaned in a little closer.

Mitch noticed the badge clipped to Thompson's belt when he stood up. It read "to protect and serve." At his hip was a small holster with a silver chrome-and-black-trimmed pistol poking out. There was something final and deadly about the weapon. No doubt it was loaded, and no doubt it had been used over the years. Carolyn reached for Mitch's hand under the table and squeezed it tightly, bracing herself for what was to come.

Carolyn happened to be sitting just to Thompson's left, and when she glanced down and looked at the briefcase at his feet, she noticed a red file sticking up above the rest, labeled "Rachel and Evan Turner Homicide." Next to it was a blue folder labeled "Daniel Turner." How could these three lives be reduced to a few file folders? She shuddered to think of the pictures they might contain, and hoped nothing of that sort would be shown to the group. Then she realized that she needn't fear anything of the sort, but she was getting used to having crazy thoughts. The room was thick with anticipation as Thompson began to speak.

"I was going to meet with just the family members down at the station, but due to the influx of media in town, I asked Tom if he and Anna would be kind enough to let us meet here."

"We're happy to do it," Tom replied.

"I'll start at the beginning, and I invite you to stop me to ask questions at any point. According to the statement given by Maryann Turner, who is Danny and Rachel's adopted daughter," he paused as he glanced at her, "and, as you know, Rachel's cousin, the last time she saw Danny Turner alive was at approximately 7:30 p.m. on the night of Tuesday, November 16, when Mr. Turner left the Turner home to drive to a Steve's Sporting Goods store that he managed in Copley for the stated purpose of firing Logan Vonda, an employee who was caught stealing by use of the video monitor.

"Previously that day, according to Maryann, Danny called and requested that she come to the Turner home to pick up his and Rachel's two boys, Evan and Christopher, and bring them to her apartment for the night. Danny asked her for this favor because he told her that Rachel would be coming home late from Cleveland, and he wanted her to get a good night's sleep because she was scheduled to start her new job the next day, meaning Wednesday morning.

"Maryann arrived later than planned, at approximately 7:00 p.m., by which time Rachel was just a short distance from home. Rachel arrived home at approximately 7:15 p.m." The detective paused and asked, "Maryann, am I correct so far?"

"Yes, inspector, and he also kissed her on the cheek and congratulated her on passing the exam."

Silence.

Then Pete looked at her and said, "You can't be serious!"

Maryann nodded and then slammed the table, crying out, "That lying phony, how could he?" Detective Thompson let the moment pass without comment.

Then he continued. "Maryann told us she didn't notice anything strange or different between him and Rachel. It seemed just like any other night, without any particular tension. After Danny left to go to Copley, Rachel and Maryann decided the boys would not go to her apartment that night."

Thompson paused for a moment and wiped his brow. "Could I trouble you for a glass of water, Mrs. Schroeder?" Anna was quick to jump to her feet and fetch the water. Once she was seated, Thompson took a large sip, cleared his throat, and was about to start again when Sam interjected.

"So, you're saying Danny thought the boys were going to be with Maryann when he went to go fire this store clerk?"

Thompson thought for a second and said, "We can presume that, but we don't know for certain. I will try to present the facts as we know them based upon the information provided to us by the people who were participants. I would prefer to avoid making presumptions, but it's likely you are correct."

Detective Thompson continued, "At approximately 8:45, when Maryann left the Turner home, she drove past Rayburn Senior Center, and saw Danny and another man, whom she recognized as Logan Vonda, sitting in Danny's truck, talking and apparently drinking coffee." Thompson turned again to Maryann. "They were in the parking lot facing the street, according to our notes; is that correct, Maryann?"

"That's right," she answered. "I didn't think much of it at the time, except that I thought it was weird that if he had just fired Logan over in Copley, that they would be sitting together in Danny's truck, just down the road, but I forgot about it in a minute and just went home. If only I would have pulled in and asked what was going on!" Pete and Sam assured her she did the only logical thing she could do at the time.

"No," Maryann protested, "I should have known something was fishy. Danny had had to fire a lot of guys over the years because someone was always doing something to get fired, and I knew it was probably true about this guy Logan, because I'd worked with him one summer, and I knew he was into petty stuff. When he had to fire someone, Danny would do it nicely, but he would always walk the guy to his locker, make him pack up, promise to send the last check, and get him out of the store as soon as possible.

"For a second I thought about turning into the parking lot, but then I figured I would embarrass Logan, so I kept on driving. If only I would have pulled up! If only I would have insisted the boys stay at my place that night, at least Evan . . ." Maryann shook her head furiously, got up, and ran into the kitchen, followed by Anna.

Before starting again, Thompson paused and looked at the faces around the table. Mitch stared at him impatiently, but was uncertain he wanted Carolyn to hear the rest of the story because he knew the worst was yet to come. With Maryann and Anna gone, she was now the only woman remaining at the table. Her nails were digging into his palm, so he lifted her hand and clasped it between his hands. He could feel her body shaking uncontrollably.

"According to the statement by Vonda, shortly after the store closed at 7:45, Danny met with him privately, accused him of stealing from the cash register, and told him he was fired. At first Logan denied it, but then he admitted it and promised to pay back the cash. According to Logan, Danny said that it was out of his hands, that his brother and boss, Tony, had seen the video, and they had a strict policy of firing anyone caught stealing. He begged Danny not to fire him, and finally Danny said something like, 'Okay, there might be another way,' and said he should get in his truck and follow him back to his neighborhood."

"I'm sorry to interrupt, Detective," Tom said, "but if Tony saw a surveillance video of somebody stealing, we would have had to fire him, even if he did offer to pay it back. That's the store policy."

"That may be the policy, but that isn't what happened on Tuesday night, if you'll let me continue, Tom." Thompson was starting to get concerned that they were getting off track, and he was the type of person who needed to follow procedure.

For his part, Mitch began to wonder what all of this had to do with how Danny wound up killing Rachel and Evan, but he kept his mouth shut.

"So," Thompson continued, "after they arrived at the parking lot in the senior center, Logan climbed into Danny's truck. He said that Danny seemed like a different person, and had even bought him a cup of coffee. Then Danny changed his demeanor again and started yelling at him, according to Logan. Logan calmed Danny down and asked him to tell him about the idea he had mentioned back at the store, thinking Danny wanted him to obtain drugs for him. When he suggested he could take care of Danny if that was what he wanted, he says Danny just started laughing hysterically, and then said something along the lines of, 'It's gonna take much more than that.'"

"Why would this guy care so much about losing a crappy job at a sporting goods store?" Pete asked. "I'd just go down the road to another store and get a job."

"Logan isn't too bright," Tom answered, "and he had been working at Steve's for a long time, so the job was important to him."

Mitch thought he saw something the cops had overlooked, and that this might be a good time to mention it. "So, isn't it possible this Logan Vonda guy helped Danny murder Rachel and Evan? Why did Danny then commit suicide? How do we know this guy is telling the truth and that he didn't commit the murders and then stage Danny's suicide?"

Carolyn nodded and added, "I agree, that makes much more sense."

All the people who had known Danny for years warmed to this explanation, and they tried to persuade Thompson to pursue this possibility.

Thompson took a gulp of water and glanced around the table. He then said, "I know how hard this must be for all of you, or maybe I don't, because I've never had a family member or close friend commit a heinous crime like this. We have explored Logan Vonda's role, and we are fairly confident he didn't participate in the murders, but not 100 percent certain yet. However, I can tell you with certainty that Danny committed these murders and then took his own life."

There was a collective feeling that their hope that Danny might in some way be redeemed was being peremptorily dismissed. Mitch spoke again for the group. "All we are saying is that it's very suspicious that this Logan guy has admitted to plotting a crime with Danny, and that it's confusing to us that he is getting off scot-free, while Danny, who isn't here to speak for him—"

"I assure you there is much more to this story that you don't yet know," Thompson interrupted. It was obvious his patience was wearing thin. "I have tried to explain this in the way in which it unfolded because the details of the actual murders are very difficult, or, to be blunt, they are exceptionally unpleasant. Once you have heard all the facts, I assure you it will become apparent that Mr. Turner committed this crime."

He glanced at his watch. "So please, be patient and let me continue."

CHAPTER 10

Midnight

Deep into that darkness peering,
long I stood there,
wondering, fearing
—*Edgar Allan Poe*

THOMPSON HAD BEEN reading from a report that had been provided to him by the officer who interviewed Logan. He now picked up the folder with Danny's name on it. "I know that some of you are aware that Danny spent time in jail for a particularly brutal crime that he committed with his brother." Except for Tom Schroeder, all the people at the table had grown up in Cuyahoga County and were aware of this, and so they just kept silent in reaction to the comment. Without knowing it, they had come to a tacit agreement not to mention this incident. But Tom was shocked.

"What do you mean, Dave? Are you saying that Danny and Tony went to jail for killing someone?"

"No, the individual was not murdered, but Danny beat him with a tire iron, and had it not been for his brother stopping him, it is almost certain he would have killed the man."

Tom was befuddled. Danny in jail? He knew about Tony, but always presumed he was busted when a kid for selling pot or something benign like that. Tony would say he'd made some mistakes as a teenager, but he was upfront about it, and said that's what had convinced him he had to change. Tony alluded to that time as a life lesson that had contributed to his success. Tom didn't know what to make of the fact that it actually had been a serious and violent crime.

"That's really hard to believe, Dave, because Danny just doesn't, I mean, didn't have a temper. When did—"

Mitch jumped in. "It's true, Tom. Danny and Tony broke into some guy's house one night to crack into his safe and steal money. They didn't think anyone would be home, so it wasn't like a home invasion or anything, where they intended to harm someone. But it turned out the son of the owner was asleep in the house, and then Danny beat the crap out of him, and the guy wound up in the hospital, seriously injured. There was some other guy involved, but he was killed in a car accident trying to escape."

Tom just sat back, stunned, and let out a long, slow breath. At that point, Anna and Maryann returned, and asked what they were talking about. Tom told Anna he would explain things later.

"And the testimony," Thompson added, "was very explicit about the fact that Danny completely lost control of himself and was vicious in his attack. So, while that in itself isn't proof that he committed this crime, it does make what I'm about to tell you much more plausible.

"When Logan and Danny were sitting in the truck, he told Logan he wanted him to help fake a jewelry heist at his house so he could make an insurance claim of thirty thousand dollars, which he said he would share with him. Vonda told us he declined getting involved with a fraudulent insurance claim, but agreed to go to Danny's house with him and fake the robbery. He didn't think that was really a crime. So they agreed to leave Vonda's truck at the senior center and drive to Danny's house together.

"According to Logan, they arrived there at approximately 10:15, and Danny told Logan to wait in the garage for him. He also made Logan hand over his phone, saying he wanted to be sure Logan didn't tell anyone what he was doing. According to phone records, Danny made several phone calls in the next few hours, including one to his brother and several to Logan's friends, in which he claimed that he had fired Logan, and that Logan had threatened to kill him."

"But doesn't this Logan guy also have a record? Why should we believe what he has to say?" Pete asked.

"He does have a minor record, but his statements check out." Thompson replied. "When you're dealing with a crime of this nature, it's not surprising for the witnesses to be people with dicey backgrounds. We know Logan Vonda isn't a Boy Scout, and we haven't yet totally cleared him. This is an ongoing investigation. However, the fact that we have been able to verify that Danny made these calls indicates he was attempting to frame Vonda and create an alibi for himself.

"Then, according to Vonda, Danny went inside the house and told him he would come back to the garage to get him once Rachel fell asleep. At around 11:30, he came back and told Logan to break the glass at the back door of the garage, to make it look like a break-in, and then he went back into the house."

Carolyn, like the rest of the group, was totally confused. They all looked at each other impatiently. Now the detective was coming to the difficult part.

"At around 1 a.m., or some time shortly afterward, Danny returned to the garage again, and told Logan that there was a change in plans. He never really planned to steal jewelry; in fact, there wasn't any jewelry to steal. Instead, he wanted his help in killing Rachel."

"Whoa, whoa, whoa!" Now Mitch was totally nonplused. "I know it's reported that Vonda stayed in the garage all night. Who in God's name would simply hang around when somebody tells him he wants help killing his wife? That sounds like total crap to me. That's when anyone would just pick up and leave."

"Well, Logan says he stayed because, when he refused to help Danny kill Rachel, Danny then said something like, 'Did you think I was serious? I was just putting you on, dude,' and Logan was convinced that he wasn't serious about killing her," Thompson answered and continued.

"However, he started to get 'freaked out,' to use his term, because Danny wasn't acting like himself. The last time he appeared at the door, he had seemed calm and had turned on the garage light. This time he seemed jumpy and wild-eyed, shouted, and stood in the dark. He refused to give Logan his cell phone, and then he abruptly went back into the house. Logan says that at that point he got spooked; he found a pipe sitting in the corner, placed it on the passenger seat, and then fell asleep. He didn't wake up until around 4 a.m., when Danny opened the garage door.

"We believe that Danny committed the murders sometime between midnight and one o'clock, prior to when he asked Vonda to help murder Rachel."

Everyone at the table was speechless, confused, and dubious about the whole picture, but no one interrupted Thompson.

"Vonda said that he next saw Danny around 4 a.m. At that time he appeared to have showered and changed his clothes and his demeanor was very different. He seemed very calm. Vonda asked if he could have his cell phone back, and Danny gave it to him, along with Rachel's car keys, and told him to leave her car in the lot at the senior center. So Logan left, and then discovered several voice messages concerning the calls Danny had made to his friends. He then got into his own car and drove to his manager's house, and they called Tony Turner, who was on vacation in Italy."

Now Sam had to speak up. This was his sister and nephew who had been murdered. He generally didn't trust the cops, and this was clearly an example of a small-town force blowing an investigation. He was apoplectic that they would believe such an outlandish story. Additionally, they were clearly overlooking one very important and obvious fact. He tried to maintain his respectful demeanor without success as his question turned into a statement and then an accusation.

"Officer, it's hard enough to believe that somebody would just take a nap with all this craziness going on, but, excuse my language . . . how the *hell* can you believe this Vonda creep would sleep through the sound of several gunshots? The house isn't that big. Come on, this is total nonsense."

He rolled his eyes and looked around the table for support. Before anyone could respond, Thompson replied abruptly.

"Well, that's the point I'm coming to. There weren't any gunshots." Thompson was dreading telling this part of the story to the family, but the moment had finally arrived.

⇢═◎ ◎═⇠

Mitch tipped his chair back, curled his fingers behind his head, and started to realize what the detective was alluding to. Perhaps the rumors he'd heard earlier that morning were true. The rest of the people around the table must have heard the same rumors, but no one wanted to accept that Danny might have beaten his wife and child to death, as the news reports contended.

Now they were completely silent, save for Maryann, who said softly, "I didn't want to believe it when I first heard it." Carolyn stared at her without a clue. Then she turned to Thompson, touched his hand, and said, "What are you trying to tell us?"

"Listen, I know this isn't going to be pleasant to hear, and if anyone wants to leave before I go further, please do so." No one moved. "As awful as a simple gunshot, multiple homicide would have been, this wasn't that. This was much worse. It's easily the most horrific crime scene I have ever encountered in my career."

"Perhaps it's time for you to tell us the details," Pete said in a quiet, dull monotone. No one wanted to go there, but everyone knew they had to.

"Both victims were brutally stabbed and beaten in a manner that is commonly referred to in a homicide investigation as 'overkill,' meaning the victims would have died had they only incurred a fraction of their wounds, but the killer continued to stab and bludgeon them in an excessive and frenzied manner. I'm sorry to have to be so graphic, but there is no other way to say it."

Carolyn simply stood up and walked out the front door without bothering to collect her coat. Mitch went after her and brought her back inside; he asked Anna to take her to the kitchen and sit with her for a few minutes. Then he returned while Thompson was starting to describe the crime scene.

"At some time, but definitely after midnight, Danny went upstairs to Rachel's room with the intent to bludgeon her to death. She was apparently sleeping at that time."

"Bludgeon her with what?" Mitch asked.

"Are you familiar with the furniture in the house?" he asked Mitch.

"Yeah, I guess so."

"Then you might recall that there was a brownish lamp in the living room that had a very heavy base. Danny cut the cord with a small kitchen knife, removed the lamp shade, and used that as the primary weapon."

Despite the fact Carolyn was repulsed by what she overheard while sitting in the kitchen, she walked back into the dining room to ask the question that was on everyone's mind at that moment.

"Did Rachel ever know what happened?" She prayed that at least it had ended quickly. Dear God, she thought, if only she could have been given that small gift.

"I'm afraid she did. Though Danny probably thought that one blow to the head would have been sufficient to kill her, it wasn't. She apparently fought back with all her strength, and might even had been able to stand up, but Danny then used the knife he had taken from the kitchen and stabbed her. The knife was not very big, only around two inches long, so at some point Danny grabbed a pair of scissors off the sewing table and overpowered and stabbed Rachel with those." Thompson was purposely withholding some information because he knew it would be too upsetting to the friends and family, and tried to move on.

"That's the long and short of it. The—"

"Did Rachel at least not know it was Danny?" Carolyn interrupted, as her bar was lowered yet another notch.

"I'm afraid it's almost certain she did. This struggle went on for several minutes, and even though we suppose the room was dark, she must have recognized his voice, and there's no doubt there was a great deal of shouting between them, which is likely what caused the children to wake up. Many items in the immediate region were knocked to the floor, so there was clearly a pretty fierce struggle. Additionally, the victim had many defensive marks on her arms, and what we presume to be Danny's skin under her fingernails. She was fighting for her life, and there's no doubt she knew her attacker."

"How long did it take?" Now Carolyn needed to know.

"Given the number of stab wounds, I would estimate more than a minute, but less than two minutes."

Mitch spoke up, asking a question he had to ask, having to do with that odious word he'd just learned, "overkill." Dreading the answer, he barely could form full sentences.

"Number of stab wounds? How many, where . . .?"

Thompson paused before answering, pretending to look through some papers. That particular fact had been the topic of much discussion between the officers at the crime scene, and it was emblazoned on his mind. "There were approximately forty stab wounds, some to the torso, but many to the face and neck."

Sam and Pete leaned against each other as brothers will and wiped tears from their cheeks. The sounds of sniffling and nose-blowing filled the silence. Anna had thoughtfully placed a box of tissues within reach on the table. There was something about that last part of the last sentence that seemed to get to everyone. It was all too much. Anna, a reader of P. D. James, Patricia Cornwell, and Ann Rule, knew to ask about the piece of information Detective Thompson had glossed over.

"Officer, what was the official cause of death?"

"A combination of multiple stab wounds, a severed carotid artery, and numerous blunt-force traumas, including a broken jaw. The severed artery alone could have caused death, as well as the trauma to the head, had she been left unattended, but in combination, death occurred at the time of the attack." He thumbed through some papers. "The medical examiner hasn't completed the autopsy yet, but my notes say that the victim suffered a severed left carotid artery that resulted in exsanguination—which means bleeding to death—so that will likely be the official cause of death when the autopsy report is completed."

As Thompson was speaking, Carolyn peered out the picture window and tried to focus on the trees in the Schroeders' yard. Her eye landed on the house across the street. What an ugly yellow color the owners had painted it. Who would do that? A car motored by, and two teenagers on skateboards invaded the soccer game in which the Schroeder kids were engaged. They all started shouting with their kid voices. It sounded good. For a moment, she found some solace in the normal things of life. Then, as if on cue, a flock of five or six crows descended upon the front yard and started arrogantly parading around like a bunch of gangsters busting their way into rival territory.

She could sense Detective Thompson was struggling to relate the facts with as much compassion as possible, and she felt sorry for him, but was repulsed nonetheless by the litany of words that were being uttered regarding her best friend, "the victim." Phrases like 'blunt force trauma," "severed artery," "exsangu-something," "autopsy," "medical examiner." The scene outside at least offered a mild distraction and provided some reassurance the world was still humming along despite the horror being discussed within these walls. Then those damned crows had to appear. She felt herself starting to slip away.

She knew they had yet to discuss Evan. What a sweet little boy. She pictured his cherubic face. He was always laughing, and so easygoing, even as an infant, even on the day he was born. She remembered the first time she held him, just a few hours after his birth. He came into this world on a wintery night in December, almost eleven years ago. Danny had a great story about that night, and how their beat-up old Camry went skating down Mayfield on the part that bottoms out at Chagrin River Road. Danny's imitation of Rachel freaking out was hilarious. He said he didn't know Rachel could curse like a construction worker until that night. When they got to the hospital, the nurses rushed her into the delivery room and Evan made his appearance in no time at all. He was never any trouble his whole little life, and Rachel and Danny were glowing that night.

Now all three were gone.

⊷═◉ ◉═◅⊶

Dave Thompson had over twenty years on the force, and naturally he'd seen things and done things no one should ever have to see or do. When he was a patrolman, the single worst assignment had been delivering bad news in person. There is nothing quite like the look of horror a cop gets when he appears at someone's door unannounced and asks to be admitted in order to convey some information. Several times people had slammed the door in his face, or, after letting him in, they had run away and hid in the house before he could speak. The task was always awful, but when it concerned the death of a child, it was brutal. His wife knew it took a toll because she would hear him rise some days at three in the morning.

Dave had a son right around Evan's age. When he entered Evan's room, and turned on the overhead light, he saw the same Cleveland Browns poster that James had hanging above his headboard, in almost the exact position Evan had placed his.

The child in the bed looked as if he had been tucked in for the night, but his face was almost unrecognizable, and the blanket covering him was soaked a sickening purple. The people around the table now staring at him expectantly hadn't seen him lurch outside the Turner residence and lose his breakfast yesterday morning. They looked at him with a mixture of fear and anticipation, needing to know, but wishing to leave. He didn't think he would ever be able to escape the image that was embedded in his mind. Now, for the first time in his career, he wanted to bolt. Instead, he asked for directions to the bathroom, and excused himself.

When he returned, the discussion abruptly stopped. It was evident that Evan would be the next topic of discussion. "I do not think it's necessary," he started, "to go into the degree of detail I did in the case of Rachel's death."

Everyone around the table agreed.

"Officer," Carolyn began, "do we know why Danny killed Evan?"

"We can only speculate on that matter, of course, but based upon the physical evidence, and some comments from Evan's brother, it appears that Evan attempted to stop Danny while he was attacking Rachel, and he lashed out, possibly because he thought it was Logan Vonda behind him."

The detective was hopeful no one would ask the next obvious question regarding the amount of injuries the boy suffered, which were very similar to his mother's. Thankfully the next question moved on to Christopher.

"Dave," Tom said quietly, "do we have any idea why Danny *didn't* harm Christopher?"

"We really don't, Tom, but as you know, because you were the first to mention it, there was a blood impression on Christopher's back, which we presume came from Danny pushing him into his room. It is very likely that Danny simply came to his senses and was able to stop at that point."

"Or that God intervened," Anna suggested.

"If He did, He arrived too late for Rachel and Evan," Sam said, but instantly regretted he had opened his mouth.

"Well, we don't know," Thompson continued, "but we do know that Christopher said he went back to sleep afterward, and he was clearly in a state of shock when Tom found him." Thompson didn't think it necessary to mention that the eight-year-old likely attempted to rouse his brother and mother, because blood was found on his hands and under his fingernails.

"I'm sorry, everyone, but I really do have to get back downtown." Dave handed his business card to Maryann, Pete, and Sam and promised to be in touch with any other relevant information, and then quickly said his good-byes. After Tom closed the door behind him, he exhaled for the first time in the last hour and relished the cold air on his face.

Then Dave Thompson drove right past the station house, to his own front door, snatched up his little boy, and held him until he squirmed free.

CHAPTER 11

Boots, Shoes, Hands, and Feet

Go out into the darkness,
And put your hand into the hand of God.
—Minnie Louise Haskins,
"God Knows"

ONE FEBRUARY MORNING when Joanna Larson was eleven years old, she went outside to shovel the snow off of her parents' driveway. Today was her father's birthday and this was going to be her present to him. She had planned to purchase a pair of shoes, because he'd mentioned that was what he needed, but she was only able to amass three dollars and the shoes cost seven. Technically, they were work boots, not shoes, and, as the year was 1962, boots could be purchased for seven dollars, because a 3 Musketeers bar cost a nickel.

She was frustrated and angry with herself for not being able to buy the boots, because she hated to disappoint him and knew how important they were. Now the only gift she had was the card she had made with a picture of the boots pasted inside, along with the promise they would come in the near future. A few weeks before, when she'd seen the advertisement in the *New York Daily News* featuring a black-and-white drawing of the boots, she had shown it to her dad and declared she would find a way to purchase them. The advertisement had been placed by the Thom McCan store on Flatbush Avenue and had warned that the sale price was for a limited time only, so the pressure was on.

In order to motivate herself, she had clipped the drawing out of the newspaper and displayed it on her dresser drawer. She would pick it up and look at it whenever she was tempted to leap on her bike and ride down the block to Mr. Schultz's store. Schultz's was a wonderland that contained every comic book or candy bar known to mankind and naturally Joanna was a regular customer. Mrs. Schultz got a kick out of her, so when she was sent on a mission to buy a loaf of bread or a bottle of milk, she would usually emerge with a free licorice stick along with her purchase.

The fact that she didn't have a gift for her dad other than the card caused her great anxiety. She knew her father was planning to find a job, and without a pair of work boots, this would probably be impossible. However, he had chuckled the day before when she'd delivered the bad news.

"Oh, Joanna," he'd said, "you're so sweet, but I'll get the money to buy a pair of shoes soon." Her father had been touched by his daughter's sincerity. "And don't worry about me finding a job. I just heard yesterday that something was going to open up at the Sunoco station in a few weeks." But Joanna did worry, because her mother worried, and always would say her father had a hard time keeping a job because of his heart condition.

So that is how she came to be in the backyard, shoveling snow, when the event that would alter her life forever occurred.

Her dad's green and white 1956 Chevy Bel Air was safely tucked away in the garage, but it had snowed heavily the night before and there was close to a foot on the ground. Joanna planned to cut two paths from the garage to the driveway, so that when her dad pulled out he would be able to glide down the driveway the Larsons shared with their next-door neighbor and head straight out onto the street. This proved to be harder than it looked. She was exhausted after shoveling only one path not even six feet long, and realized that her wool mittens made it next to impossible to grip the shovel's handle. So she took a break for a minute to try to figure things out, toying with her breath in the frosty air.

Mike and Joan Larson rented the apartment on the first floor of a two-family attached building, and the bedrooms were at the rear of the house facing the garage where Joanna now stood. The bedroom her mother and father shared was right above the basement door. Her mother was up already, preparing breakfast, but her father was asleep, and wasn't expected to rise for another hour or so, which gave Joanna enough time to surprise him with a pristine driveway. She hoped he wouldn't be awakened by the sound of the shovel scraping the ground and then peek out from behind the curtain and ruin her surprise.

She was looking at his window and thinking about how pleased he would be, and what a big deal he would make of her handiwork, when suddenly she felt a tingling come over her body. It was almost as if she could feel her father's presence, but she knew he was still in the house, asleep. Then she noticed a blue haze that appeared to emanate from the top of the window. It quickly grew into the shape of a large, slender bubble that began to dance back and forth as if blown by the wind, while it continued to grow brighter and larger. Finally it broke free of the window and shuttled into the air until it reached the roof line, and then rapidly flew upward through the sky until it became a speck and disappeared into the clouds.

She dropped the shovel and ran toward her front door and into the house. She was overcome by the certainty that her father had just died. Once she was inside, she shot past her mother who was standing at the kitchen sink and threw open the door to her parents' bedroom. The room was dark, and she saw her father lying there, his back to her, on his side, his hands folded under his head, facing the window.

"Daddy! Daddy!" she yelled and began to leap onto the bed.

Just before her feet left the floor, her mother grabbed her around the waist and harshly whispered "Shush, Jo, let your father sleep. It's his birthday." Then she dragged her out and closed the door.

"What's the matter with you? Can't you see he's sleeping?" her mother asked, annoyed.

"Mom, I know something's wrong. I saw this big blue balloon come out of the window and go into the sky!"

"What are you talking about, sweetie? What do you mean about a big balloon?"

"A big blue balloon! It flew away and took Dad with it!"

Joanna's mom squatted down on her haunches and looked into her little girl's eyes. Joanna had a vivid imagination and often saw strange things and said even stranger things. "Don't worry. Dad is okay. Just let him sleep a while longer, and we'll get him up when the waffles are ready."

Joanna held vigil in the kitchen, watching her mother make the batter and pour it into the waffle maker, and repeatedly asked after the status, until at last her mother said breakfast was ready. As soon as her mother opened the door to the bedroom, Joanna jumped off the kitchen chair, hit her knees, and prayed with all of her might. She pointed the tips of her fingers straight to heaven as the nuns had taught her, and repeated under her breath, "please God, please God," over and over.

The next thing she heard was her mother screaming the words she feared the most. "Oh, my God! Mike, Mike, wake up! Oh, no! He's all blue!"

-→▐═◉ ◉═▌←-

The tradition in that part of Brooklyn at the time was for Roman Catholic families to hold a wake for several days. Joanna thought it was silly that they called it a "wake," when they knew the person in the casket was not going to wake up. It seemed to her that everyone just sat around and whispered, and left as soon as they could, but the family members stayed throughout the hours the funeral home was open. This became the new normal for Joanna, and she found that she would regularly inspect the floral arrangements and meander over to kneel beside her father as often as possible. She wanted to make certain she did not miss one second that she could look at her dad, even though he really didn't look like himself. She was filled with dread at the idea that in just a few days they would put him in the ground, and she would never see him again.

Her dad had treated her like a princess. He had loved to lift her up onto his lap, and tickle her belly or make a silly sound blowing on her neck. Whenever she would come home from school or he would enter the house at the end of the day, he would make his first glimpse of her seem like a celebration. He had always made her feel special, and so she wanted to do something for him—but she couldn't, and, on top of that, now she never would be able to buy him those work boots, so she felt she had broken her promise. She did the little things she could, such as straightening his tie, pressing down the handkerchief in his suit pocket so it would lie flat, and adjusting the rosary beads in his hands, though they didn't move at all. This last thing she didn't like to do because his hands felt so cold and hard. In real life, her dad had hardly ever worn a suit, but here he was, all dressed up in the dark suit he saved for special occasions, such as weddings and christenings.

Mr. Crook held the front door for Joanna and her mom at the end of the evening, and they heard the click of the locks after he assured Joanna he would take good care of "Mr. Larson" that Saturday night. Joanna thought it was odd that someone would have a name like that, but right there on the sign it said "Crook's Funeral Home." So Joanna and her mom held hands and walked home together in silence. The snow had started to melt, but a wind was blowing, and Joanna worried her dad might not be warm enough.

Her mother was not yet ready to sleep in the bed she had shared with her husband for the last sixteen years, and so she climbed in with Joanna in her little bed, and the two women held each other until they fell asleep.

That night Joanna dreamed she saw her father walking through a forest, wearing the same dark suit he had on now. He was walking down a path, and kept turning his head and calling to her. But he had to go somewhere, so he kept on walking fast, taking extra big strides. She chased him; sometimes he would disappear behind the trees and sometimes he would briefly reemerge, but he kept walking. She kept chasing him, because she could tell he was saying something important. Then he started pointing to the ground, but she couldn't understand what he was saying because he was too far away. Suddenly she was right next to him. He had to be somewhere soon, so he wasn't able to stop, but he turned to face her and said, "My feet are so cold; I don't have any shoes on." And sure enough, she could see his bare feet kicking up the snow as he walked down the path and around a bend and disappeared. Then she woke up. Since it was almost morning, she went into the kitchen and filled the kettle with water to make some oatmeal for herself and a cup of tea for her mother.

In a few minutes, her mother called to her from the bedroom. "Joanna, sweetheart, come here. I can't start this day without a hug from you."

Joanna was thinking about telling her mom about her dream when the whistle on the kettle blew. "I'll get it, Mom."

When they sat down to breakfast, Joanna broached the subject.

"Mom, is Dad wearing shoes? I mean, now, at Mr. Crook's?"

"Yes, he is. Don't worry; I took care of that with Uncle Jim yesterday."

"But how do you know for sure?" Joanna wasn't easily dissuaded, and she was always one to insist, particularly when she knew she was right.

"Your uncle brought a pair of dress shoes he had at home, and we gave them to Mr. Crook, with a pair of socks. So you see, it's all been taken care of."

"But how do we know he put them on Dad?"

Her mother reached over and took Joanna's little hand in hers; she knew what was going on. "I know you're upset because you were going to buy your dad a new pair of shoes, but he is with God now, and also, we made a point of getting Dad a nice pair of shoes. It really is okay."

But Joanna wasn't convinced, so when they got to the funeral home that morning before the official opening time, she asked Mr. Crook about it.

Despite his surname, Crook was a kindly old gentleman, who understood how difficult it was for a child to lose a parent. He usually counseled parents not to bring children as young as Joanna to the viewing, but Joan Larson had insisted her daughter attend, and so he wasn't surprised by the question. It was the type of thing children always asked.

"Mrs. Larson," he said, "I wouldn't normally do this, but I can see that Joanna is very concerned, so perhaps we should just open up the lower part of the casket for a second to reassure her." Mr. Crook knew things like this could stay with a child for a lifetime, and since it was so simple to show her, they walked over to the casket, and he lifted the lid that covered the bottom portion.

Much to the amazement of Mr. Crook and Joan Larson, Mike's bare feet were sticking out of the bottom of his pant legs, white as marble. Mr. Crook, clearly very embarrassed, blushed and then turned angry.

"I'm very sorry. There must be some mistake. I didn't er—dress the body . . ." He closed the lid and stormed off, blathering to himself and promising to return with the shoes and socks.

Joanna began to cry at the sight of her father's bare feet, and her mother brought her over to the chairs reserved for the family and sat her down. "Joanna, how do you know these things?

"I don't know, Mom. I just do."

"I guess I'm just going to have to start believing you when you tell me things like this. I'm so sorry I didn't trust what you said, but it just sounded so . . . so crazy. Then again, it also sounded crazy when you told me Dad was gone, and I just kept on making breakfast."

"It's okay, Mom, you didn't know. I'm just glad Dad's feet will be warm."

After a few minutes, Mr. Crook returned. He was visibly upset, and was stammering.

"I don't know how to tell you this, but apparently, by some mistake, the shoes were thrown out."

Joan, who was normally mild-mannered, was incredulous, and stood up to speak to Mr. Crook in a hushed but firm tone. "Mr. Crook, I can't believe you would not put shoes on my husband in the first place, and then just throw out the shoes we gave you, and not tell me. What are you going to do about it?"

Mr. Crook took Joan by the arm and led her away from Joanna, who trailed right behind. "Please understand, Mrs. Larson," he said, looking at his watch, "we are going to open the doors in five minutes. We'll have to purchase another pair, but with today being Sunday, and the department stores closed all day, and mass scheduled for ten o'clock tomorrow morning, there may not be time. But I will do my best to find another pair, somehow."

"Mr. Crook, that's not good enough. My husband is not leaving here unless he has socks and shoes on!"

Before he could answer, Joanna spoke up. "I know! I'll go home and get the shoes Daddy always wore. They might be scuffy, but no one will know, except for us, and they'll probably be more comfortable anyway."

Somehow there was a logic to this that even the grown-ups could understand. Unbeknownst to Mr. Crook and her mom, Joanna now realized that this was exactly how things were supposed to turn out.

Unlike today, back then an eleven-year-old child could walk three blocks down a street on a Brooklyn morning, and let herself into her apartment without a parent having to fear a thing, so Joanna was allowed to go on this mission alone.

"Hurry back, Joanna," her mom said as she buttoned her coat and gave her a kiss.

After Joanna reached home, and let herself into the apartment, she hesitated before opening the door to her parents' bedroom. She took a deep breath and finally forced herself to go in, going immediately to her dad's closet without looking at the bed. She gasped when she saw his shirts and pants. The first thing she noticed was the brown and white flannel shirt he had been wearing last Thursday night. She held it to her face and basked in his scent; closing her eyes, she felt the rubble of his beard when they kissed for the last time.

She knew the shoes were on the floor of the closet somewhere, but it was dark, so she groped around among his personal belongings: a stack of magazines and books, a transistor radio, a toolbox, and a box containing the sort of personal miscellaneous memorabilia one collects over a lifetime. She dug through the disarray and eventually her hand landed on the shoes.

They were as old and worn as she remembered, and so she dragged a kitchen chair over to the closet and reached up on the shelf to retrieve the box that held the shoe polish and rags that were stained black and brown. She sat in the chair and put her hand inside the shoes, and she rubbed and buffed until they looked as good as new. She knew her dad was there with her, and felt his hands on her shoulders the instant she put her hand in his shoe. She didn't want this time to end, but knew her mother needed her to return, and so when both shoes were finished, she put everything back in order and prepared to leave.

I guess God really does have a plan, and I don't have to understand it or agree with it, she thought. She knew her dad was in that room and not really in the box sitting at Crook's Funeral Home. Before she closed the door, she looked back and broke the silence, saying, "Good-bye, Dad. Don't worry about me, and don't worry about Mom, because I'll always take care of her."

That night, after all the visitors were gone, Mr. Crook opened the casket again, and Joanna and her mom watched while he slipped on the socks and shoes.

"I guess you got to give Dad a pair of shoes after all, honey," her mom said as they reached their front door. But Joanna already knew that.

→≡◉ ◉≡←

By the time Joanna was ready to go to college, she had grown into a beautiful young woman, with the dark coloring of her father, complemented by the soft features and blonde hair of her mother. She had dated a few high school guys but was a very serious student, as were the majority of the boys who also attended Stuyvesant High School. Almost all of the guys were science geeks, but Joanna was focused on literature, history, and the study of religions. Joanna was one of the first young women to be admitted to Stuyvesant, probably the most prestigious high school in New York City. The courses were very demanding, which suited Joanna's temperament.

Her gift to see things and know things was, at times, unsettling. By now, however, it had become a part of her routine. Sometimes it was very beneficial. When she insisted her mother go to the doctor for a checkup, Joan followed her direction, because by now she had accepted the fact that Joanna had a sixth sense that was very powerful. The doctor said it was fortunate that she had come in for the checkup, because he caught her cancer early, and her doctors were able to successfully treat her.

When some of her relatives heard the stories about Joanna, they asked her to do things like pick the winning horses at the racetrack or the team that would win the World Series, but she always pretended not to know such things. She knew her gift was special, but it also brought great responsibility.

One day she was walking from the subway to her apartment in Greenpoint, when she was drawn to a young man walking ahead of her on the street. She couldn't see his face, but she knew he was very angry. *Angry about what?* she thought. Then she heard his mind: *I know she's cheating on me. I'm going to beat the hell out of her as soon as I get home.*

She immediately threw herself on the ground. "Help, mister. Help me!" she cried. He stopped and turned around, and was tempted to keep going, but instead he came over to her.

"Are you okay?"

"No, I'm not. Could you please help me up? Could you walk me to that bench over there?" She pretended to limp and moaned in great pain.

When they got to the bench, she raised her head and looked him straight in the eye. "Your wife is a good woman. She loves you very much, and she is faithful to you. You shouldn't hurt her."

The man blinked at her. "How did you know . . . ? I don't get it." But she had succeeded in slowing him down, and he sat next to her on the bench and thought about what she had said.

Joanna was used to this sort of reaction by now, and she knew it was better not to try to explain, but simply to help. "Trust me, sir, I know. You're lucky to have such a good wife. I know you think she is interested in the man who lives in the apartment below you, but she isn't. You should tell him to leave her alone, and he will. He'll be afraid of you."

They sat and talked for the next fifteen minutes, and finally he thanked her, and headed home in a completely different state of mind.

This sort of thing happened from time to time with Joanna. In a flash, she could see the two different directions this man might take. If he took the path of kindness, forgiveness, and trust, he would go on to live a fulfilling life of hard work that would allow him and his wife to move to the suburbs, raise several children, and one day be surrounded by a large, loving family. If he chose the path of mistrust, hate, and violence, he would be in jail by nightfall, his wife severely beaten and almost dead. She would divorce him, and, after his release from jail, he would grow into a lonely and bitter old man. It was almost as if two movies ran in her head simultaneously.

On this occasion she had been successful, but it didn't always turn out that way. There were many times when she would envision someone about to perform a dreadful act, but found herself incapable of intervening and altering the course of events. God gave us free will, she reasoned, but God also permitted evil to exist in the world, and when the enemy was determined, he was a vicious adversary. These times were excruciatingly painful for her, both physically and emotionally. As the years went on, she learned to sense when she was outmatched, and, with rare exceptions, she would step out of the situation.

As a teenager, she had struggled at times. She was proud of her gift, and would forget that it wasn't something she had earned, that it didn't make her better than others. At times pride would overtake her. Once, she told a friend about her gift (referring to it as a "power"), and the girl challenged her to prove herself by curing her brother, who had been born with a club foot. Joanna was tempted to do so, and tried, but she drew a blank. Disappointed, her friend accused her of being a fraud.

At dinner that night, she told her mother about the incident, and Joan knew the time had come for a serious discussion.

"Joanna," she said, "you and I both know that you have been given a very special ability, but it's only through the grace of God that you have it, and so it's not to be trifled with. I don't know why you were given this talent, but it's clear that God selected you because He knew you would know how to use it properly. *You* can't heal anyone; you can only petition God to heal someone. I don't know why He seems to hear you when He doesn't hear others, or why He allows you to know things that others don't, but—"

"But, maybe God wants me to heal others like the apostles were able to heal people in His name after Jesus was resurrected!"

"That may be so, Joanna, and if you are so directed, then so it will be. But I can guarantee you that unless you are humble and quiet about this gift, it will be taken away. God knows that you will be tempted by pride and the desire to be admired and loved by others, and I am sure He does not want you to succumb to those temptations. Remember that the Devil is alive and well and does his work through others who may not even know they are being used."

She knew her mother was right, and there it was, the part that scared her the most. The Enemy.

--->===◎ ◎===<---

Joanna felt a direct connection to God, but, despite her upbringing, she couldn't persuade herself to believe in any particular religion. As she matured into a strong woman, she was offended by the fact that most religions were begun and run by men, and that women were never treated as equals. She studied the Bible, but found that some of the sections, particularly in the Old Testament, treated women in a disrespectful manner, and she understood how some of those beliefs were used over the years as a justification for subjugating women.

However, in the New Testament, she was touched by the suffering of Jesus's mother, Mary, and the faith she showed when the angel Gabriel came to her to tell her she was going to have a child. Because Joanna also experienced supernatural occurrences, she could appreciate how lonely Mary must have felt when she was mocked and treated as an outcast. An unmarried pregnant woman is still shunned today, so imagine the criticism Mary had to endure! She also loved Joseph because he embodied the concept of a man who trusted and protected both his wife and child, though in the natural, other men must have considered him a cuckold.

But the woman who really spoke to Joanna was Mary Magdalene, because it was through her that Jesus was able to demonstrate one of the primary lessons of forgiveness. In many ways the story about Mary Magdelene was similar to the one about the woman who was accused of adultery. He drew the line in the sand, and encouraged those who were without sin to cast the first stone. Of course that meant no one could throw a stone. Forgiveness was difficult, and sometimes it seemed impossible, but if everyone in the world practiced it, then there would be much less pain and suffering in the world.

Before Joanna left for college, she decided to confide in a pastor to whom she naturally gravitated, who seemed to be a learned and patient man. She was convinced he would listen to her situation carefully and advise her. Much to her astonishment, he not only listened, but also confided to her that he, too, had a similar ability, and said it had been both a blessing and a curse in his life. He warned her that she would be tempted to use her ability for personal gain, and that it was a dangerous thing to do.

"Joanna," he admitted, "I know this because I made that mistake, and I suffered for it. I am indeed grateful that I was visited one day by an angel who led me to see the true meaning of this gift, and that I should be guided by a simple and honest prayer."

Then he handed her a card with a prayer on it, and told her to memorize it, and to rely on it whenever she needed guidance. She knew the prayer and had recited it many times, but from that point forward, it became the guiding principle of her life:

Lord, make me an instrument of Thy peace;
Where there is hatred, let me sow love;
Where there is injury, pardon;
Where there is error, truth;
Where there is doubt, faith;
Where there is despair, hope;
Where there is darkness, light;
And where there is sadness, joy.
O Divine Master, Grant that I may not so much seek
To be consoled as to console;
To be understood as to understand;
To be loved as to love.
For it is in giving that we receive;
It is in pardoning that we are pardoned;
And it is in dying that we are born to eternal life.

The "Prayer of Saint Francis" said everything she needed to know as she began her journey toward a life of ministry.

⊷⊷⧫ ⧫⊷⊷

After she graduated from the University of Chicago, Joanna studied at the Chicago Theological Seminary, and spent several years as a visiting assistant pastor at several churches in the Midwest. She returned to

Chicago to open a home for battered women, and decided that would be the focus of her work. She was repulsed at how often men would take advantage of women because they were stronger and larger, and how vulnerable these women and their children were. Joanna, on the other hand, was fearless. She thought nothing of placing herself between a man filled with hate and righteousness and his wife and child, and sometimes—but not always—could tame the wildest of beasts. She had purposely chosen a dangerous profession.

In 1995, she moved to Cleveland to join the ministry of the man she had met and married, who had devoted his life to working with young men who had been abandoned by their fathers, which was his experience. The cycle of violence had to be broken, and so she and Richard grew their ministry in a tiny church they purchased from the city for a dollar on Fifty-fifth Street. They were surrounded by crime and drug dealers, but neither of them feared for their own safety. They were guided.

Richard helped Joanna learn how to balance her gift with her responsibilities as a pastor, mother, and wife, but it concerned him that sometimes she would be taken with a particular problem and wouldn't let it go, despite the personal toll it would take on her. A lifetime of this work had aged her prematurely, and her hair had turned so light, it was almost luminescent. Perhaps her physical challenges were the price she was to pay for her gift. However, if God chose her to intercede in a particular situation, she knew not to question His wisdom, although it had become more difficult in recent years. And that was her plight on the morning of the Turner family murders.

-→⥱ ⥲←-

All through the night, Joanna kept pushing Danny to forget about his insane scheme and to drive away with the young man waiting in the garage. At one point, he had a moment of clarity and decided to forget about his absurd plan. Joanna rejoiced that she had finally reached him, but then he abruptly turned around, rushed into the living room, and cut the cord to the lamp. He decided in that instant that it was too late to turn back. How would he ever explain cutting the cord to Rachel and the kids?

Danny began to walk up the stairs, the cord dragging at his feet, convinced he was past the point of no return, unaware of the dark figure at his back, urging him toward the horrid actions that would soon result in so much misery.

When it was all over and she sat by the window early that morning, trying to let the cool breeze assuage the pain that racked her body, she felt she had in some way failed. Perhaps it was too late now to do anything for this family. Perhaps she should ignore this particular problem. Perhaps it was really none of her business. The agony and horror that filled this world were much bigger and stronger than she was. Perhaps she was too old and tired to take on this problem. Better to leave it for someone younger.

And then she saw her father's smiling face in the reflection in the glass, confident and happy, and she was reminded of the amazing healing power of the Lord. She laughed when she recognized the true author of her doubts, and how skilled he was at subtly encouraging her to quit. But she saw it for what it was: just another devious trick.

Don't worry, Dad, your scrappy little girl won't give up without a good fight, she thought, and then she said in a bold, loud voice: "Okay, now I'm ready."

CHAPTER 12

A Thread of Light

To love and win is the best thing;
To love and lose, the next best.
—*William Makepeace Thackeray*

AFTER DAVE THOMPSON drove off, the group sat in stunned silence until Tom came back into the dining room, and they were sure they were alone. Pete was the first to speak.

"Well, I'm grateful he was so open with us, but it still feels like there's a lot of unanswered questions," he sighed.

"That's for sure," agreed Mitch. "You'll never convince me that Vonda just sat out there in the car all night, didn't hear anything, and fell asleep. It doesn't add up."

Mitch heard himself speaking and felt disingenuous as the words came out of his mouth. In the back of his mind, he knew that it was somehow easier to focus on the mysteries surrounding the crime than on the awful brutality of Danny's actions. While it was true that there was probably more to the story, there was no escaping the fact that Danny had killed his wife and child and then committed suicide, in each instance in the most gruesome way imaginable. Playing detective created an artificial wall that provided a bit of a respite for the group, however, and so they all indulged.

After a few minutes of rehashing the meeting with Detective Thompson, the group moved on to the particulars of the funeral service. Because Rachel's older sister, Terry, hadn't been heard from in several years, and no one knew how to contact her, the burden of making all the decisions regarding the service, burial, and other issues had fallen on Maryann, Pete, and Sam. Pete and Sam admittedly had had very little contact with Rachel, Danny, and the kids over the last ten years, so their role was a bit removed. It was really Maryann, as the adult child, who would bear the brunt of all the ugly choices to be made over the next few days.

Of course, there was the big, fat elephant that had shoved its way into the living room, and had sat there huffing and puffing, ignored until this point. Sam, who was never one to avoid a conflict, bluntly brought it up.

"So, are we going to have a service for just Rachel and Evan, or should we include Danny, also?" There it was. Had the mother, father, and child died in a car accident, there would be no need to ask the question, even if the father had been driving drunk, and had caused their deaths. This was a whole other set of circumstances, however.

Maryann was adamant. "There's no way in the world that I would ever agree to include Danny in the service with Rachel and Evan. I already spoke with Tony and told him that, and he said that he was okay with it. He was disappointed, for sure, but he said he and his parents would make the arrangements for Danny later next week. He also said that he wanted to pay for all of the burial expenses for Rachel and Evan. I told him he didn't need to, but he insisted."

"Boy, that must have been one awkward discussion." Pete said. "You really have to let the rest of us do some of this stuff, Maryann."

Maryann suddenly looked so young to Carolyn (she was only twenty-two, after all), and so she took her hand and said, "I agree; just tell us what you need us to do. Anything."

"Well, Carolyn, I was thinking of asking you to do the eulogy for Rachel at the service. Of all of us, you were the closest to her, and I think that's what Rachel would have wanted."

Carolyn looked over at Mitch and he was nodding and smiling, and so she smiled for the first time that day, and said, "Maryann, I would be proud to do that. I'm afraid that I won't be able to get through it, but I'll do my best." Her response made it clear to Mitch that he needn't mention the very vivid dream he'd had that morning.

"Thanks, Carolyn, and one more thing, if you don't mind. The police told me that we could go to the house later today to select some clothing for Rachel and Evan and get some photos of them to display at the church. I was planning on going over there around three, and I would really appreciate it if you would help me pick out her dress and something for Evan to wear."

Carolyn gasped at the idea of going to the house so soon after the murders, and was surprised the police would allow them to visit an active crime scene. "Are you sure they will let us do that?"

"That's what the sheriff in charge told me. He said we could only go on the first floor, though, and could only stay a few minutes," Maryann replied.

"Do you mind if Mitch comes as well?"

"No, of course not."

"Maryann," Mitch said, "why don't we come by and pick you up a little before three, and we'll go over together?" Mitch imagined there would be television crews staked out in front of the house and didn't want her to have to face them alone.

After they discussed a few other particulars, it became apparent that it was time to leave, though everyone resisted making the first move. Paralysis had set in due to the fact that there was something so grim and unnatural about the tasks that faced all of them, Maryann in particular. Her eyes had taken on a permanent glaze, and her movements seemed robotic. Carolyn found it hard to believe that Maryann, the little girl who had already known such tragedy in her young life, now had to carry this burden. At least they would be able to help her through the visit to Danny and Rachel's house later that day. Now Maryann displayed maturity beyond her years yet again.

"Thanks so much," she said to Tom and Anna, "both of you, for letting us meet here, and for arranging the meeting with Dave Thompson. It would have been horrible to have gone down to the police station and put up with those awful reporters."

"Maryann, it's the least we could do," they said almost in unison.

When Mitch and Carolyn climbed into their car, they simply sat there, immobile, trying to absorb and process all that they had learned in the last few hours. When they had arrived, they had been under the impression that Danny had snapped and shot his wife and child and then himself. The details Dave Thompson had shared moved this tragedy into a whole new realm. Carolyn sat quietly, staring ahead, exhausted, perplexed, angry, sad, unable to process the enormity of the events that had taken place over the last forty-eight hours. The complexity of emotions left her with an overwhelming feeling of dread. A dense fog had descended, and at that moment she couldn't imagine ever again feeling an emotion that might be described as "normal," let alone something presently as foreign as "happiness." Mitch looked over at her and thought she was probably in shock. *This must be what shock looks like,* he thought. *What if she never comes out of it? What if she sinks deeper?* He realized that the impact on his wife would be much more severe than on him. He felt helpless and frightened.

"Are you all right?" he offered, expecting her to nod mechanically that she was. Instead she looked directly at him and said, "I don't think I will ever be 'all right' again, Mitch," and she turned to continue her silent vigil. This was not good. Mitch always needed to fix things, and right now things were very broken. When he suggested they go check in at the hotel, Carolyn vehemently shook her head from side to side. So they continued to sit there in silence.

And then Mitch remembered an incident, just a few years ago, when Frankie was six months old, and Mitch had stupidly placed him on the kitchen table in his infant seat while he was making a snack. The game was on and it was halftime. Mitch was watching their three boys, and he figured he'd whip up a sandwich just before the second half. His sixth sense told him he shouldn't place the baby on the table (okay, Carolyn's rule was that the infant seat should *never* be placed on the table), but he reasoned that he was just a few feet away, and it would only be for a minute or two.

He kept up a running dialogue with the baby, glancing at him every few seconds to keep him amused and make sure he was okay. He didn't notice, however, that Frankie's rocking had caused the chair to creep to the edge of the table. In the instant it took to cut the sandwich in half, the chair tipped over and he smacked his head on the tile floor just before Mitch could grab him. That awful crunching sound would haunt Mitch for years.

He picked Frankie up and screamed for Carolyn. At first the baby was wailing, and then he suddenly stopped crying and went silent. When Mitch and Carolyn felt the back of his head they were convinced serious damage had been done, and so they rushed everyone into the car and Carolyn raced to the hospital while Mitch sat in the backseat and begged his son to cry or make any noise at all, but he just looked at his father with a terrifyingly blank stare.

After the CT scan, the specialist said there was indeed a fracture, but the only thing they could do was to wait and monitor the progress. If his brain swelled, they would have to operate, but there was a possibility he would be fine and it would heal naturally. However, it was obvious the entire medical staff was mightily concerned at little Frankie's total lack of responsiveness.

Mitch and Carolyn were beside themselves with worry, but all they could do was wait and pray. Then Mitch realized that he should call Pastor Tim, Tim McConnell, the associate pastor of their church. The indefatigable Tim immediately agreed to drive directly to the hospital, despite the fact he was on another ministry call over an hour away, way up in Bainbridge, and it was now snowing heavily and well past ten o'clock when they reached him.

Mitch and Carolyn were sitting quietly when they heard a flurry of activity, accompanied by shouts of greetings, and presumed Pastor Tim must have arrived. They immediately felt better as soon as they laid eyes on him.

Despite being a small man, he seemed larger than life, partially due to his perpetually ebullient smile and relentlessly positive demeanor, and partially due to his shaggy black hair and bushy beard. Everyone at church adored the man and always joked about how much he resembled one of Jesus's apostles, which in fact he was.

It was around midnight when Tim arrived, hurriedly brushing the snow off his shoulders and stomping his boots. They thanked him for coming out so late at night, particularly with the roads in such poor condition. Tim pooh-poohed this, threw his overcoat and scarf on a chair, and immediately went to the patient's bedside. He gently kissed Frankie on the forehead and bent close to him, whispering. The baby appeared to be sleeping soundly.

Carolyn and Mitch were explaining how things had happened and Frankie's medical condition, when Tim suddenly lifted up his head, looked at them with a broad smile, and said, "He's going to be fine." Almost laughing, he added, "All we have to do is pray."

Right then there was a shift in the room. The atmosphere changed, and Mitch and Carolyn tentatively started to laugh along with Tim, though they didn't know why, and it made absolutely no sense at all.

"Pastor Tim!" They turned to see one of the nurses, an attractive, middle-aged black woman, who had helped to get Frankie settled a while before. She immediately caught him in a clinch and burst out laughing. "I'm so glad to see you, Tim. You're just what the doctor ordered!"

"Billie, it's been ages! How are you? Are you still singing at Redeemer?"

"I sure am, Tim! And will be for as long as the Lord blesses me with another breath, you can bet on that!"

They caught up on old acquaintances, and then turned their attention to the baby in the bed. Mitch was a bit dumbfounded, and didn't know what to say, so he immediately put his foot in his mouth.

"Well, I figured that when all else failed, it was time to call you, Tim!"

Despite the bone-crushing foolishness of his statement, Tim put both hands on Mitch's shoulders and kindly said, "But talking to God is the first thing you should always do, and I'll bet you've already been doing a lot of praying. All you have to do is have a little faith, so let's get to work!"

The four of them circled the bed and placed their hands on Frankie, and Tim began to speak, his voice echoing down the hall. He appeared to be speaking to God as if He were standing right there in the room.

"Jesus, we ask that you heal this beautiful little boy, Frankie, completely. We ask that you find it in your all-encompassing mercy to touch him, and allow him to be restored to perfect health. We know that you have it within your power, Jesus, to do that which appears to be impossible. We have seen your incredible healing powers so many times and know for certain that they are real, and that all we need to do is ask that you come to our aid, right now, on this night, here in this room. We feel your presence, Jesus, and we know that it is only through your mercy that the hand of every doctor is guided every day, every minute, throughout the world, and that you need only say the word, and this innocent child will be healed. We believe in the depths of our souls that you will answer our prayers. Amen."

There were four sets of wet eyes as they all mumbled "amen," accompanied by the voices of those who had gathered outside the door to join in the prayer.

For the next hour or so, Mitch and Carolyn could hear Tim stopping at each room, regardless of the faith of the parents, to pray, laugh, and encourage, until he finally went home to be with his family.

At around three in the morning, while Carolyn napped next to Frankie's bed and Mitch fretted while walking aimlessly up and down the corridor, Frankie awoke and started to cry. It was the sound they were waiting to hear.

The next day he was given a clean bill of health, and was released shortly after the morning rounds. It took a while for Carolyn to forgive Mitch for his carelessness, but they knew they had been granted a valuable experience that was not to be taken lightly or ever forgotten.

So now, sitting in silence next to Carolyn, Mitch said, "Do you remember what Pastor Tim said that night at the hospital?"

She looked down, and a hint of a smile crept across her lips.

"All you have to do is have a little faith," she said, to which Mitch replied, "So let's get to work!"

They prayed together for the next few minutes, and began to remember that, despite all the terrible events that had taken place, there was still hope. God *does* exist, love *is* stronger than fear, and faith is the willingness to accept that which we cannot possibly understand, either in the case of grace or the difficulties that come into our lives.

They finished and Carolyn said she was ready to leave. Finally, a small thread of light had broken through the darkness.

→→■◎ ◎■←←

Mitch and Carolyn checked into their hotel, and went downstairs to the restaurant to order lunch, which neither of them ate. They were just trying to do some normal things before the next step in the process. Carolyn called her mother, who told her that the boys were doing fine and that she should take her time, and come home when she and Mitch were done with what they had to do. *So strange,* she thought. *As parents, we protect, love, forgive, worry about, and correct our kids. They love us in return and have absolute trust in us. What could possibly have caused Danny to go so wrong? Could it really all be as simple as cashing in an insurance policy? Was there another woman involved?*

Maryann was sitting on her front steps, smoking a cigarette, when Mitch and Carolyn pulled up in front of her apartment building. Mitch was tempted to ask her for a smoke, but he had quit over ten years ago, and he knew Carolyn would be furious if he started up again. Perhaps he would borrow one a little later if he knew for sure that Carolyn was preoccupied.

"Oh, no, I can't believe it!" Maryann said when they turned onto Caves Road and saw the TV trucks lined up. Before they were even able to emerge from the car, there was a swarm of reporters poking microphones in their faces.

"Are any of you family members? How are you related? Do you know why he did it?

"*Who are you?*" one particularly smarmy fellow demanded. Obviously their deadlines for the evening news were looming and they had yet to get a statement from the family.

While they pretended to be working as industry colleagues, of course each reporter secretly hoped for an exclusive with a family member, and once he had that someone alone, in front of the camera, each jackal was confident he could break that person. The method was to sucker in the family with a few sensitive questions, and then go in for the kill. The coup de grace would be a three-second clip of a distraught family member in tears that the producer could play over and over as a tease, while the announcer advised viewers to stay tuned in order to see the important, exclusive interview.

Mitch and Carolyn huddled around Maryann and pushed their way up the driveway. A cameraman tried to press his lens between them to get a shot of Maryann's ashen face, and Mitch instinctively pushed it away. A few enterprising reporters had enlisted a neighbor to provide them with information about the family, and they apparently knew who Maryann was. It only took a few seconds for those reporters to jump into the fray.

"Hey, Maryann, look over here! Why do you think your father did it?"

"Maryann, what are the funeral arrangements?"

"Is it true there was a big insurance policy?"

Finally they reached the front door and were greeted by Sheriff Dandridge, who was lifting up a stretch of yellow tape that read "Caution, Crime Scene" so they could step under it more easily. A few uniformed police officers ordered the reporters to stay off of the property, which had the effect of creating an invisible wall around the front of the house, but didn't stop them from hovering in the front yard.

Sheriff Dandridge looked to be in his sixties, and just about ready for retirement. In fact, he had just been thinking to himself that it was too bad he hadn't taken retirement before this mess. He was your classic string bean, but only stood around five foot seven, and his long, narrow head was topped by what at first looked to Carolyn like a beige cowboy hat. When she saw the badge in the center of it, however, she realized it was part of his uniform, which was a dull khaki color. Another blue-uniformed officer stood beside him, like a sentinel. There was some pretense they were observing a certain amount of protocol, but in reality everyone was faking it. Dandridge knew he and the rest of the force had never experienced anything like this before.

Dandridge was wearing a very grim look on his face, but he also appeared perplexed, frustrated, and a little out of his depth. The cameras and the reporters in particular scared him. He knew that thanks to the Internet, one little slip-up could instantly be transmitted around the world, and then replayed over and over for years to come. So he had stood in front of the cameras only once that morning, in order to convey the basic information to the reporters, and had declined to provide any other details for the rest of the day—only adding to the mania of the massive collection of media professionals desperate for any nugget of information.

Once inside, Mitch pulled back a curtain; it was only then that he realized just how many people—reporters as well as onlookers—were in front of the house. It appeared their mad dash into the house had just provided the highlight of the day, and everyone seemed to be buzzing around frantically. Then Mitch remembered where he was and why he was there.

He turned and looked across the foyer, at the yellow caution tape the police had crisscrossed from the banister to the wall at the base of the stairs to prevent anyone from setting foot on the steps. Mitch glanced up into the darkness of the second floor. He could see that the door to Rachel and Danny's room was shut, and for an instant it seemed a shadow moved across the hallway. A sense of foreboding hung in the air. It was then that he had a palpable sensation that he could taste the evil that permeated the house. He was overcome by a desire to rinse out his mouth. Perhaps this was why Dandridge looked so spooked.

"Well, you can go anywhere you like on the first floor," the sheriff said as he took his hat off in the presence of the ladies. He was a gentleman in an old-fashioned sort of way, and clearly was very concerned about Maryann. He had a reedy voice with a slight Southern twang.

"Please accept my condolences," he continued. "I can't imagine what y'all are goin' through. And those reporters outside . . . I recommend that you take whatever photos you need and sort through them at your convenience, and if there's clothing downstairs here, you can take that as well." He knew no one wanted to stay there longer than necessary.

"Sir, thanks so much for letting us do this," Maryann replied in a barely audible voice. Carolyn led her into the living room where she knew Rachel kept her photo books, a box of slides, and several framed photos as well. They would find what they needed in no time at all. She hoped that Rachel had left a few of her nicer dresses in the closet downstairs near the entrance due to the prohibition against going into the bedrooms—not that she had the slightest desire even to glance up the stairs. She didn't want to linger. There was a repulsive sweet odor she had never smelled before and certainly never noticed in Rachel's house in the past, and it was causing her to feel nauseous.

Mitch still could not understand why they were permitted into the house at all, and presumed it was due to the small-town, suburban environment; however, it also spoke to the fact that the police had already judged Danny and found him guilty. They clearly were convinced he acted alone; otherwise they at least would have prohibited anyone from walking on the floor in the area that led from the garage into the kitchen and the path up the stairs. He shook his head in wonder, and hoped the police knew what they were doing.

He walked across the dining room and into the kitchen as if led by an invisible cord that had strung itself around his waist, and he opened the door that led to the garage. To think that Danny had stood in this very spot just two nights ago, debating whether or not to murder his wife. If only he had come to his senses and, if for no other reason than self-preservation, realized he would never get away with it. He could have walked into the garage, driven that dope Logan to his car, and called it a night. Aside from everything else, his decision had been downright stupid. Danny must have presumed that he would be able to lure Logan up to the room after killing Rachel, and then make it look as if he had killed Logan in self defense. Or perhaps he had been out of his mind. Or perhaps something had had him in its grip.

Mitch closed the door but still couldn't shake the ominous feeling that had consumed him the minute he walked in the front door. He had the feeling he was being watched by someone, and indeed he was. The silent cop had followed him without so much as a harrumph to announce his presence. As the sheriff walked into the kitchen, Mitch's eye caught three kitchen knives that were lying next to a wooden block.

"Sheriff, were the knives out like that when you first discovered the crime scene?"

"I'm afraid they were, but we have no idea why they were left out, or why Mr. Turner chose to use such a small knife. None of it makes any sense to me."

"That's exactly what I was thinking," Mitch replied as he went off to look for Carolyn and Maryann.

He found them chuckling over a picture of Rachel in a Halloween costume and chose not to interrupt their brief moment of levity. Instead, he turned into the study that Danny used as his office. It had a TV in it, and didn't really look as if much work got done there. Indians and Browns pennants lined the sides of the TV, and the walls were adorned with family photos. There were three empty Budweiser bottles standing on the coffee table. The desk was littered with bills, which Mitch mechanically thumbed through. Some were opened, and some were months old, unopened and disregarded. He sat in Danny's chair and opened a drawer that was crammed with junk, and noticed the Tony Robbins workbook from the seminar to which he'd sent Danny. He had intended it to help Danny get on top of things like managing his finances, being truthful, taking logical risks, and opening up to his friends, but the program hadn't been a fit for him. Most of the pages were empty, but under the heading of things he needed to improve, he had written, "Have to increase my earnings at least 20 percent next year in order to provide for Rachel up to her standards." That was certainly a strange thing to say, and betrayed a hint of resentment toward his wife.

He pictured Danny sitting at the desk, surrounded by bills that were multiplying like the mops and pails in *The Sorcerer's Apprentice*, deciding that he had had enough, and needed a way out. Mitch wondered if Danny's financial problems had driven him over the edge. He thumbed through the book, and noticed something written in the notes section: "If they don't find out you did it, then you didn't do it." Mitch closed the book in disgust and went to see if Carolyn and Maryann were ready to leave. He found them talking with Sheriff Dandridge. They all turned and looked at him when he entered, and he had the feeling he had just been the topic of their discussion.

"Mitch," Carolyn started, "Sheriff Dandridge thinks it would make sense if the family made a statement outside to the press, so they'll back off a bit, and we think you should deliver it."

"Well, I'll do it, but I don't think they're going to call off the hounds just because they get a statement. They're going to want to ask questions."

Sheriff Dandridge responded, "I'll stand out there with you, and make it clear that we're not taking any questions. Just read it, and at least some of them will have something to deliver to their bosses, so maybe some of them will leave. By the way, uniformed officers will be stationed here all night to make sure no one sneaks in."

⊷⊶◉ ◉⊷⊶

That night, when they got back to the hotel and turned on the TV, Mitch saw himself standing next to Sheriff Dandridge, with Carolyn and Maryann in the background.

Dandridge stepped up to the group of microphones arrayed in front of him. "Okay, now, the family has decided to make a brief statement, and has asked a family friend, Mitch Bianci, to read it. We will not be taking any questions after that."

Mitch and Carolyn sat on the edge of the bed, and watched the television, feeling a bit like they were in a movie watching a movie of themselves. How did they go from obscurity just hours before to being on national television? Mitch watched as he nervously tugged at his collar and then stepped forward. He cleared his throat, but as he began to read, he felt a thwack of emotion rain down on him, and his voice began to tremble.

"Rachel and Evan Turner were two of the nicest people you could ever hope to meet. Rachel was a hard-working and loving mother and a supportive wife, and Evan was a ten-year-old who was known for his remarkable good nature, love of sports, and the love of his family.

"This is a tragedy beyond our comprehension, and it is of course compounded by the fact that the person who committed the crime was their husband and father.

"We have no idea why this happened, and can offer no explanation, and know nothing more than what has already been reported in the media. So we ask that you please respect the privacy of the family, and that everyone pray for Rachel and Evan and for all their remaining family members.

"We have no further comments at this time. Thank you."

The assembled reporters collectively began to shout questions, and then the picture cut back to the anchorman, who recounted the details of the crime and showed the photos of Danny, Rachel, and Evan that were being bandied about in the media. The broadcast then cut to a few special reports at various locations. Mitch and Carolyn sat watching numbly until the report regarding Danny's suicide came on, and then they were physically taken aback.

An attractive blonde woman, bundled in a winter coat, was speaking into the camera, while a hubbub of police activity took place in the distance behind her.

"Hello," she said, "this is Jennifer Wilson reporting for Channel Five Nightly News. I am standing at the edge of Nicholson's Quarry, which is the location where the final act of the Turner family tragedy took place Wednesday morning at approximately 7:30 a.m. It was here that Danny Turner, the husband and father of the murder victims, took his life in a very spectacular and gruesome manner. This next segment may not be suitable for young viewers, so we suggest that you take that into consideration."

The image on the screen cut to a close-up of what appeared to be a gravel road that came to an abrupt end at the edge of a cliff. The massive twin boulders that teetered on the precipice created a corridor that looked to be about twelve feet wide. The opening didn't appear menacing at all until the camera panned down into the watery ravine that was perhaps one hundred feet below. One clip showed the police engaged in attempting to remove Danny's Escalade, a car in which Mitch and Carolyn had been passengers countless times. The next shot scanned across the terrain, where there appeared to be a body covered by a white sheet.

At that moment the announcer said, "Though the final report has not yet been released by the medical examiner, the police did confirm that the cause of death was a gunshot wound to the head." It was then that Mitch and Carolyn turned away and each began to sob. Suddenly, Danny's humanity was front and center, and regardless of what he might have done, he was still their longtime friend, and their anger turned to grief, which only increased their complex of emotions and confusion.

"Turn it off, Mitch. I can't watch this anymore."

⭑⟶⊨◉ ◉⊨⟵⭑

Because the funeral service was taking place the next morning, Carolyn had no choice but to write Rachel's eulogy before she went to bed, despite the fact she was bone-tired. Mitch took a notepad out of his briefcase, and they began to discuss what she would say.

Carolyn had found Rachel's diary at the house, and she was thumbing through it for inspiration, when suddenly she cried out, "Oh, no! I can't believe she said that!"

"What? What did she say?" Mitch grabbed the book from her, and saw the words that had sent Carolyn into a tizzy.

"Carolyn did a lot of great things for me, but the best thing she ever did was to introduce me to Danny!"

"Mitch, that's the truth! If I had never introduced her to Danny, Rachel would still be alive! In a way, it's all my fault." She pounded her fist on the table in front of her.

"That's ridiculous, Carolyn! She and Danny fell in love with each other, and they had a great life together for a long, long time. What Danny did is on Danny, and nobody else."

"Well, that may be logical, but seeing it in black and white, in Rachel's handwriting, is just too much. I wish I hadn't seen it, but I was thinking it all day."

"They loved each other, and they made two beautiful children, honey. We'll probably never know why this happened, but we do know that what happened was outside of our control. You can't blame yourself; that's just crazy. Don't let that diary bother you."

"That's easy for you to say, Mitch. You don't have to live with this."

"Honey, let's just try to calm down. This day has been all too much, and we have to try to keep our heads on straight. Besides, we have to start writing this, now, so we need to get started."

↤⟶ ⟵↦

Carolyn didn't finish until almost three in the morning, by which time Mitch was stretched out on the bed sound asleep. Carolyn's head began to dip as she started to nod off over her writing, but she insisted to herself that she needed to make just one more improvement.

"Go to bed, girlfriend. I think it's perfect!" She lifted her head expecting to see Rachel standing there. Her voice was so clear and vibrant, and so alive. Of course, Rachel wasn't there; however, Carolyn followed her friend's advice and went to bed.

She was asleep within seconds of shutting off the light.

CHAPTER 13

Courage and Wisdom

If in Christ we have hope in this life only,
We are of all people most to be pitied.
—*1 Corinthians 15:19*

IT HAD BEEN prescient of Mitch to arrange for a 7:30 wake-up call, because they were both sound asleep when the phone rang. They called for room service and hurriedly prepared for the day ahead while the *Today* show blared in the background. Carolyn changed the channel the instant Katie Couric began to introduce the segment about "the terrible double homicide in the Akron area." Both she and Mitch were starting to loathe the way the media was milking the tragedy that was so real and personal to them. Fortunately, Reverend Kirkpatrick and the police department had promised to prohibit any television cameras inside the church, but there would doubtless be a crush outside, and there was no way to keep the reporters out of the building.

Carolyn asked Mitch to read the eulogy she'd finished writing after he had fallen asleep, and he did so over breakfast.

"I think it's beautiful, honey. It's straight from your heart, and I think the way you end it will reach everyone. I know Rachel will be remembered for how generous and loving she was, and you know that firsthand, so it's truthful and honest, as it should be."

"Well, I just pray I can get all the way through it. I still don't feel as if any of this is real, but I know today is going to make it seem final."

"Just take your time, and take a deep breath whenever you need to. People will understand that this is a very hard thing to do, but you can do it. I know you can. You just have to hand this over to God, and have faith that it will be fine."

Mitch continued to be concerned about Carolyn, but he was hopeful that after the funeral, when they returned home later that day, they would at least get back into the rhythm of things. He hoped that she would be able to move on, but he feared he was deluding himself.

Rachel had been a daily part of Carolyn's life since they had met back in high school. They wouldn't make a move without consulting each other, whether about little things, such as which color curtains to buy, or more serious matters. It wasn't the same for Mitch and Danny, not by a long shot. Carolyn had been as close to Rachel as she was to anyone in her life, barring her immediate family. Rachel could always be counted on to get Carolyn out of a funk, or to help her stop fretting about whatever was plaguing her. They would calm each other down when one of them would conjure up the sort of frightening scenario mothers create in the middle of the night. Minutes after picking up the phone, Rachel would have Carolyn laughing at herself, or she'd share some ridiculous story or juicy gossip and, before Mitch knew it, all her concerns would fade away.

Mitch's heart was broken as well over this tragedy, but his defense mechanism allowed him to compartmentalize things. He was mainly dumbfounded by Danny's actions and, frankly, furious at him. It turned out there had been a pretty hefty insurance policy on Rachel, so his motive might have been money. But if money was the problem, why couldn't Danny just swallow his pride and ask for help? It was a sort of open secret that Rachel had caught him cheating on her a few years back, and every once in a while Rachel would make some oblique reference to it, but they seemed to have weathered that storm.

He wouldn't rest until he found out what had caused Danny to do what he did. No matter how many times he played it over in his head, there were still just too many unanswered questions, beginning with why he did it, why he thought he could get away with such an idiotic idea, what Logan had to do with it, and how he possibly could have murdered his own son and abandoned his eight-year-old son to deal with the devastation he had wrought. And, hanging over all these questions, was the one that was so loathsome that he couldn't allow himself to go there—the manner of death. The sheer carnage.

There was no doubt that everyone attending the service, as well as the community at large, was vexed by the same unanswerable questions. An unspoken fear lurked just below the surface: *if such horrible things could happen to an apparently happy, suburban family, then could they happen to our family?* Wives looked at their husbands a little askance, and, within the privacy of their own four walls, parents reassured their children that they were safe.

Mitch and Carolyn were running late when they got their car out of the garage to go to the service; they then got stuck in traffic and made a wrong turn. So the church was already brimming with people when they arrived. Most of the seats were taken, and the side aisles were in the process of filling up. As soon as they entered, however, they saw Maryann waving to them to join her in the first pew with the family members. Christopher was sitting between Maryann and Danny's brother, Tony; Tony's wife, Emily; and his parents.

"I was starting to get worried about you guys," she said as she sat back down.

Mitch answered, perhaps a little defensively, "We're really sorry, but it seemed as if everyone was out on the street driving five miles an hour, and then we got lost. Crazy for a Monday morn—"

"It doesn't matter. You made it, and that's all that counts."

Mitch and Carolyn nodded a silent hello to the Turner family and Mitch reached over to shake hands with his old friend Tony. They weren't so far removed from the days when a game of hoops and a few beers were all they needed for a great night. They gripped each other's hands for an extra-long time. Their mutual expressions seemed to say, "How did everything go so wrong so fast?" Steve and Debby Turner wore the expression of parents who were thoroughly shattered. They appeared perplexed and worn out, with Debby experiencing a depth of grief that could only be reserved for a mother and grandmother. She would not allow herself to escape the conviction that she was somehow responsible for this tragedy.

Christopher edged past Maryann so he could hug Mitch and Carolyn. Danny and Rachel had always insisted the Bianci boys call them by their first names, and so the Turner boys in turn called Mitch and Carolyn by their first names. Christopher tried to offer some encouragement.

"Carolyn, don't look so sad. One day we'll see Mom and Dad in heaven and it will be just like it used to be."

Carolyn noticed that his dark blue suit was a bit too large for him, probably because Maryann had had to find something quickly off the rack that couldn't be altered in time. His red tie was also a bit too long, probably borrowed from his uncle. He was a little boy, dressed like a man, having to do something no one should ever experience. Christopher didn't dare tell anyone, but he too suspected he had done something to cause his dad to do what he did.

"Oh, Chris," Carolyn said as she pulled him onto her lap. She kept repeating his name and hugging him, before handing him over to Mitch, who pretty much did the same. There are times when there just aren't any words that can, or need to, be said, and this was certainly one of those moments. Chris looked over Mitch's shoulder and noticed Evan's little league teammates, decked out in their jerseys. He waved to them and then returned to his seat, because it was obvious the service was about to begin.

The scene before the altar was gut-wrenching: two caskets, one a matte white with golden handles adorned with a spray of pink roses and baby's breath. The other was light blue, and covered with a baseball jersey that simply read "Evan." That box looked tiny by comparison. For some reason, Carolyn was reminded of a duckling trailing its mother. All eyes in the church were trained on this simple setting. Over to one side, there were slides of the Turner family, enjoying the beach, Christmas season, birthday parties, baseball games, and other benchmarks of family life. The slides changed every few seconds, and repeated numerous times while everyone sat and whispered to one another or stared at the screen, lost in their thoughts. Included was the high school photo of Rachel kissing a smiling Carolyn.

Finally Reverend Kirkpatrick approached the pulpit. The screen discreetly went dark and the incidental organ music gave way to the staccato notes that introduced Schubert's "Ave Maria." The singer, an attractive young woman whose face was framed by long, wavy dark hair, gently placed her fingers on the shoulder of the pianist in an apparent attempt to steady herself, and together they performed the simple yet beautiful paean to the mother of Jesus and all mothers.

As the last note resolved into silence, Kirkpatrick stepped forward. He had spent the previous few days wrestling with just how to officiate at this service. Funeral services were a regular and important role of the clergy, and he'd performed more than he could remember, but the circumstances of this occasion were without precedent in his experience. He knew the Turner family only fleetingly, and so he would have to rely on others to a great degree. That was not uncommon. Even some long-time parishioners only spoke with him directly in any meaningful way when they had to bury a loved one. He had long since gotten over the feeling of duplicity in not knowing the people he was shepherding into the next world. It was no secret that the ceremony was for the comfort of the living as well as the benefit of the souls of those who had died, not to mention the positive impact on his ever-challenging budget.

But of course today was different, and so the usual bromides he had learned in theology school, which were perfectly suitable for people who had passed on of natural causes, or even young people who were taken suddenly, would not suffice. These deaths fell into a whole other category that he had never had to contemplate before.

Kirkpatrick had been in favor of including the father, but emotions were raw and he had been rebuffed, so he had made arrangements with Danny's parents and brother for a separate service. It would have taken great courage to broach this topic at the service, and some would doubtless have seen it as inappropriate or at least in bad taste, so he'd accepted that Danny would not even be mentioned. However, the pastor was deeply conflicted and had been praying all morning for guidance.

After reciting the twenty-third psalm, and reflecting a bit on how it was the role of all of those assembled to aid the departed with their prayers, and to support the family members with their actions during this difficult time, he concluded with these words from John 1:1: "The will of God will never take you where the grace of God will not protect you." The words rang hollow as they left his mouth.

Carolyn was stung by the inadequacy of this sentiment as well, because it spoke to the very heart of the question she could not answer. Why hadn't God protected Rachel and Evan? This stuff about God never giving people more than they could handle was refuted every day by all the misery in the world. If He got the credit for all the wonderful things in the world, why wasn't He also responsible for all the suffering? She awoke as if from a trance when she heard someone calling her name and realized the pastor was motioning for her to step up to the altar.

Mitch squeezed her hand and helped her rise. For an instant, she felt like she was walking in quicksand and wouldn't be able to make it up the stairs. Then she turned and found herself standing in front of the microphone, looking out upon a sea of mournful faces. Though she knew Rachel's body lay before her, her essence was by her side.

"One of the reasons we are here today," she began "is to honor and celebrate Rachel for the lady she was, what she stood for, the legacy she left, and the hope that we all should share because we were blessed to know her, albeit not for long enough. Mother Teresa once said, 'We cannot do great things on this earth, only small things with great love.' To me these words personify who Rachel was as a mother, wife, sister, and friend.

"My name is Carolyn Bianci, and I am privileged to say that Rachel was my best friend since ninth grade. I'll never forget how she was one of the first people to reach out to me and offer her friendship at the new school I was attending. We made an immediate connection and developed a bond that continued to grow over the past twenty-six years. I knew that in Rachel, I had a friend for life. We shared a lot of our lives together because she was so willing to invest her time and heart into her friends. I love her and miss her dearly.

"I have always had a great sense of admiration for Rachel because she had a few more obstacles placed in front of her at an early age than most people do. But as you all know, Rachel was never the type to settle. She always demanded more of herself and always wanted the best for her family and her friends. In addition to raising her two wonderful boys, Evan and Christopher, of whom she was so proud, she opened her home to Maryann without hesitation because of her love of family and her enormous heart for others. Just yesterday, Maryann shared with us that she wouldn't be the woman she is today if it hadn't been for Rachel's involvement in her life."

Carolyn looked up for a moment to connect with Maryann. She had her arm around Christopher and his head rested on her shoulder. He looked at Carolyn with an expression of trust, hope, and expectation.

After their eyes connected, Carolyn paused, took a deep breath, and continued.

"Rachel had such a beautiful spirit and a unique ability to always focus on the positive instead of the negative. Rachel always looked for the good in everything and in everyone and accepted others unconditionally. As a result of this, she was truly rich in the sense that she had experienced real gratitude in her life.

"Rachel talked frequently about the friendships she developed here in Akron and how grateful she was for her inner circle of friends. After spending the last three days here in Akron with this wonderful group of people, I can easily see why she felt so blessed to have developed these relationships.

"They say if you can find one true friend in your life you are blessed. We are all so blessed because, in Rachel, we were privileged to have that one true friend. Matthew, chapter 5, verses 14–15, tell us, 'You are like a light for the whole world. A city built on a hill cannot be hid. No one lights a lamp and puts it under a bowl; instead it is put on the lamp stand where it gives light to everyone in the house.' Rachel has always been that bright light to all of us.

"My husband, Mitch, is forever reminding our three boys that decisions shape our lives and ultimately shape who we become as individuals. We all have a question before us today, and that question is: what meaning will we attach to these events? If we choose tragedy, we all will lose. My challenge to all of us today, myself included, and what I would like to leave everyone with, is to take that piece of Rachel that we were so fortunate to experience and to hold it forever in our hearts. By allowing it always to inspire us to be better mothers, fathers, and friends, we will carry Rachel and Evan's light forward."

Reverend Kirkpatrick thanked Carolyn, and asked Evan's fifth-grade math teacher, Mr. Suder, to say a few words about his student. Suder was a short-statured, older fellow nearing retirement, who was known for his big heart, good cheer, and love of children. He talked about how Evan always had a smile on his face, and recalled his wonderful, infectious laughter, raising a chuckle when he told the story of the day Evan discovered the joy of mathematics. After a poor grade on a test, he suggested to Evan that if by some fluke he didn't make it to the major leagues, he was sure to have a great career as a statistician, and then explained to him was that was. Evan quickly became an A student from that moment on. His voice then turned somber as he expressed the sadness all the teachers felt over the fact that Evan would not have the opportunity to continue to share his gifts. He then pulled himself up to his full height, apologized for the folly of a math teacher attempting to read a poem, and launched into Emily Dickinson's "Because I could not stop for Death." His rich, stentorian voice gave way to a whisper by the time he arrived at the last sentence.

Reverend Kirkpatrick rose to end the service. Listening to the last two speakers, he had felt a shift come over him. He knew he would forever regret his actions this day if he did not summon the courage to at least make mention of Danny. He hesitated, looked out at the congregants, and noticed a woman with luminescent white hair sitting in the last pew, who seemed to know what was on his mind. This somehow gave him the reassurance he needed. He cleared his throat and began to speak without the slightest idea of what he was about to say, but confident that God would give him the right words.

"We have spoken of Rachel and Evan, but have not mentioned Danny." He felt the congregation rustle uncomfortably in their seats and perceived a collective gasp. The reverend was quite aware that many people in town, including some of the elders in his church, had vehemently objected to the idea of including Danny in the service in any manner.

"However, I would be remiss if I did not at least remind us all that he, too, was a child of God, and that he, too, has passed into another life, prematurely, and will be missed." Steve and Debby Turner looked down and then back up at the reverend with deep gratitude. To them, of course, Danny was their little boy, and would always remain so.

"Most faiths embrace the concept of forgiveness, but for those of us who are Christians, we know that Jesus told us to 'above all else, love one another,' and that His words on the subject of forgiveness knew no bounds, even right up to the moment He uttered His very last few words, when He asked His father to forgive those who had persecuted Him because He knew they did not understand what they were doing. I ask that you each search your own hearts and attempt to find that same forgiveness, not only for Danny, but for anyone in your life whom feel you need to forgive, perhaps beginning with yourself.

"When Jesus was asked how we should pray, he spoke the words we now call "The Lord's Prayer." So, please let us all stand, and hold the hand of the person next to us, and as we recite these words, I pray we set aside our grievances and listen with an open heart as if we were hearing them for the first time."

Initially, when the group stood and reached out to one another, the discomfort was palpable; yet by the time the end of the prayer was near, the timbre had escalated and the sanctuary reverberated with these familiar words:

"And forgive us our sins, as we forgive those who have sinned against us, and lead us not into temptation, but deliver us from evil, amen."

At that moment, a collective sense of hope descended on the group, and more than a few grievances were put to rest.

CHAPTER 14

Homecoming

My mind is like a bad neighborhood;
I try not to go there alone.
—*Anne Lamott*

THE FUNERAL WAS a desultory affair, made more so by the gray sky that threatened snow and the wind that whipped through the field and fluttered the canopy over the gravesite. Carolyn stood alone for a few minutes as Mitch helped to carry Rachel to her final resting place. After the ceremony concluded and the group dispersed, Mitch waited patiently while Carolyn took one last look into the open grave, and the cemetery workers began their chores. She realized it was time to leave when she noticed the practiced gaze of the crew chief that was intended to make it obvious this was not a spectacle intended for mourners.

"There's something I'd like to do before we head back home," Mitch said as they trailed the last few cars out of the cemetery. Carolyn stared at him without saying anything, so he continued, "I'd like to go over to Nicholson's Quarry, to the place where Danny ended it all."

"Why would you want to do that? Haven't we seen enough horrible things over the last few days?"

"I guess you could say I'm curious, and maybe it's that, but I also feel as if we haven't properly said good-bye to Danny yet."

Carolyn let out an intentionally disingenuous laugh. "Good-bye? I'm not so sure he deserves any more of a good-bye than he's gotten."

"Well, I think we should try to keep in mind what Reverend Kirkpatrick said at the end of the service. Danny was a human being too, and our friend, and while it may be a little early to forgive him completely, I think we at least should try," Mitch replied.

"Mitch, I know that's right. And I pray that I will one day get there, but right now, I'm not there yet."

"Okay, I know what you mean. But do me a favor, and just indulge me." And off they drove to the ravine.

-→⊫◉ ◉⊨←-

The *Akron Beacon Journal* had printed several photos of the area, as well as a map pinpointing the exact location, so they expected to find a crowd when they arrived. They drove down a winding road for several miles and eventually came upon the spot. It was somewhat more obscure and out of the way than they had imagined, but they knew they had found it when they turned a bend and came upon a single police car parked in front of an opening between two boulders that were decorated with the now-familiar yellow crime-scene tape. The media had apparently moved on to the next juicy story, and so Mitch and Carolyn were alone with the police officer who was assigned to the site, save for one other car. He turned out to be the same uniformed policeman they had met the other day at Danny and Rachel's house.

Officer Ellis seemed relieved to have some company, and unlike at their previous meeting, was quite talkative. Because he knew Carolyn and Mitch were close friends of the family, he allowed them to walk to the edge of the cliff and peer over the precipice. The impression from the impact of the Escalade was fairly obvious, but the vehicle had been removed, and after just a few days the image was already somewhat obscured by leaves and other greenery. By next spring, the spot where Danny's car had settled would be an overgrown jumble of weeds and branches, and by the end of the decade, a new subdivision would be under construction and the Turner murders mythologized into just another local legend. But at this moment they were still very raw.

The officer gestured toward the pathway between the two large boulders.

"The owners of the quarry have agreed to put a metal fence between the two rocks. They're afraid this might become one of those popular places for people to come and, ya know—"

"Drive or jump off? You mean sort of like the Golden Gate Bridge," replied Mitch, ever the architect.

"Yeah, I guess that sort of thing," Ellis replied. "Out here, it'll probably also become one of those places where teenagers congregate when they're bored on a Friday night and dare one another to do stupid things. It's a pretty steep drop. It will be tempting to kids with nothing better to do," he said, scratching his head.

Mitch noticed Carolyn clutching one of the boulders and leaning over to stare into the ravine. He hustled over to grab her. "Whoa, honey, that's not a safe place at all." There was something about the look in her eye that scared Mitch, so he pulled her back. She broke free, fell to her knees on the gravel, and started pounding the ground.

"Why, Danny? Why? Why? Why?"

Mitch kneeled next to her with his arm around her and let her cry it out until she was finally ready to leave. The embarrassed police office retreated to the squad car and pretended to be otherwise occupied.

An hour later, when they reached the interstate, they both breathed a sigh of relief at the sight of signs promising they were headed in the direction of Chesterland. They were looking forward to seeing the boys, and just being in their own home. They each craved some semblance of normalcy; Carolyn thought about taking a long, relaxing bath, and

Mitch was anxious to put on his running shoes and run for several miles along his usual path.

⤙⫸ ⫷⤚

Much to the amazement of Mitch, Carolyn, and everyone who was close to the Turner family, Christopher adjusted remarkably well. He moved in with Maryann and her new husband, and his grandparents saw him almost every day, so he certainly didn't lack attention.

Mitch and Carolyn stopped over to visit with them from time to time, and were delighted to see that Christopher seemed happy and at peace with things. He talked with Mitch and Carolyn about his mom, dad, and brother, and about what had happened, but the tragedy didn't seem to preoccupy him. His interests had more to do with the then and now. Carolyn and Mitch were somewhat relieved. While they were not convinced that Christopher was out of the woods, thus far he was doing remarkably well. Fortunately, Maryann wanted them to stay involved in Christopher's life and they were determined and happy to do so. Things were not so sanguine in the Bianci household, however.

An outsider looking in would have assumed life had returned to normal, but that was far from true. Things were starting to come apart at the seams.

Mitch had returned to his role of running XAI. The biggest change in his work life was that he now had to travel a great deal, because his firm had successfully landed the Superfood Supermart account Mitch had been pitching the day he was abruptly forced to leave the office when his father-in-law called. He was required to go to Portland, Seattle, or San Francisco at least one week out of every month, because the first six stores were scheduled to open simultaneously in those markets the week before Thanksgiving—right around the one-year anniversary of what

Mitch and Carolyn had euphemistically taken to calling "the events in Akron."

Mitch welcomed these changes; the challenges work provided engaged him intellectually and architectural problems provided a great distraction from bleaker thoughts. His newfound travel schedule gave him a fabulous excuse to get out of the house every few weeks and forget about the issues at home. In his mind, those issues all centered around Carolyn's inability to shake her grief. She was an expert at hiding her true feelings from everyone in the world except Mitch, and so, in the privacy of their home, a pall was cast, and little by little it was starting to take a toll on their marriage. However, the issues didn't all originate with Carolyn.

Mitch was confused and frustrated by the way things were. He had grown weary of encouraging Carolyn to put things behind her, the way he had. He'd read the books on the various stages of grief, as had Carolyn, and they had each attended a few meetings of a support group that was held at a local church. Upon occasion she would be fine for a few days, or even an entire week, and then something would happen and she would be brought right back to the moment when she had learned of Rachel's death. She hardly ever slept through the night anymore, seemed distracted all the time, and, of course, cried regularly. And he noticed that she did not want to leave the house by herself, not even to run a few errands. Some of her behavior was downright scary.

One day in March, he stopped at the house unexpectedly in the middle of the afternoon, right before the boys were due home from school, and heard her in the basement listening to that final phone message from Rachel on the answering machine. The fact that she was listening to it was understandable, and he could appreciate why it was so important to her, but in the five minutes Mitch stood there, he overheard her replay it at least ten times. He could hear her weeping, but chose to head back to the office rather than try to deal with it. Of course he felt terribly guilty about abandoning her, but by now he was beginning to feel it was fruitless to attempt to comfort her. Lately, when he would talk to her about how things were starting to deteriorate in the family, they would simply wind up arguing. A few times in the last month, she had simply forgotten to get Frankie off the school bus, and she'd been called to pick him up back at school. For a conscientious mother like Carolyn, this would have been unthinkable in the past. Thus far, most of these issues had been fairly minor, but they were increasing in frequency, and he was frustrated by his inability to get her to talk honestly about what was going on with her.

So, a mile down the road, he turned the car around and came home, ostensibly to comfort her, but in actuality to catch her in the act of doing something that he felt was pretty bizarre. He hoped a confrontation might cause a breakthrough.

"Carolyn, what are you doing down there?"

"Nothing, I was just cleaning up," she said as she shoved the answering machine beneath the couch while Mitch bounded down the stairs.

"Were you listening to Rachel's message again?"

"No, what makes you think that? I hardly ever listen to it anymore, you know that!"

"Actually I don't think that's true and it bothers me that you're not being honest with me about it." He glanced down and saw the edge of the answering machine peeking out from beneath the couch. She grew furious when she followed his line of sight and realized she had been caught.

"Okay, Mitch, so I did listen to the message. What's so bad about that? It's just comforting to hear Rachel's voice. You don't understand what I'm going through. Why do you have to be such a bully about it?"

"Don't understand? All I've been doing is living this nightmare since that day last November. It hasn't been easy on me either, but I'm determined to move on. It's really sick and unhealthy to listen to that tape over and over." He was shouting now and so she shouted back.

"I don't listen to it over and over. I just listened to it once, and I hav—"

"That's a lie. I was standing upstairs before and heard you play it about a dozen times!"

"You think I'm sick? What about you creeping around checking up on me in the middle of the day? Why don't you just leave me alone? You can't think about anybody but yourself! You don't understand what I'm going through and you don't even try!" She pushed past him and ran up the stairs.

Mitch started to follow her, with the intention of winning the argument, when it dawned on him that he *was* being a bully. He was doing more harm than good and he needed to back off. This wasn't one of those problems that he could wrestle to the ground and solve.

Later that night, after they had given each other the silent treatment through dinner and long past the time they had put the kids to bed, Mitch finally saw the light and apologized. He felt bad about their argument earlier in the day, and knew he had only made matters worse. He knew that at times he could be impatient, and that was not going to help matters.

"Honey, I have to tell you honestly that I'm worried about us in general, and I'm worried that things are never going to get better," Mitch started. "You seem to be living a double life. You try to keep it together for the kids and the neighbors and even your parents, but behind the scenes and with me, well, it just seems like you're never going to get over this. And now things are starting to happen that, well, just aren't good. Half the time you don't seem like you're even here."

She winced at him, and was about to jump on the "double life" comment, but backed off when she saw that he was genuinely concerned. "I know that's what it looks like, Mitch, but I think I'm getting better, and

I don't know what else to do. I can't just wipe Rachel and Evan out of my mind. And sometimes I can see Danny doing that, you know, that night, and I get so damned angry at him, that I want to kill him! I'm going as crazy as he must have been, because I start to think about their last minutes, over and over, and I can't get these horrible pictures out of my mind."

"Doesn't it help to pray about this, honey? And what about that women's support group at the church?"

"Are you kidding? You see that closet over there?

"Yeah. What about it?

"When I can't stand it anymore, that's where I go and kneel on the floor and ask God to let me stop thinking, and stop hating and being so angry all the time. I must do that six or seven times a day, but I still can't let go of this. It just seems like the world is such an awful place with so much misery. So hopeless and ruthless and random. Then I start to think that something awful is going to happen to you or one of the kids. Particularly the kids, to tell you the truth.

"Sometimes I start to feel a little bit better, and even start to believe everything is okay and that Rachel and Evan are in heaven, but then I think about Christopher and what he went through, and how devious Danny was and how selfish. It's like this merry-go-round that I'm on and I can't get off of it. I can't stop thinking about it.

"And the support group means well, but actually, well, they're mainly a bunch of women who have had awful things happen, like their kids dying, or husbands who walked out on them, or abusive husbands, and I leave there more depressed than when I walked in . . ."

Mitch looked at her and felt completely helpless and frustrated. He didn't know what to do but it was obvious that he couldn't just ignore things and hope for the situation to improve by itself.

"I really think you should see someone about this, Carolyn, and soon."

"What good would that do? No shrink is going to bring them back or make this pain go away. This isn't like the *Dr. Phil* show, where you just get fixed like magic!" She looked at Mitch and his heart sank because he knew she was right, but he was scared, so he insisted and finally she agreed to get some counseling.

Their family doctor recommended she see the psychiatrist who was affiliated with the group, and the following week she had her first session. He was a thoughtful man, who listened carefully to her story, nodded sagely, responded with an occasional *hmm . . .*, and constantly jotted down notes. At the end of the session, he set up another appointment and sent her off with prescriptions for a cocktail of antidepressants, sleeping pills, and anti-anxiety medications. Carolyn filled the prescriptions and, when she arrived home, lined up the bottles in a neat row in front of her on the kitchen table. It looked as if she was starting a small pharmacy of her own.

⊷⊨⊚ ⊙⊨⊰⊷

If Mitch thought Carolyn was leading a double life by sinking deeper into depression while putting on a happy face for everyone in the world but him, he would have been astonished had he been able to step back and honestly see the insidious influence the murders were having on him. But that was hardly possible, because the darkness was creeping into his life in imperceptible increments, unbeknownst to him, in much the same way it had crept into Danny's life. They say you are only as sick as your secrets, so clearly Mitch was sinking fast, because his secrets were multiplying at warp speed and were hell-bent on leading him to destruction.

First the door was nudged open just a crack—just enough to reach him right where he was most vulnerable. That voice in his head started to tell him it wasn't fair that he was being put in this position. After all, he was a man who had achieved a great deal from humble beginnings, and now he had to worry that his partner in life might be going off the deep end. Other men didn't have to put up with such things and, frankly, he deserved a better life than he had at the moment. His marriage was feeling less like a marriage every day; he shouldn't have to wait forever for Carolyn to get back to her old self. As it so happened, recently someone had come into his life who appreciated him, admired him for his success, and was cheerful and fun-loving. He didn't mention it to anyone, but she began popping into his mind more and more often.

Mitch couldn't deny his attraction to Jennifer Brueuer, the young vice president of marketing for the Superfood Supermart. To a man, the guys were gaga over the clever, slender blonde with the dry British wit and fashionable outfits. They would all smile slyly to one another and yuck it up like schoolboys whenever Jennifer walked out of the room, though she was way ahead of them and accustomed to that sort of reaction from the boys. Mitch imagined she had a special fondness for him. Whether she did, or whether she was playing him—getting her way when it came to important design decisions or other areas where Mitch would normally assert his authority—it didn't matter. He felt powerful when Jennifer would clap with glee and peck him on the cheek when the big man caved in to one of her requests.

So it wasn't surprising that, increasingly, he enthusiastically anticipated his West Coast trips. It was all harmless, after all, and he deserved a break from the cloud that had descended over his home in Chesterland. At one point, for an instant, it dawned on him that he was thinking the same sorts of things Danny had mentioned that day they built the deck—that stuff about just pointing your car in some new direction and driving off to a new life. But he quickly dismissed that thought for the nonsense it was.

Lately, he felt that if he and Carolyn weren't talking about the kids or the bills or some upcoming social obligation, they didn't really have

much to say. Then somehow things would come back to the events in
Akron. The concept of the two of them just having fun seemed totally
alien. Even his father-in-law noticed something was wrong.

"When's the last time you two went out on a date, just the two of
you?" he asked Mitch, as he and the boys took their seats at Cleveland
Stadium on opening day of the baseball season.

"Not since before all that stuff went down last fall," Mitch replied.
"I suggested it a few times, but I almost have the feeling that we wouldn't
have anything to talk about except for doom and gloom. She just hasn't
been the same since then."

"You think I can't see that?"

"I didn't know it was that obvious. Carolyn's pretty good at hiding
her feelings."

"And what about you, Mitch? Are things okay with you?"

"Sure," he lied. What could he say? Had he answered truthfully, he
would have said, "Now that you ask, Pops, there's this little matter of a
very hot Brit that I'm getting to know pretty well, who makes me feel
like a man again, and we're always at the same hotel and I don't know
where this is going to lead, but I see trouble brewing. But, hell, it's not
my fault because it's all harmless, and I deserve a little female attention."

Instead, he switched to the safe subject of sports. "Who'd they say
is starting for the Indians today, Pops?"

And then there was the other obsession he hadn't mentioned to
anyone besides Devito, the private investigator he had hired to track
down Logan Vonda. He was convinced the conniving creep had had
a lot more to do with the crime than had been revealed. This ate at
him like a burr under his cap, for months, but in April, he was truly
astounded, insulted, and incensed when the inquest was held and it
was concluded that Danny had acted alone. No charges would be
brought against Vonda. Mitch was furious, but Carolyn didn't care to
discuss it.

"It doesn't matter, Mitch. It's over with, and whether that guy helped him or not, Danny did it. Let it go!"

But he wasn't so easily dissuaded. The same Tooterville police officials who had allowed hordes of people to stomp all over the crime scene had also convinced themselves they had solved the case within twenty-four hours. It was over and done with, as far as they were concerned. Apparently they felt it was totally logical for someone to relinquish his phone, wait around in a car, and even take a nap after his friend announced he was going to murder his wife and then disappeared into the house to do just that. The picture the cops painted was of someone who'd simply been at the wrong place at the wrong time. A poor, innocent sap. A hapless fool. How could anyone have expected him to walk next door to a neighbor and report that a crime might be taking place? Let sleeping dogs lie.

Well, Mitch didn't think that way. His experience had taught him that when the pieces didn't fit into place there was always a reason. His staff hated it when he said, "If you are not 100 percent certain, then you are 100 percent wrong! I don't want excuses. Solve the problem. Period. End of story." Unbeknownst to Mitch, one of the junior architects did a spot-on imitation of him giving that particular lecture, right down to the flourish he would brandish when sending the underling on his way at conclusion of his tongue lashing.

But the Logan Vonda mystery wasn't so easily explained. So Mitch decided that he should have a chat with him—except he had apparently departed from the suburbs of Akron and disappeared. Mitch was determined to find him and so had written a few hefty checks to the private investigator in order to track him down, but thus far, he hadn't had any luck. Then one day his cell phone rang and things started to fall into place, along with an amazing stroke of luck.

"Hi, Mitch, this is Devito, Charlie Devito. I think I have something for you." The burly detective had spent a few decades with the Cleveland

PD and then left under suspicious circumstances. However, the guy came highly recommended and was known as an absolute bloodhound, even though he was admittedly a bit rough around the edges.

"Great! What is it?"

"This Vonda scum has a rap sheet as long as my grandpa's nuts, so I figgered it was only a matter of time before this jerk got hisself nailed for doing something stupid, and sure enough he did."

Mitch tried to contain his excitement. "What did he do this time? Where is he?"

"Well, he got pinched for trying to scam some old biddy out of a few thousand bucks by telling her he was a friend of her grandson's and that he needed the money to bail the kid out of prison. Wooda got away with it if the bank teller didn't smell something fishy and start asking questions and then Vonda bolted."

"And did they catch him?" Mitch could smell his prey.

"Yeah, he went back to his girlfriend's apartment and they tracked him down a few days later. The guy's not too bright, ya know."

"No, apparently not," said Mitch. "Anyway, where is he?"

"It seems he got out on bail, but he's not allowed to leave the state."

"And which state is that?"

Then Mitch got his nice surprise. "Oregon. The guy was last seen in Portland—"

"You've got to be kidding me! I'm going there in a week! Where does he live?"

Devito hesitated, and then caved. "By law, I'm not supposed to give you his address. But what the hell, you're payin' for it. Just keep your mouth shut, ya hear?"

"You got it." And with that Mitch found out exactly where to find Logan Vonda. Now the question was whether or not the guy would be willing and able to answer some of the questions that had been nagging at Mitch for so long. He wanted to look this petty thief in the eye and finally learn the truth, and if he was guilty, he was going to do something about it.

→⊨◉ ◉⊫←

Naturally he didn't breathe a word to Carolyn about having tracked down Vonda. The fact that he had a trip planned to Portland gave him the cover he needed. If he found out anything useful, he'd just say he happened to run into Vonda; if not, he'd never have to mention it to her.

He drove directly from the airport to the address where he expected to find Vonda. Now that he was just a few miles away, it dawned on Mitch that he didn't actually know what he was going to say to the guy, or what he hoped to accomplish. It was also possible that Vonda would refuse to speak with him, and would tell him to get lost.

By the time he reached the second floor landing of the ratty walk-up Vonda lived in, he was starting to doubt the wisdom of his plan. Feeling his heart beat faster, it became very apparent to him that this whole thing could go terribly wrong. But he had come this far, and he couldn't back out now.

Standing outside the door, he heard a man and a woman loudly hurling insults at each other inside the apartment. When he knocked on the door, everything suddenly went silent and someone turned off the television. Mitch presumed that when a guy like Vonda received an unexpected visitor, it usually wasn't good news. In response to the silence, he knocked again, and then said, "I'm looking for Logan Vonda. Is he home?"

After a few seconds of silence, a female voice spoke from behind the door. "Who's there?"

"Does Logan Vonda live here?"

"Who wants to know?"

"Listen, my name is Mitch Bianci, and I'm looking for Logan Vonda. Is he there? I was a friend of Danny Turner's."

He heard the two of them whisper conspiratorially, and then the door pulled back a few inches and two eyes peeked out at Mitch. "What do you want? I know who you are. I got nothin' to say to you. Leave me alone."

"Listen, Logan, I only want to talk with you to get a better idea what Danny did that night. I know you weren't to blame. How about we go across the street for a cup of coffee?"

The door opened a little wider and Vonda stuck out his head. He was obviously frightened and obviously high. "I got nothin' more to say. I said it all to the cops."

"Just come out for a minute. I'm not looking for trouble; I just want to settle some things in my mind, and I'll pay you for information." With that the door chain came undone, and Vonda stepped out onto the landing and lit up a cigarette.

"Okay, whaddya want to know?"

Now that he had the long-awaited object of his manhunt in front of him, Mitch realized he had been obsessing over a poor, pathetic wreck of a kid, chasing him all the way across the country, and he was probably nothing more than the cops had figured. A dupe. But Mitch had him in his sights, so he pressed on.

"Why do you think Danny asked you to come to his house that night?"

Vonda was obviously nervous; he repeatedly took off his baseball cap, ran his fingers through his unkempt hair, and put the cap back on. He had told this story many times, yet he was acting like someone who was afraid he was going to slip and say the wrong thing.

"Didn't you hear what I told the cops?"

"I did, but I wanted to hear it from you, because, well, you know the whole thing seems sort of crazy, and Danny was my good friend. I'm just trying to figure out what set him off." Mitch was still suspicious of Vonda, but he had just identified exactly what was driving him. It was that unknowable "why" question.

"I don't know for sure. I only know what he told me, and that was just some made-up stuff, but it's probably just like the cops said. He wanted to make it look like I did it, and then he was gonna use that shotgun on me after he killed Rachel, and say it was self-defense, or make it look like he was trying to save his wife and had to kill me."

"But you must have gone into the house at some point, didn't you?"

"No way. No, man, I didn't! After Danny said he was gonna kill her and then went back inside, I wasn't gonna set foot in there. And before that, I was just supposed to be outside trying to make it look like a break-in."

"Okay, but I don't get how you could have just gone to sleep after he said something like that, even if you thought he didn't mean it. How do you sleep through all the screaming and yelling that must have been going on?"

"You want to know the truth?" Vonda looked defeated and a bit embarrassed.

"Yeah," Mitch said. "That's exactly what I want."

"I had a few Oxys I'd been saving because I thought I would be going home, and I wanted to pop them there. When Danny went back in the last time, I swallowed them and nodded off."

Of course, Mitch thought, *that makes perfect sense. It probably* is *the truth. How obvious.*

However, there was one other issue that gnawed at Mitch.

"Just one last question, Logan. After he told you he was going to kill Rachel, why didn't you do anything, like go to a neighbor's house and call the cops? You might have been able to save their lives."

"Don't you think I wish I did? Don't you think I've thought about that a million times? Not a day goes by that I don't think about it and wish I'd done something different." Mitch obviously had struck a nerve, and Logan looked away and wiped his eyes.

"Hey, I'm sorry, Logan. I didn't mean it the way it sounded. I was only—"

"Danny was my friend, too, ya know!" His face had gone totally flush and a vein popped on his forehead. "I saw him almost every day for eight years, and we had lotsa good times. Everybody liked him down at Steve's and he was always pretty cool with me, even though he was my boss."

He threw down his cigarette butt and stomped on it. "So, why didn't I run to the neighbor's house and start banging on doors? I don't know! I guess the only answer is that I was scared, and so I copped out and told myself he wouldn't really do anything to Rachel."

That's the simple truth, Mitch thought. Now that he was looking Logan in the eye and could see him for who he was, he felt a bit guilty for browbeating the guy. He was simply a scared kid caught up in the drug world who was just another victim in this whole sordid series of events.

Mitch had learned a few more details, but really nothing more than what he already knew: Danny did what he did, for whatever selfish motives, and followed through on an incredibly stupid and deadly plan. There would never be a plausible explanation for his behavior.

Mitch thanked Logan and offered him a twenty-dollar bill. "Not necessary," Logan muttered. Mitch shook his hand, and then headed to the Pearl district of downtown Portland to the work site, where he was scheduled to meet with his team and the lovely Jennifer. He felt like a fool for wasting all this time, money, and anger on someone who was just another fellow traveler, and a much less fortunate one at that. There was something about recognizing the common thread of humanity in Logan Vonda that made him feel ashamed of himself, and he started to awaken to how far off the beam he had gone.

And then there was that other matter. How silly he had been to engage in even a mild flirtation, when he had an amazing wife like Carolyn at home who loved him and desperately needed him.

He drove a mile or so and then could not go on. Pulling over to the side of the road, he cut the engine. For the first time since all this horror and tragedy had started, he allowed himself a good cry. And then he surrendered and babbled out a prayer of his own making.

"Oh, God, I'm so sorry and I don't know what to do, so I'm giving this one up to you. I don't know how I've gotten so far away from you over these last months, but I know I've been lying to myself about a lot of things. All I've done is get more and more miserable, letting myself get eaten up by anger—at Danny, Vonda, the cops—and wanting somebody to be punished for this. I know, Lord, that I've been so selfish and self-righteous that I haven't been able to see what I've been doing. How one lie builds on the next, and how secrets like the ones I've been keeping are leading me to a very dark place. I want to see the light again, Lord. Help me to be the sort of spouse that I want Carolyn to be and I know she is. I know she needs me now, Lord, and I pray that you will lead me so that I can help her, and help us all to start healing, so we can be happy again. Amen."

He felt exhausted and drenched with sweat. Leaning back against the headrest, he closed his eyes and took a deep breath. He had a sense that God was trying to speak to him, and that, for a change, he should just shut up and listen. As he became more and more relaxed, he felt a lightness, as if he were falling. Instead of fighting it, he simply handed himself over to whatever it was that was taking him. For the first time in a long time, he stopped grasping for control and felt a newfound sense of freedom. The conviction that he was about to discover something important was leading him, and he simply followed it. His last conscious thought was, "This must be what it feels like when God answers your prayers"

He was not asleep. In fact, he felt more awake than he ever had. He knew he had entered a different realm. He glanced down and saw two tiny feet that he recognized as his own childhood feet, bare on the soft, lush, green grass. They felt connected to the earth. He came upon a clearing in the woods on a warm summer day and instinctively knew his way, though he had never been there before. He could see all around with utter clarity, despite the fact his eyes were closed. Just ahead a brilliant ray of sunlight broke through an opening in the trees and illuminated the soft grass, displaying a bright green patch that had been prepared for him. He stretched out and rested his head on the fluffy ground. The sun was warm on his face. He watched the images dancing on the insides of his eyelids. Blue, black, and white speckles moved side to side and twirled against a red background. In the distance he could see the figure of a woman who spoke to him. Her voice sounded familiar and comforting, and yet he knew they had never met.

"You are free because you are not alone and never will be alone, because you are one with every other human being as they are one with you. Be guided by love, and it will destroy all fear. Trust in God. He has much greater plans for you than you could ever possibly imagine. You must accept that you are forgiven and then you will be able to forgive others. God is in you and you are in God. God is everywhere, in everything and in everyone."

⇥⊙ ⊙⇤

On the other side of the country, Carolyn sat opposite the array of bottles filled with pills that promised to remove her anxiety, help her overcome her sadness, and allow her to sleep—perhaps for a long, long time. There was something comforting about this pharmaceutical oasis, where all this pain wouldn't be able to reach her. The doctor had made it sound so inviting, like flipping a switch and making the incessant noise in her head just stop. Disappear. Relief was simply an arm's length away. She had avoided taking the medication for some time, but the sleepless-ness and sense of foreboding were starting to overwhelm her. She felt herself sinking fast, but something told her to wait.

She walked over and sat in Mitch's chair near the sliding-glass doors. He called it the "most comfortable chair in the world," and loved to sit in it. It was his corny joke, but now she wanted to hear him say it. She had an overwhelming need to feel his presence. All these months of confusion and conflict had torn them apart and left them unable to see the tremendous love they shared. She flashed on the night her dad had waited up for her and, in her best Dad voice, said to the silent room, "He's a keeper." That brought a smile to her face. She hadn't realized how good it could feel to smile. It was as if her face had been frozen since November. She started to chuckle; for some reason, the squeaky noise that came out of her sounded totally ridiculous and hilarious. Then she laughed so deeply and loudly, and for so long, that eventually tears of joy rolled down her cheeks and she had to gasp for air to catch her breath, which only made her laugh more.

At that instant, she was startled by the sound of someone knocking on the glass door a few feet away. She looked up to see a strikingly beau-tiful woman with brilliant white hair, gesturing for Carolyn to unlock the door and allow her to enter. Certain she was in a dream, she did as instructed. It was not until their hands touched that Carolyn discovered that the woman was indeed very real, and very much alive.

Despite the fact they were strangers, they silently clung to each other as if they were long-lost sisters, and then stepped back and looked deeply into each other's eyes, holding hands as women often will. Carolyn was confused, speechless. Then Rachel whispered in her ear and told her what to say.

"I'm Carolyn. What's your name?"

CHAPTER 15

What a Difference a Day Makes

God whispers to us in our pleasures,
speaks in our consciences,
but shouts in our pains.
—*C. S. Lewis*

JOANNA SMILED BECAUSE she knew Rachel had reached across into the sphere of the living and had reassured her dear friend. It brought a sense of ease and comfort to both women.

Even though Joanna had seen countless people respond to her with a look of utter astonishment, it still delighted her when someone was genuinely awestruck, as Carolyn was at that moment. Her expression was priceless: a mixture of child-like wonder and confusion, but not fear, despite having just invited into her home a stranger who seemed to have appeared out of nowhere. At such times Joanna had to remind herself to keep her ego in check; she was simply a messenger.

"Hello, Carolyn, my name is Joanna, Joanna Larson, and I am so happy to meet you!"

"Do I know you, Joanna? I think I do! You look familiar and I could swear I've heard your voice before."

"Actually, no, we've never personally met until just now, but I've been thinking about you a great deal." Joanna's beatific smile put Carolyn at ease. Logically, she at least should have been apprehensive; instead, she was burning with curiosity. Something important was happening here, but she didn't know what it was.

"I don't mean to be rude, Joanna, but—"

"Why am I here? And why have I been thinking about you given that we don't know each other?"

Carolyn nodded her head, and Joanna replied, "Well that's a perfectly reasonable question to ask someone who comes knocking at your back door, imploring you to let them in!" The absurdity of the whole situation suddenly struck both women as so totally ridiculous, they were both reduced to uncontrollable laughter. It reminded Carolyn of being a teenager with Rachel and how they would laugh at the most ludicrous situations without a care. When they were finished, Joanna said, "Well, since I'm now in your house, may I sit down?"

Slightly embarrassed, but still reeling from the sense of absolute joy, Carolyn said, "Oh, of course. How thoughtless of me; can I get you something, Joanna?"

"I would like a glass of water if you don't mind. It sweltering outside."

Joanna sat down at the kitchen table, folded her hands, and shut her eyes for a minute. Then she reached into her handbag and started searching for something.

While Carolyn poured the water, she glanced at her guest, trying not to appear too conspicuous. She couldn't take her eyes off of her, however. She thought Joanna to be one of the most exceptionally beautiful people she had ever seen. Aside from the color of her hair, which was pulled back into a ponytail and almost reached the small of her back, there was something distinctive about her smooth, olive skin, and her extraordinarily wide and brilliant green eyes. Though she had the demeanor of a cleric, she was fashionably dressed in jeans and a bright pink T-shirt, accompanied by an open flannel shirt that was tied at her belt buckle.

She was one of those people who looked much younger than her actual age, or perhaps her hair made her appear older than she actually was. Carolyn guessed she might be around thirty-eight or forty at most.

Just as Carolyn sat down at the table, Joanna found her wallet, produced her driver's license, and slid it across the table toward Carolyn.

"Everyone always wonders how old I am, and no one believes me when I tell them," Joanna said with a laugh, accompanied by a girlish grin and just a hint of smugness.

Carolyn pretended she hadn't just been pondering that very question as she scanned the license for the date of birth.

"You were born in 1950! That can't be, Joanna! That would make you . . . fifty-five!"

"You're so right! But don't say it that way! That's not so old! She said, pretending to be offended.

Carolyn went on to make a fuss about how young Joanna looked; she then talked about her own age, her religious upbringing, and how she was married with three kids, born and raised in Cuyahoga County, and had gone to John Carroll. She concluded by confiding that she and her husband had been going through an exceedingly difficult time of late.

She was normally a very private person, particularly with strangers, so she was a bit bemused and surprised by her candor. Carolyn thought perhaps she had said too much, too soon, but she felt so comfortable with Joanna. However, she backed off a bit and tried to change the subject.

"I don't know why I just dumped all that on you, Joanna. I just met you!"

Joanna answered with her angelic smile and said the words that truly stunned Carolyn, but were intended to allow them to shift to the true purpose of her visit.

"Oh, please don't worry about that. Haven't you figured it out yet? I was sent here to help you." She looked down at the row of prescription medications that Joanna had lined up like soldiers and completely forgotten about.

"Oh those? I was just looking at them. I really wasn't going to take them. The doctor said they would make me feel better. . ." She scooped them up and put them on the counter behind a loaf of bread, and cursed herself for leaving the pills out on the table and for announcing that a doctor had prescribed them for her. But then how was she to know all this would happen when she innocently sat down in Mitch's chair just a few minutes ago? And what was that Joanna had said about being sent here to help her? Things were happening very quickly.

She looked at Joanna quizzically. "What do you mean sent here to help me? Who sent you?"

--→■◉ ◉■←--

Mitch shook his head in an attempt to clear the cobwebs. The last thing he remembered was sitting in the rental car and praying intensely, and then he must have fallen into a deep sleep. He recalled having an incredibly powerful dream. He had a vague recollection of a woman speaking to him and telling him something important. What was it? He saw himself walking through a forest, lying in a clearing, staring into the sun— but before that, he had plunged through the earth to some secret place.

"Whew! Man, was that ever something." He strived to recall the details, but they eluded him. However, he was brimming over with a sensation of having just been freed, but from what he didn't know. He felt lighter. There seemed to be a wire running from his forehead directly to the tips of his fingers and toes. He didn't know what had happened, but whatever it was, it felt fantastic. When he glanced outside the car, at the ground, trees, and sky, the colors were vibrant and rich. Some inner source directed him to sit still, and simply observe things and wait.

The scent of freshly mowed grass wafted into the car. He could smell summer. He could hear summer. The array of dissimilar sounds that burst forth from the city street coalesced into a rhythmic symphony that was perfectly in pitch. Mitch had practiced meditation and prayer throughout his life, and at those times he felt a connection to his soul, but this was distinctly different. He successfully ignored his natural desire to understand what was happening and basked in the experience of utter calm until it started to dissipate.

He was about to turn on the ignition when a butterfly fluttered past the windshield, disappeared out of view, reappeared, and perched on the steering wheel. He leaned in closer to study this gorgeous creature, who simply stood her ground and observed the incredulous human before her.

Her wings were a brilliant orange, tipped in strokes of black, against a powdery white background that was daubed with blue speckles. Mitch was astounded.

"Boy, you sure are beautiful! I never realized . . ."

Then his inner voice gently interrupted: "Now would be a good time for silence."

When she finished showcasing her remarkable good looks, the butterfly zipped back out the window and into the ether.

Mitch shook his head, looked straight up, and shouted, "All right, God. I get it! Caterpillar to butterfly! You really *don't* have to make things *that* obvious!" He'd heard that God had a sense of humor and now he had proof of that.

As he drove to the hotel he mused about the many stories of transformation that were in the Bible. Doubting Thomas; Saul, who was knocked from his horse and became Paul; Jacob, who wrestled with the angel all night and was transformed into Israel by the morning. He chortled and thought, *You know, Mitch, perhaps you should learn how to receive a gift graciously instead of always being so suspicious! Just say, "Thank you, Lord!"*

He desperately wanted to speak with Carolyn. He had so much to tell her, but he didn't know what to say or where to begin. He doubted he would be able to pull her out of the funk she was mired in back in Ohio. He also had to admit that he was afraid that talking out loud to anyone about this experience would somehow shatter it. *What if she laughs at me?* he thought.

But now his new inner voice pounced with a ready dose of wisdom, interrupting the thought pattern that had been his companion for so many years. "Stop trying to figure everything out," it advised. "Stop doubting and fearing and start healing!" Mitch loosened his grip on the steering wheel and began his journey home.

--→▮◉ ◉▮←--

Joanna knew she had to choose her words carefully when answering Carolyn's question regarding the identity of the person who had directed her to come knocking on her door that morning. She knew that sometimes even faithful people could be frightened by the authentic presence of God in their lives.

"Carolyn, haven't you been speaking to God every day, several times a day, asking for help?" Joanna leaned forward and for the first time Carolyn noticed the cross dangling from the chain around her neck.

"Yes, that's true. I've been going through a very difficult time for months. It all started last Nov—"

"I know about the pain that you and so many others have suffered since that terrible day—"

"It was all over the news," Carolyn interjected.

"It was, my dear, but I'm speaking about a deeper knowing. Tell me, when you are upstairs, in your sacred spot, on your knees, you believe that God hears you, don't you?"

"That's what I'd like to believe, but every day I just fall right back into sadness and grief and I can't stop all those horrible thoughts." Then Carolyn looked at Joanna quizzically.

"Wait a minute. How do you know where I pray upstairs?" She felt a little insulted at the invasion of her privacy. "Who are you really, Joanna?"

Joanna threw back her head and laughed. "You are too polite, Carolyn. I was wondering when you would get around to asking that! Let's just say that I have a very special gift. Sometimes I think of it as more of a responsibility that I have been given. But I believe—no, I know—that God has selected me to help where I can. Though sometimes I'm not able to help, which, I'm sorry to say, was the case with Danny. I just couldn't reach him. He was beyond my ability to help that night." She looked away and thought about the moment she was literally driven to her knees that morning in November.

"So, you're telling me that you knew Danny, and tried to stop him from doing what he did?"

"Yes and no, Carolyn. I'm sorry if I'm confusing matters. Let me start by answering your first question. What I'm going to tell you will sound very strange, but I know that you too are a woman of faith, and that we share the belief that Jesus is our Lord and Savior, is that right?"

"Absolutely!" Carolyn said. They each felt their connection deepen.

"So to answer your first question: God sent me. And to answer your second question . . . I know about your going into your bedroom, and speaking to your Lord in the quiet and privacy of your closet, because God has shown this to me for a purpose."

Carolyn began to allow herself to feel some sense of relief. Was it really possible that this stranger could help her, or was she so desperate for relief that she would allow herself to believe even something this preposterous? It occurred to her that Mitch would probably have her committed if he could hear this conversation.

"I truly want to believe what you're saying, Joanna, but I think you can imagine that this is a little much to take in. Who are you really, and how could you possibly know these things?"

So Joanna talked about her childhood and told her the story of her father dying on his birthday, and the blue bubble rising to the sky, and the shoes and the bare feet. She recounted those extraordinary and bleak February days in 1962 when she discovered what she later came to describe as "the knowing." She shared her stories of stumbling as she learned how to use her abilities, and the battle that she had raged with her ego. She talked a little about being called to ministry—how at first her personal calling had directed her to work with women who were in danger from abusive men, and how then, after she'd met and married Richard, together they had decided to minister to young men, to try to stop the problems before they began.

"So you see, Carolyn, I am just a simple woman who has the ability to help sometimes, but not always. For instance, I can look at someone and know that he is at risk because Satan or evil spirits have him in their grip. Sometimes I can help, as I did with a young man earlier this morning, and other times, free will takes over and then a person may make the very worst decision."

"Joanna, my husband Mitch and I often talk about all the other options Danny had right up until the final moment when he stood at his kitchen door, looking out into the garage . . . but, I'm sorry, you probably don't know what I'm talking about."

"Actually, I do. And I want to tell you much more than I have, but not right now. It's important that your husband be part of the conversation. I know he has been suffering in his own way. So, let's meet again when we can all be together. I suspect I've already given you more than enough to think about!"

"I would like to have Mitch there, but I'm so anxious to learn more. I'd like meet again soon, but he's away on a business trip and won't be back until the weekend so—"

"In Portland, yes, I know," Joanna replied.

Carolyn's jaw dropped, and before she could say anything, Joanna continued.

"Don't worry. We'll get together the day after tomorrow. I would like the two of you to come downtown to Cleveland and visit our church, so we'll have a chance to speak at length."

"But Mitch won't be back yet," Carolyn insisted.

Joanna began to gather her belongings. "Don't worry, my dear. Things have a way of changing as the universe directs. It's a spiritual contract, and it's out of our control. You don't mind if I leave by the front door, do you?"

"Of course not, but . . . you mean you drove here by car?"

"Well, how did you think I got here? I didn't fly!"

They walked to the door and hugged again on the front porch.

"Carolyn, it's been so nice to meet you." She scribbled on a piece of paper. "Here is my number. Call me after you speak with your husband. And feel better! God has heard your prayers."

"Help is on the way!" she added with a smile as she turned and walked down the steps.

"I can't tell you how much better I feel already, Joanna. Thank you so much!"

Carolyn stood at the door while Joanna climbed into her fairly battered blue minivan. "I'll see you soon," she shouted as she watched Joanna wave, pull away from the curb, and finally turn the corner.

She shut the door and leaned against it. Then she remembered something she'd heard a television minister say that morning. It hadn't made sense at the time, but it had stuck in her mind all day: "You can't find God, because He isn't lost." It was a silly little play on words, but then the preacher had made the connection with patience and doing things in God's time.

The man had said something else that struck her: "Faith is easy when things are going your way, but you need to work for it when you are in the midst of your own storm."

He had gone on to talk about the famous section in Mark where Jesus is asleep in the boat with his disciples. A storm comes along and the disciples panic, but Jesus simply calms the waters. *How true it is that our faith faces the greatest test when we're in the middle of difficult times,* Carolyn thought. In less than an hour, Joanna had restored so much of her faith.

She was on her way to call Mitch when the phone rang. Now she was starting to have visions of her own, because she knew with absolute certainty that it was her husband calling, and of course she was right.

"Hi, Mitch," she said, as she picked up the receiver. "I have something really important to tell you."

"Hi, honey. That's exactly what I was going to say to you!"

"Okay, you can go first, but I have a feeling you're going to tell me you're coming home tomorrow, right?" Carolyn couldn't wait to hear his reaction.

"How did you know? Are you a mind reader now or something?"

And then they both laughed. Laughter was something they hadn't shared very often in recent months. Mitch thought Carolyn sounded like her old self—maybe even better than her old self.

"No, I'm not a mind reader, but someone just left who is just about the most amazing person I've ever met. Her name is Joanna and—"

"Wait a minute, Carolyn. Stop there. Does she have really white hair? Almost glowing?"

"Well, in fact she does. But how would *you* know that?"

Then Mitch tried to describe the experience that had taken place after his meeting with Logan Vonda. He knew his words were inadequate, but he took a leap of faith and tried. Carolyn could tell that Mitch had been through something powerful and listened intently. He sounded like a different person, but she sensed she was hearing the real Mitch for the first time in her life. She closed her eyes and could clearly see him sitting on the terrace outside his hotel room, gesturing and talking with his hands in the way he always did when he was excited. She sat cross-legged in his chair, and listened as he rambled on until he had said everything he needed to say, concluding with, "I know that probably sounds completely insane to you, but I just have this feeling that I'm different now."

"Mitch, I was just thinking that you sound like a different person. That's sort of how I feel after meeting with Joanna."

"So tell me about this Joanna."

"Oh, where can I begin, Mitch? I was sitting in your chair—where I'm sitting now, by the way—and I looked up because someone was knocking on the glass doors, and there she was!"

"You mean she just appeared there? You didn't meet her someplace? You let her in? Why?"

"To tell you the truth, it seemed like the most natural thing to invite her into the house, and as soon as she stepped in, we gave each other a big hug!"

Then Carolyn told Mitch as much as she could about the beautiful woman who had simply stepped into her life unannounced and had somehow relieved so much of her grief with the things she said and the way she said them. Carolyn told Mitch a few of the things Joanna couldn't possibly have known unless she had some ability that went far beyond the rest of them.

"And, you know, even when she was telling me that she had been sent by God to help us, it seemed so normal and natural. I have to admit that I feel better than I have since Danny killed Rachel and Evan."

And there it was. She had said it out loud and it hadn't hurt her. She felt a little stronger for it.

Mitch also took note of the fact that Carolyn hadn't used a euphemism, and that she seemed filled with joy rather than misery. He was thrilled to have his wife back, and if this woman could do that, he would be eternally grateful. He wanted to accept that this Joanna person was the real deal, but, despite his experience earlier in the day, he wasn't convinced.

"Well, I'd really like to meet Joanna. If she is who she says she is, she'll be able to explain a lot about what Danny did and why he did it."

"That's what we're going to do tomorrow."

"Okay, then I'll get on the red-eye tomorrow night and meet you at Hopkins in the morning."

"Okay, honey. Oh, and I forgot to mention what Joanna said I needed to tell you."

"Yeah, what's that?" Mitch steeled himself for some prosaic, feel-good slogan like "stop and smell the roses," or "God will be there just in the moment you need Him." The old Mitch was trying hard to make a comeback, but was dealt a serious blow.

"She said to tell you the butterfly thinks you have beautiful eyes."

Chapter 16

An Open Heart

Let us forgive each other,
only then will we live in peace.
—*Tolstoy*

CAROLYN DROVE TO Hopkins to pick up Mitch, and then they headed straight to downtown Cleveland for their meeting with Joanna. They were thrilled to see each other. Somehow it felt a bit like they were on a first date because each had undergone such a dramatic emotional shift. Because she had already met Joanna, Carolyn had some idea of what to expect, but despite the fact Mitch remained in the sway of his transformative moment in Portland, his protective nature caused him to worry that perhaps Joanna was just a well-intentioned kook, or worse.

However, there was no denying the fact that they were both ignited by the sheer thrill of leaping into the unknown together, and were now consumed with a childlike sense of adventure.

Of course, their adult sides attempted to assert authority and perform a reality check. Any rational person observing the situation would say that this all seemed more than a bit bizarre, and of course he would be correct. However, this was not a dream from which they would awaken at the end with some remnant of having visited another world. This was real life, and within just a few hours they would discover that this ordinary Wednesday morning would be the most defining few hours of their lives.

As Carolyn exited the airport, she found it impossible to contain her excitement.

"Mitch, I really feel like what we're doing was meant to be," she said. "I mean, how could it be that you went through what you did out in Portland at exactly the same time I was meeting with Joanna?"

"I know, honey, but I have to admit that this is pretty weird, and I don't think we should get our hopes up too much. I don't really know what to expect from this woman, but I'll admit I couldn't get her out of my mind all the way here. But then I couldn't remember. . . . What exactly did she say she could do for us?"

"Well, she said that she sometimes knows what's in people's minds when they are at turning points. And that she can communicate with people who have passed on. She said she was actually in contact with Danny on that night, and seemed very sad about not being able to stop him."

"Come on, honey! Do you really think all that could be true?"

"I do. I can't really explain why I believe that, but I think when you meet her you'll be convinced as well." They had now exited the interstate and were headed into downtown Cleveland.

They sat in silence for a few minutes. The break was what they needed. This was a lot to absorb.

"Anyway, Mitch, what have we got to lose by just meeting with her?"

"You're right," Mitch replied, and thought about all that had happened yesterday morning and laughed at how quickly he had forgotten. Caterpillar to butterfly. "You've got the wheel, honey, and I'm just going along for the ride!"

"Well, we've either both gone nuts or we're driving off into another dimension!" Mitch made the requisite *Twilight Zone* music as they headed down Fifty-fifth Street and slowed to a crawl so they could check the street numbers.

They were not far from their destination. Joanna had mentioned they would be driving through some pretty rough neighborhoods, and indeed they were. Around them they saw abandoned buildings, empty lots, a bodega, a liquor store, and boarded-up storefront windows with signs from another era. It was the middle of summer, so there were a good number of people out on the streets, particularly teenagers sitting on steps to escape the heat and see what opportunities might come their way that day.

"Whatever else we might think about Joanna, Mitch, the fact that she chooses to live and work in the inner city and help young men is certainly admirable."

"I can't argue with that," he answered.

"That must be it," Carolyn said, pointing to a stone church on the corner that fit the description Joanna had given her. "Beautiful gray stone with a red door" was how Joanna had described it. The building had been lovingly restored. At one time, it must have been the center of the community. On this day, the positive energy that emanated from it was palpable.

"Man, she's a beauty." The architect in Mitch admired the stonework while the little boy gyrated with anticipation. Was it really possible that Joanna could explain what had happened that night?

The church that Joanna and Richard had resurrected turned out to be a fairly large building with a bell tower, numerous stained glass windows, and two magnificent oak doors that were painted a deep red. Mitch noticed "1897" engraved into the cornerstone to the left of the steps. He had a passion for visiting churches and suspected this one would not disappoint.

The original name of the church had been sandblasted off the area above the doors and replaced by the name of the present congregation. Large, elegantly chiseled letters proclaimed the building to be "The Church of Forgiveness," with smaller type announcing "All Sinners

Welcome". This wasn't just a temporary saying meant to entice pass-ersby, but rather a permanent mission statement.

They were greeted at the door by a tall black man with a gray pony-tail and piercing blue eyes, who was supervising the installation and refurbishment of a collection of used pews. He stuck out his huge paw and said, "Hi, I'm Richard. You two must be Carolyn and Mitch. We've been expecting you."

Richard introduced his two workers, who were his and Joanna's teenage boys. They both had the same remarkable olive coloring and sharp good looks of their mother, though one was blond and the other sported an Afro.

Richard volunteered to take Carolyn and Mitch through the church to the garden, where Joanna had said they would be able to meet in private.

As they walked down the center aisle, Mitch was awestruck by the glorious crucifix that was suspended high above the altar and domi-nated the interior of the church. It was surprising not simply because the figure of Jesus was so frighteningly realistic, but because the fine detail and color had been rendered so exquisitely that it could have stood proudly in the Vatican—yet here it was in a little church in Cleveland. It was a riveting work of art that could only have been divinely inspired.

Mitch and Carolyn paused in front of the altar and respectfully made the sign of the cross as they continued to peer up at it.

"Amazing, isn't it?" Richard said.

"Fantastic," Mitch replied. "How long has it been here?"

"It was part of the original church, so that would make it something like one hundred and twenty years old. It's survived two world wars, the Depression, Vietnam, the riots in the '60s, and Lord knows what else over the years.

"The church was abandoned for a decade before we took it over. I guess it provided shelter for the people who needed it, but it was pretty ripped up by the time we came along. Joanna and I knew we had found our church the minute we walked in, looked up, and saw Jesus beckoning to us. We knew we had come home. Sometimes ya just know, ya know?"

Mitch and Carolyn nodded as Richard led them through a door to the left of the altar where they emerged into a flower garden that greeted them with an explosion of color. The brilliance of the colors was particularly stunning in contrast to the drab setting on either side of the backyard.

Richard laughed when he saw their reaction and said, "I don't know how she does it, but anything she touches just seems to grow and grow. Joanna says it's all the conversations she's had with the flowers over the years! Well, there she is. I'll see you later."

Joanna stood near a stone picnic table that was set behind a trellis adorned by all manner of grape vines, ivy, roses, clematis, and an assortment of climbing plants that all strained skyward. It created an extraordinary passageway to what appeared to be a shady grotto that was bathed in dappled sunlight. Mitch was immediately reminded of the sacred place to which he had been drawn in his dream.

She was dressed almost exactly as she had been two days ago; the only difference was that this time the shirt beneath the tied flannel was dark blue rather than pink. Mitch was surprised by Joanna's appearance. Though Carolyn had told him how casually Joanna had been dressed the other day, he still half expected she would be decked out for the occasion in a flowing gown and that her hair would be blowing in the wind. Passing her on the street, one would never guess she was a minister. However, she was every bit as striking and memorable as Carolyn had described.

Mitch and Carolyn both reached forward to shake hands at the same time, and Joanna clasped both their hands together and vigorously shook them in an up-and-down motion. Mitch was musing that he had never felt such soft yet strong hands when Joanna said, "Mitch, it's so nice to meet you. And Carolyn, you look even more beautiful than you did when we first met."

"Well, thanks for the compliment, Joanna. But I think the first time I must have looked a mess because I was totally in shock!"

They all laughed politely and chatted about their surprise meeting as Joanna offered them a seat at her table and poured lemonade for everyone. Once they were seated, they waited for Joanna to speak, but she just folded her hands in her lap and sat silently.

Normally Mitch couldn't stand the awkwardness that came with a gap in the conversation, but he had learned the other day that keeping one's mouth shut was the only way to listen to God. The world was anything but silent. They all sat still and enjoyed the sounds of the flowers rustling, the birds singing, the wind whistling, and the city in the distance. Soon Mitch realized he could hear the beat of his heart.

After a few minutes Joanna broke the silence. Mitch and Carolyn opened their eyes when they heard Joanna's voice.

She held her hands in front of her in the form of a cup and began to pray.

"We thank you, Lord, for bringing the three of us together this morning in the beauty of your garden, so that we might be one with your Holy Spirit. We share the faith that through your goodness and mercy you will allow us to discover the truth. Lord, I humbly ask that you allow this messenger to be blessed with the words that will bring healing to Carolyn and Mitch, so that they may in turn help others as they continue their journey of hope and forgiveness and, in so doing, glorify your name. We ask this in Jesus's name, Amen.

She looked at Mitch and with her eyes invited him to speak.

"Joanna," Mitch said, slightly above a whisper, "I know you know what happened with our friends, and how this has impacted our lives, and there is no doubt we are in need of help. The other day, you told

Carolyn about yourself and your background, and of course she told me, but to tell you the truth, I'm still confused. So would you mind telling us a little more about how you're able to help us? I guess I'm asking how you know these things."

Joanna answered in a slow and methodical manner. "Perhaps I should tell you what I am not. I'm not a medium, but God sees fit to use me as an intercessor. So God allows me to use the gifts He has given me to intercede and pray for those in need, which is the focal point of who I am and how I help others. Sometimes I am permitted to do things that most earthly men or women wouldn't understand. For example, I'll be in the presence of someone living in heaven and they will speak to me, and I'll hear their voice. And I will receive their message and their words and be able to share them with others. So the truth is that I am simply a messenger, and I will answer your questions if I am able."

"Thank you, Joanna," Carolyn replied. "Then I guess my first question would be about Rachel. I have felt her presence so many times, but it's just so hard to believe it's real, and so I don't trust it and then I convince myself that I'm just imaging things."

"Well, Carolyn, given that Rachel was such a big part of your life for so long, and that she left so abruptly, it's only natural that you would feel a connection with her. Why would it be so hard to accept that her soul lives on and that your soul lives on and that they sometimes intersect? Don't you still feel the same love for her that you always did?"

"Of course I do, but—"

"But like all of us you struggle with faith, and God understands that and forgives us for that—as He does all of our mistakes, much in the way a loving parent will forgive her child over and over. So, trust that this is true, and, if you do, it will become easier over time for the two of you to find each other."

Carolyn took a leap of faith. "Joanna, when we met you said that Rachel had spoken with you. Did she? Do you know where she is? Is she at peace?"

"Yes, yes, and yes. The first time she spoke with me directly, you and I were in the same room with her."

"How can that be? We were never together with Rachel!" Carolyn feared that if Joanna could be mistaken about such an obvious fact, then perhaps everything she had told them was wrong. Mitch was shocked at Carolyn's vehement response.

Joanna smiled at the confusion she had caused.

"I'm sorry for sounding so mysterious, Carolyn. Let me explain. The day we three were together was the day Rachel and Evan were buried. I decided to attend the service because I knew the pastor would need encouragement."

"You were in the church that day?"

"Yes, I was. Sitting in the very last pew, near the center aisle."

"And Rachel spoke with you? What did she say?"

"She told me to thank you for saying such nice things at her service and that she was very proud of you."

And then she added, "You know that Rachel was standing next to you at the altar, don't you?"

"I did have that feeling at the time, but I was afraid to believe it."

"And you know that she sometimes speaks with you in your dreams?"

Mitch interjected, "You've told me that, honey."

"Yes, she does come to me in a dream. I see her walking with Evan. Holding hands and walking together. They look like they're at a beach or someplace near water."

"That's because she wants you to know that she and Evan are safe, and at peace, and she wants you to move on with your life and enjoy yourself."

Carolyn dabbed her eyes. She was hearing so much; it was hard to take it all in. But something was bothering her and she had to get it out.

"Joanna, I really appreciate what you are doing for us, and I don't want you to think I doubt you, but I was thinking last night about what you said the other day."

"Said about what?"

"You said you knew about my praying so much, that God had heard my prayers and sent you. If that's true, I don't get why . . . why He'd care enough to send someone to help me get over my grief but would allow something so horrible to happen in the first place. If God cares enough to help someone who's grieving, why didn't he stop Danny?"

Mitch excitedly jumped in. "That's the big question, isn't it? Why did Danny do what he did? I hardly ever saw him without a smile on his face. I knew him for a long time and never once saw him lose his temper. He did do some things he shouldn't have, like cheat on Rachel, and he didn't work that hard, or manage his finances, things like that. But to actually murder your wife and child! Where was God then? I just can't believe it!"

"Okay, Mitch. I know you're upset, and you have a right to be. I know you've had a burning desire to learn the answer to these questions, and I have a great deal to tell you about what happened that night, and I will tell you soon, but I ask that you slow down and do one thing first."

"What's that?"

"I want you to finally forgive yourself." The instant she said the word "forgive," she reached across the table and gently touched the middle of his forehead with two fingers.

Mitch felt a jolt at her touch. In the time it took for a single beat of a pulse, the blame, guilt, and shame he'd been carrying about the murders seemed to be lifted. He instinctively reached out to touch Carolyn.

"So, Carolyn, do you have any of the same thoughts Mitch has had? Do you think that in some way you are to blame?"

Carolyn nodded, and could hardly speak at first, but finally blurted out, "Rachel didn't tell me everything, but she told me enough. I just didn't try hard enough. I was going to have dinner with her that night, but I didn't even bother to call her back after she left her last message."

"Carolyn, would you like to know what Rachel has to say about that?"

She gasped, put her hand to her mouth, and nodded.

"She wants both of you to know that Danny did what he did because he was betrayed by the Devil, and that neither of you are to blame, and neither is Danny. But in order to understand that, I have to explain what happened that night. Do you want me to continue?"

"Okay," they answered in unison. Mitch couldn't comprehend why Danny was not to blame, but he certainly could not stop Joanna at this point, though nothing could prepare him for what he was about to learn.

⇥▨◉ ◉▨⇤

Joanna took a deep breath and appeared to be listening to a distant voice. She rolled her head slightly and began. Mitch started to ask a question, but she quickly shook her palm toward him to warn him off. Her demeanor had completely changed.

"Danny's easygoing nature was a mask for passivity and was the result of deep-seated fears . . . fear of not being good enough, fear of failure, and, in the end, fear of not being loved. That's what drove him always to be 'nice' so that he would always be liked. But Danny, as we all do, had plenty of anger. The fact that he wore a mask to disguise it didn't make it any less powerful or real; in fact, keeping it hidden only made it all the more explosive when it finally came out, which anger always, inevitably will. You might say he was like a volcano that finally erupted.

"Because he thought of himself as unworthy, he tried to compensate by lying, cheating, and pretending to be something he wasn't. At times, he fought with the Devil, but he lost again and again for many years.

"He lost because he didn't fight his desires. He did not pursue Godly wishes. He made gods of the earth. And since no man can serve two gods, Danny had to choose.

"Danny stopped trusting God. Without trust, there is no faith. If we trust God, and allow the seeds to be planted, our faith grows . . .

"Satan tempts us with our own imperfections. He lures us through our wounds, our shame, and our self-doubts. He has no power on his own but uses those imperfections—our human frailties—against us.

"Danny forgot that he had the love and support of his Creator and the people in his life. Then he began to let the Devil seep into the caverns of his mind. Over that time Satan established a foothold in Danny's mind and once that darkness came over him, all his hope was gone.

"We do have free will. Yes, we do make mistakes. Yes, we all experience darkness. But yet, we are given faith. We're given hope. God is the heartbeat of mankind."

⇥⊜ ⊜⇤

With that, Joanna went silent. Mitch and Carolyn looked at each other, but had no idea what to do next. Eventually Carolyn summoned the courage to speak up.

"Joanna, are you okay?"

She nodded her head, and indicated she was, but kept her eyes closed. "Would you like me to continue?" she asked. "Do you want me to tell you what really happened that night?"

"Joanna, if you know," Mitch said, "then tell us, so we can at least try to understand."

She opened her eyes and looked at them for the first time in several minutes. "Are you sure?"

They were shocked by her question, and neither Mitch nor Carolyn knew what to say, so they sat mute.

She was clearly in great pain. "I'm sorry. This is bringing it all back. And each time I go through something like this, it steals a part of me. I want to help you to understand, so you can begin to heal, but you must promise me that you will trust that what I'm going to tell you is the truth, even though in the natural it will not make sense. You must promise to use what I'm going to tell you to spread the message of hope and forgiveness despite the fact you will be scorned and ridiculed."

Mitch and Carolyn agreed despite the fact they didn't truly understand what they were agreeing to. Mitch prodded her slightly.

"Joanna, if you're ready to continue . . ."

A cloud passed before the sun; the brilliant morning was washed in gray and the air turned chilly. Joanna hesitated. It was as if some force in the garden was trying to prevent her from speaking. As before, her expression changed: the lightness was swept away and was replaced by a pained expression. She took a deep breath and began again.

"Listen carefully."

Then silence. She seemed to be trying to hear a faint voice, to watch something though her eyes were squeezed shut. She spoke slowly and carefully at first.

"Two angels appeared at Danny's bedside the night before and said, 'Do not do what you are about to do.' Those angels attempted to convert Danny's thinking, to show him there was another way. But Satan's powerful lure was impossible for Danny to resist.

"At that moment he was given the opportunity to choose between darkness and light. In his confusion, it was the darkness that appeared to be the truth.

"I said, 'We always have free will, Danny.' That's what I tried to remind him of, but I knew he wouldn't listen.

"All through the next day he struggled with his decision. I seized the opportunity to push him toward the light. I prayed intently all day and all that night. At one point, that night, very late, he decided to forget the plan, and told that young man in the garage that he was only joking. For a moment I thought we had won. Then the darkness overtook him, pushed him toward the lamp, and shouted, 'Just cut the cord, Danny. Just cut the cord so you will be prepared. You can decide what to do later.'

"But the instant he sliced the cord and picked up the lamp, he was prodded up the stairs. The dark shadow stood behind him and whispered in his ear, 'It's too late Danny; the cord is cut.' He swung the lamp at his side and the cord dragged on the steps. Then he stood outside the door. Now the darkness gave him one last nudge: 'Danny, it's too late to turn back. How would you explain cutting the cord to Rachel?'

"It works a million times a day all over the world. A tiny nub of truth that makes a lie seem real.

"After Rachel, he lashed out at Evan. He was told he was doing the best thing for his sons, and he believed it. This was too much for me! I begged God to stop him, and fell to my knees, and perhaps I was heard. I will never know for sure.

"I'm sorry to have to tell you he was on his way to kill Christopher, too, when finally God sent an angel who blocked Christopher's doorway and told Danny, 'Stop! No more! Stop! You are not taking this one!' It was those words that brought Danny to his senses and caused him to spare Christopher."

Joanna put her head in her hands and began to weep. Mitch and Carolyn jumped up to comfort her, thanking her not just for today, but for what she had done that night. She looked exhausted, but quickly began to recover. A breeze swept through the garden and chimes softly sang. The clouds moved past the sun and the summer warmth returned with a passion.

Joanna looked up at them and wanly smiled. "Thank you, but please stop fussing over me. I'm fine."

She reached into a bucket of gardening tools that sat next to her, found a pair of clippers, walked to the edge of the garden, and selected a brilliant white rose.

"Please take this. I want the two of you to have it. I ask only that when you arrive home, you turn to Luke 23:34 in your Bible and place it between those pages forevermore. It's a symbol of innocence and purity, and it's meant as a reminder that love is truth and will always conquer darkness.

"What I'm about to tell you is the part of the story you will probably find incomprehensible, upsetting, and possibly even reprehensible. That's because it's the complete opposite of what most cultures believe and what you have been taught your entire life. All I ask is that you keep an open mind and ask God to guide you to an answer. If you choose to accept it, then perhaps this rose will provide you with the courage and wisdom to share this story with others."

⇥⟊ ⟊⇤

A few moments later, Joanna seemed restored to the vibrant woman who had greeted them earlier that morning. Her green eyes had regained their sparkle and the color had returned to her cheeks. She smiled mischievously, and then reached behind her head to release the ribbon that held her ponytail in place, shaking her head like a schoolgirl to reveal her magnificent mane of pure white hair.

Now she spoke with the excitement and alacrity of someone with very good news to share.

"I know this will be hard to accept, especially for you, Mitch . . . and yet I believe it is absolutely true. As I said, it will throw into doubt everything you've ever been taught. But as I alluded to before, this is not something you can understand when viewing from a human or a conventional mind.

"Please try to look at what I am about to tell you from God's point of view. God sees from the inside out and He understands with perfect truth. He loves from the heart, not the flesh. And only God truly knows what is inside a man's heart. He can see all of the good and all of the bad."

Mitch suspected he knew where she was going, and Joanna was certainly right about one thing. He didn't like it.

"He has said, 'This man is your brother. I've forgiven him and you should as well. If you expect to be forgiven, then you must learn to forgive him. He is here with me.'"

Joanna then added, "I understand that this is hard to swallow, but it is the truth of God."

Mitch had listened respectfully until that point, but he couldn't contain himself any longer.

"So, Joanna, if I understand you correctly, you're telling us that Danny is in heaven? Or rather, you're telling us that God has told you that Danny is in heaven, despite the fact he murdered his wife and son and then committed suicide?"

Joanna noticed that Mitch had pushed the rose to one side of the table. He rolled his eyes and glared at Carolyn, who said, "Joanna, is that really what you're telling us?"

"Yes, that's really what I'm telling you."

Carolyn watched Mitch do his furrowed-brow thing, and knew he was about to drill down into the details. At moments like this he wasn't always the soul of tact, and so she kicked him under the table, which seemed to do the trick.

"Okay, Joanna, please don't take this the wrong way, but why would God allow a murderer into heaven? Particularly one who then took his own life?"

Joanna thought before answering, because she knew from experience that this detail was simply beyond the capability of most people to comprehend or accept.

"Mitch, when Danny went to the ravine, he was filled with remorse. After killing Evan, particularly, he could not forgive himself, and then the same demons that had just pushed him to commit these horrendous acts turned on him, viciously accusing him of having done one of the worst things any man could do."

"Well, they were right!" Mitch said.

"But Danny asked God to forgive him. He begged to be forgiven, calling out to Jesus to show mercy despite the fact he couldn't forgive himself and took his own life."

Before Mitch could respond, Joanna leaned in close and whispered, "At the very instant of death he was taken into heaven."

Joanna sat back and looked at them with great sympathy, trying to find the words that would at least give them the willingness to consider what she knew to be the truth. "Danny, like all of us, was a child of God. He was a sinner, as we are, but his Father loved him nonetheless and brought him back home. God does not view sin in different levels. That is a creation of man."

Mitch was far from convinced, and a part of him wanted simply to get up and leave. He could feel a sense of indignation at being asked to believe something that every fiber of his being screamed was wrong. It could only have been through some form of divine intervention that his thoughts failed to reach his lips before Carolyn spoke up with a more thoughtful reply.

"Joanna, truthfully, we're not ready to accept this. I know you are just asking that we keep an open mind, and we'll do that. I can't deny that something wonderful has happened over the last few days. My heart has been lifted. While I still miss Rachel terribly, and will always grieve for her, I now know that she is still with me and for that I will always be grateful. But, if I'm not mistaken, you said before that Rachel had forgiven Danny."

"That's right. She has, and so has Evan."

Joanna looked down at her hands and then back up at each of them in turn. "I understand how you feel. But I want you to consider something. And perhaps it will help you to understand the power of forgiveness. You can remain angry at Danny, you can hate him, you can hope he will rot in hell and be punished for the rest of eternity. That's your choice. But then you will stay trapped in your anger and be imprisoned by your own emotions because of a desire to see another person suffer. Ask yourself: do you want to be guided by hate, or by love?"

Mitch finally started to calm down and listen. Something Joanna had said reminded him of his experience yesterday. He knew that on a certain level, Joanna was right, but he was not yet ready to relinquish his anger at Danny.

He picked up the rose and handed it to Carolyn as they stood to leave. "Joanna, we're so grateful for how much you've helped us. I hope we don't seem like a couple of ingrates, but it's almost too much to take in so quickly. We need to go home and do as you suggest. We need to pray, and ask for guidance."

He looked over at Carolyn for confirmation. "And we promise to keep an open mind."

Joanna stood and said, "I know that, Mitch. And that's all I ask."

⇥▬◉ ◉▬⇤

Joanna walked with them to the edge of the garden, and opened the door to the rear of the church. They chatted for a few more minutes and then said their good-byes, promising to stay in touch. Joanna declined Mitch's offer of a contribution to the church in exchange for a promise they and their boys would become regular volunteers at the soup kitchen.

After Joanna shut the door behind them they circled around to the front of the church and stood alone in the sanctuary. They wanted to take a closer look at the magnificent crucifix displayed above the altar.

As a work of art, it was astoundingly powerful, simply because it was so realistic. The lifelike face of Jesus looked down in agony, and appeared to be on the verge of speaking at any moment. Despite the great suffering depicted in the eyes, the tilt of the head announced the presence of a peaceful, open heart.

"He looks as if he is one breath away from death, and yet he exudes so much love," Mitch said.

Carolyn unconsciously twirled the stem of the rose in her hand as they both looked upward. Then she reached into a pew, removed a Bible, and thumbed through it until she found the passage for which she was looking.

"Now I understand, Mitch! Do you know what Luke, chapter 23, verse 34, says?"

"No, actually I couldn't remember which one that was when Joanna mentioned it. What does it say?" He locked eyes with the figure on the cross and was drawn in deeper.

Carolyn walked over, stood next to her husband, and squeezed his hand as they both lovingly looked up into His face.

"It's the moment when Jesus said, 'Father, forgive them, for they know not what they do.'"

Acknowledgments

WRITING A BOOK is a time-consuming and complicated process, and is truly a team effort. First and foremost, my wife and I would like to thank all our family and friends who have encouraged and supported us along the way. There are too many of you to name here, but you know who you are, and we will be eternally grateful for your help. Your faith, love, and support have lifted us up through our dark times.

As if by divine intervention, John Roadfuss appeared in the midst of our storm. My wife and I will always be grateful to John for the compassionate spiritual counseling and guidance he provided that helped to restore our faith and hope.

Technically, Michael Fragnito is the ghostwriter of *The Ravine*, but through this process (and our in-depth conversations concerning spiritual matters), he has become a friend. We met Michael at a time when the direction of *The Ravine* was at a crossroad. His creativity and willingness to fully embrace our journey helped to make this book a reality.

Peggy McColl and Judy O'Beirn are my Canadian heroes—there are truly no chance meetings and I met these sisters for a reason during the early days of the book. They both have amazing hearts and have guided and supported me, not just as the professionals they are, but as friends.

Janet Kirkman is a true friend, believer, and supporter. She was truly the guardian angel of our book, and we thank her for being with us every step along the way.

Susan Scherzer and Amy Schmidt are women of great faith who speak God's wisdom. Their words of encouragement gave us the inspiration we needed at just the right time.

And of course, I need to thank Kelly, my wife, who has always been there for me . . . she is my rock.

Finally, we are humbly grateful to God, who called upon the least expected, and inspired me to begin this message of hope and restoration—not just for me, but for all of us who need forgiveness.

Join the conversation about *The Ravine* at:

Theravinebook.com

We hope you have enjoyed reading *The Ravine*, and that it will inspire you to personally explore the issues raised in the book.

Several readers have requested that we create a study guide to better aid book groups and others who wish to dig deeper into the questions of forgiveness, hope, and the afterlife. The study guide can be downloaded for free, and we invite you to use it in book groups and any other appropriate formats.

At this site, you will also find blogs by Robert Pascuzzi, upcoming events, a suggested reading list, and links to other inspirational sites. You can read what others are saying and contribute to the dialogue on our message board, as well as communicate with the author.

If you would like to purchase additional copies of *The Ravine* at bulk discount rates, please visit theravinebook.com for ordering information.

Our next book is *Hope in the Midst of Your Storm*. If you are one of the many who have been through difficult times and would like to share your experience, strength, and hope in order to inspire others, we would love to hear from you. Instructions for participation can be found at theravinebook.com. Just click on the link "Tell us your story of hope" to learn the details.

Robert Pascuzzi is available to speak to your organization or group. Please contact Robert at Pascuzzi.robert@gmail.com.

Made in the USA
Lexington, KY
16 April 2014